T0121068

If But One Wish

BONITA J. B. SALLIS

WESTBOW
PRESS®
A DIVISION OF THOMAS NELSON
& ZONDERVAN

This is a work of fiction. All of the characters, names, incidents,
organizations, and dialogue in this novel are either the products
of the author's imagination or are used fictitiously.

WestBow Press books may be ordered through booksellers or by contacting:

WestBow Press
A Division of Thomas Nelson & Zondervan
1663 Liberty Drive
Bloomington, IN 47403
www.westbowpress.com
844-714-3454

Scripture taken from the King James Version of the Bible.

ISBN: 978-1-6642-3471-0 (sc)
ISBN: 978-1-6642-3470-3 (e)

Print information available on the last page.

WestBow Press rev. date: 07/08/2021

One

ometimes you just can't go back to do it all over again.
Taking off after Ian had changed Rain's whole life. When
he'd first told her about his new job and relocation, she just
assumed that she would be going too. So, Rain left her husband
Will behind, snatched up their daughter Merry and followed Ian.
She wasn't going to lose him just because of distance.

Ian Adams had loved Will Thorpe, his former college roommate
and friend the only way he knew how, a connection by memories,
not heartstrings. It was safer that way, at least for Ian. Like a snapshot,
a thousand words later, Ian's relationships all appeared to have the
right elements. But perception, in the eye of any other beholder,
told the real story.

The affair with Will's wife Rain, happened. "Why", "Why
not", existed somewhere on the same plane for Ian Adams, good-
looking, ambitious and completely self-absorbed. His wants and
needs were one in the same. Ian had backed into, and out of the
affair with equal selfishness.

"A natural-born charmer", Ian's momma used to call him. His
daddy would just shake his head and remind his only child, "that
even snake-charmers get bit sometimes". Ian would wink at his

1

mother, and frown for his father's sake, all the while running out of the door, looking for something new to get into. Once again, there was Ian, grinning, frowning, and running out of the door looking for something, anything, new.

What a fiasco their lives turned into. Whatever it had been that Ian thought he needed from Rain, too quickly exhausted its supply. Rain had seen Ian's new job and relocation, as only a momentary intrusion, but the awful and naked truth was that Ian Adams had done what he'd always done, find 'em, fool 'em, and forget 'em, forever. Ian Adam…a lifetime member…certifiably in good-standing, of the 4F Club. The fact that Rain had been his best friend's wife did not really matter.

Truth was, that Ian never expected Rain to leave her husband, and certainly not to come to him with Merry in tow. Ian had always loved Merry, his godchild. Whenever her daddy had brought Ian along to their home, Ian would play with her as soon as he caught sight of her, but even the precious three-year-old Merry had been for Ian, just another conquest. The new job, a fresh start and his next challenge were all that Ian Adams wanted. Rain and Merry's daily and unwanted presence, wearing thinner by the moment, the building tension, tears and finger-pointing then finally the ensuing storm, came crashing in with the speed and fury of a flash flood. With no place else to go, Rain returned home to her husband Will, once more dragging their daughter Merry along, like one of the child's own dolls.

Will Thorpe, M.D., was like a comfortable old shoe, worn and familiar. Man, woman orchild, his patients liked him. He called them by name, and took the time to notice inner pain, fears and anxieties. Will understood clearly that patience made good doctors, and that good doctors made good patients. To those sick and in fear, adult or child, he was the doctor they could count on.

With a heart much too big for even his six-foot, four- inch frame, he would once again permit Rain to return, no matter how many times she had hurt him. Rain knew this. Will felt loneliest each time he returned to his empty house. He could hear the quiet echo their absence.

Home was filled with mauve, beige, open spaces and flowers in the garden.

Will and Rain had laughed and fought over the "ultra-feminization" of their first new house at 1112 Elm Street, a dream made possible, only by the generosity of Emmalyn Brown. In the end, Rain had prevailed and the soft oasis of lovely peace was unveiled. Even Will had to admit that it was much more compatible with his masculine side, than he'd thought it could be. Rain had teased that their new home would allow Will to get in touch with his feminine side.

Of all the rooms, though, Will loved Merry's bedroom the most. Rain had selected sunshine yellow accents to coordinate with pink and the room reminded him of a pink cotton candy fairyland. Mother decorated the room, the way a child does a dollhouse. There were bunny, puppy and bear families, a rocking chair and a canopied day bed with pillows in all shapes. Merry's name was spelled in soft pink cloth letters mounted on one of the yellow walls. The pique fabric Rain had selected for the bedding, resplendent with layers of lace, found itself covering her tiny dressing table and bench. Huge pink and white bunny-ear slippers peeked out from underneath the bed. Pictures of Will with Merry in beautiful fabric-covered frames covered the walls. Will found it odd that Rain had not selected any pictures of herself with little Merry to adorn the child's little "queendom". He could not bring himself to question her about it though. There were so many things Will did not understand about his wife. In time, he'd promised himself silently. Maybe in time, she would open up and share her inner secrets, secrets Rain Thorpe took great pains to keep.

A tiny-child-size computer, monitor and printer sat on her tiny white desk. Will found the miniature keyboard absolutely fascinating. Merry had learned to operate the DVD player at two years old and consequently, loved playing on her very own computer, one just like "Daddy's". That fact alone, pleased her, to no end. In amazement, Will would place his very own hands on the miniscule keyboard and simply stare at the contrast. Will had inherited his father's huge hands, a fact which dismayed him daily. He had always been ashamed of them. He was a surgeon with the hands of a farmer. Will envied the slim strong hands of Forest Wethers, Chief Surgeon of the Surgical Unit at Penrose Regional Hospital, in Bristol Point, Colorado where Will was employed. Will's hands, nevertheless, possessed a deftness and skill, akin to the finesse of a first-string violinist. In the operating room, on his table, and in his own time, they performed magic for him, the patient and for "God-Almighty".

Will's fingers were long and thick, but the skin on the top-side, was very wrinkled. Even lotioned-down, the wrinkles lay like folds of fabric. Will hid his hands whenever possible. While growing up and working in his family's small restaurant after school, he washed dishes daily, by hand, and always without gloves. He never complained. His parents made a modest living. Will never accepted wages for working there. He knew that his family loved him and that was enough. His Mom and Dad squeezed out spending money for him, whenever they could, which was not often. Will learned early on, to make do and to find pleasure in the simple things. Time and patience had become his companions.

Will had always loved interacting with people. He'd made a practice of asking the names of customers coming into his parents' restaurant. Upon their departure, he would say goodbye, always calling them by name. This never failed to surprise and delight them. Stranger to acquaintance, was, for the future Dr. Thorpe, only one hello away. The ease he felt with people translated well in medical school, especially during patient care. His parents had been so very proud when he received his medical degree and for the first time in his life, Will could come up for air. He could dare to believe that life held promises, that were his and his alone.

<h1 style="text-align:center">Two</h1>

ill Thorpe pulled into his driveway a little too fast. The car made a short "skirt" noise, as he came abruptly to a stop. Will looked around quickly, hoping he had not awakened his neighbors. It was very late. Running his hand across his face, he tried to wake up, as he got out of the car. He was tired, and badly in need of a shower. He had just spent twelve hours at the hospital. His last patient needed an emergency appendectomy, which ended up taking longer than expected. The appendix had already ruptured, and as a result, infection of the peritoneum was extensive. The patient, a ten- year-old boy named Justin Thyme, had been rushed in from his school playground by ambulance. His parents had been notified and reached the hospital almost as soon as the boy arrived at the Emergency Room. He was febrile, in pain and frightened to death. His vital signs, expectedly erratic, had not been as stable as Will would have liked. Irrigation of the abdominal cavity had to be thorough. Two hours later, it was finally over. Justin would be fine. His work day finished, Will could head home. Sleep was all he could now think about.

Will experienced a sinking feeling as he put the key into his lock. There would be no shiny three-year-old face smiling in her sleep, tucked away in her corner of the world at 1112 Elm. He used to tiptoe into her room and sit on the window seat to watch her sleep. Sweet breaths of air flowed softly out of her, cherry lips pursed, kissing angels, he often imagined.

Father and daughter had spent many a sunny Saturday morning, a rainy or wintry Sunday afternoon, curled up on the window seat, reading books, making up stories or simply discussing life, all done, of course, from the vantage-point of a well-read-to, munchkin of now, three-years-old.

Will missed Rain too. Things had not gone well for a long time before she took Merry and left. He had known that she had been seeing someone else. Will just never expected it to be his best friend, Ian Adams. Now, each time he called his wife's name in his heart, out came Ian's as well. Merry had been given Ian's last name as her own middle name. The honor of "godfather" had been bestowed upon his friend, in faith. Will ran his hands over his face, roughly this time, as though trying to wake up from a bad dream. He could not bring himself to stop the never-ending movie he played nightly in his own mind. Will turned on some music, hoping to drown those old sorrows. The steady, smooth beat of the music, violins and cries for love, carried him off to the place he wanted to be…with Rain and Merry.

Will had met Rain Meadows during his undergraduate years at Colorado State University. Rain had been a waitress at the college ratskeller, where he and Ian Adams, roommate and fellow-dreamer, ate lunch daily. Will found her quiet, but feisty. She was skittish, like a colt around him. She seemed to enjoy the verbal fencing she faced with Ian each day, several times wounding his oversized ego. She had a cool beauty that Will found intriguing. Sometimes, she hummed to herself as she was working. Will loved to listen to her. She had a wonderful throaty quality, husky, but with incredible range.

Will finally asked Rain out on a date, and one, soon leading to many. He had kept all of this from his best friend. Ian had teased

Will often about his secret new life, jesting that his new secret love must look like "Attila the Hun", if he needed to hide her from him.

Will was not as sure of himself, as his friend in the dating department, and wanted to take no chances. Ian had been merciless with their female classmates. He had changed relationships, almost as often as he changed colognes.

Shaking off this well-rehearsed reverie of the past and returning to the present, Will marched slowly up the stairs, undressing as he went along. Without thinking, he walked into Merry's room to turn on the crystal night lamp sitting on the ledge of the window seat. He had done this every night since they'd left.

Like a ship seeking safe harbor, Will hoped Rain and Merry would see the love-light beckoning them homeward. It had become a ritual born of despair.

Merry's room was on the east side of the house. Rain had insisted that Merry have an oversized room which would have east/west exposure of light. There, Merry began and ended her days with sunshine. Each morning, she would amble-up onto the pink and yellow plaid pillows covering this seat and say good morning to each of her doll babies and then say good morning to God.

Merry had no idea of who this "God" was, but her daddy told her that God was his very best friend and that he lived in a place called Heaven. If her daddy loved him, then she loved him too. Merry knew that she could not see Him, but Daddy had told her that no matter what, God could always hear her, and that if she ever needed help, she could count on Him. This seemed to be enough for her. In this room, little Miss Merry Adams Thorpe, had all sweetness and safety Will wanted the world to provide her.

Turning to close her door softly, as if she were sleeping, tired and lonely, once again, Will rehearsed those days not so long ago, when all seemed well in his life. Each moment seemed always, to bring him to Ian Adams. Had he brought Ian home so often, to fill the emotional void in his relationship with his wife?? Every invitation for Ian to visit, or stay for dinner, had been his own idea. Rain had hesitated at first, then seemed suddenly to brighten with each subsequent get-together. Will should have read the signs, but Rain finally seemed so happy. Over and again, this monologue rolled across his mind each time he went home. No new answers ever came... just the sad refrain, "if only". Ian had that effect on most women. He was handsome, amusing and illusive. In their undergraduate days, the combination had been unbeatable. Will had been amazed at how methodically Ian planned out each conquest. None of them ever lasted. Not one was ever intended to, but only Will knew that. "Enough!" growled his hungry stomach. Downstairs to make a sandwich, Will walked silently through the darkened house. Back upstairs in his nightly ritual, he carried the meager dinner to the bedroom. He turned on the television and next, the shower. He needed for the hot water to wash away his pain and the hot steam to purge Rain from his soul. His whole body ached for her.

Too tired to sleep, Will muted the television and just listened to the music he'd turned on in the living room, earlier. He headed downstairs once more, made himself a scotch and seven and after, slipped wearily onto the sofa. He lay silently sinking into the past, looking once again for answers.

Will remembered the fears he'd felt just before finishing medical school. Rain had married Will, in his last year of undergraduate study. The relationship with his new wife was foundering, even then. She seemed, however able to cope with the strains of medical school and through the rigors of his internship and residency.

Surgery had become his chosen specialty. Will wanted to be the best, and subsequently spent every spare moment, even times when not on call to assist in every procedure, any procedure, in order to hone his skill. Rain had seemed not to understand that the hard work meant that later they could have it all. Will reasoned that the sacrifice would pay off, if, Rain could just be patient. Not understanding somehow, that you cannot reason for another, he mistook her silence for acceptance. Deep, deep, down inside, like so many other times in her life Rain had really just given up. Will returned to his bedroom, finally drifting off to sleep, cursing hindsight.

The faint sound of the doorbell ringing awakened Will with a start. Groping his way through the darkness and down the stairs, he could hear the noise of a car pulling away from the house and saw the lighted sign of a taxi moving slowly down the street, as he opened the door. Merry lay sleeping in Rain's arms, wrinkled, adorable and oblivious to her mother's latest decision to return home. Without words, Will reached for his baby girl.

Rain seemed content to let her go. Husband and wife touched lightly in the exchange, but questions crowded out emotions. Dropping her bags at the foot of the stairs, Rain headed up to their bedroom, without even as much as an "I'm sorry". This scene, had been played out too many times before. Will did not say a word to Rain.

Merry roused from her sleepy reverie only long enough to feel the hand that touched her own, its smallest finger separated from the rest, as Will gently cradled her in his arms. He had always outstretched his pinky whenever he reached for Merry. It was their special sign. From the moment she could grasp, she would wrap her entire hand around this one finger. She was and would always be, his baby girl. Eyes still closed, she said simply, "hi Daddy"?

Will's eyelashes long and thick, half-covered his fully-opened and now teary eyes. The sound of her tiny voice had made the darkness alright. He had been so lonely. Gently taking off only her coat hat and shoes, pushing aside the stuffed animals, dolls and pillows, he tucked her into the middle of it all. The soft light from the window seat lamp filled the room with a quiet peace. Memories of happier times came flooding back quickly, reminding Will that pain had become too constant a companion. Tomorrow, he decided, would be soon enough to know just what Rain really wanted to do now. Will gave up the bedroom and went quietly down to the sofa in the den to make his bed there. Yawning, Rain undressed and needing to sleep, rolled over onto her side of the bed. She was not at all surprised by Wil's gesture, in fact, relieved. Rain could never imagine herself being so generous, but after all, Will was Will....

Will tossed and turned. Dream after dream invaded a night that should have brought some kind of peace of mind. At least Rain and Merry were safe, home, though for how long this time, he had no idea. Rolling over once more, determined to get some rest, he pushed all thought from his mind and drifted off. Tomorrow was already filled with too large an agenda, the hospital, his patients, and now Rain and Merry. The thought of his little love forced a sleepy smile. Somewhere between sleep and waking, Will could still feel the tiny warm hand wrapped around his right pinky. The warmth of the reunion with Merry was still very fresh. Merry was three years old, with huge brown eyes that swallowed you in wonder, as you peered into the tiny face with the rosebud lips. Her father's love and devotion had long since taught her to expect all the fullness and beauty, the world could show to her. By the age of three, she had learned to return the same with such innocence of spirit.

Sunshine and quiet awakened Merry with a start. At Ian's house, she could always hear the sounds of the tiny creatures in the woods. Sometimes she had been scared, especially at night, but this morning, she knew that something was very different. The sudden warmth streaming through the bay window with its window seat, flowered cushions and soft breeze, reminded her so much of home. Rubbing her eyes, she thought for a moment that she remembered hearing her Daddy's voice and wondered. Sure enough, when she looked around, she found herself in her very own room. Merry scrambled off the bed in a hurry. She had to find her daddy. He just had to be there this time and not just another sad dream. Rain's trip had taken its toll on her. Too many times in her sleep, she had called out to her father, but he never came. Of all she had lost, her father's loving presence had been the greatest sacrifice. Pushing the door open to her Mommy and Daddy's room, she peeked in, only to find her mother, still asleep. Maybe Daddy was in the kitchen. That was his favorite place to be. Daddy loved to cook for her.

Will quietly listened to the slap-pat of tiny bare feet running from room to room. The bed monster had apparently swallowed her socks again. He smiled. Merry was searching for him and he knew it. Will pretended to moan and groan, calling out Merry's name, smiling broadly all the while. He now listened to the "step-step" sound her little feet made, as she found her way downstairs, first going to the kitchen, then to the den, trying to trace his voice. She was home and she knew it. "Daddy?", she whispered… triumphantly tapping his arm. Merry, watching the smile on his face, laughed and scrambled up on his stomach, to help him greet his day. "Daddy?", she laughed, "its me.., it's Merry, I'm right here!" "Mommy's here too!" She proceeded to give him a great big hug. Will and Merry tickled each other until they both fell off the couch, hugging and holding onto each other, for dear life. Will bathed and dressed Merry and set her to play in her room until he too could do the same. He promised to help her make breakfast for Mommy, once he'd dressed. Merry was a good baby, spoiled by love, not things. She played in her room waiting for Will. She was a "mommy" too after all, and had to check on her own little ones. She had missed them all while she had been away.

Rain was a light sleeper. The sounds of laughter and love had floated into the master bedroom where she lay. She had heard Merry and Will starting their day together. Running off with their only child had been mean and selfish. Rain knew that Will would have let her go alone. She wasn't really sure why she had taken the baby. It seemed a lifetime ago that Ian stood together with the Thorpes, christening the precious little bundle who would also carry his last name "Adams", as her own middle name. He had accepted the honor of "godfather" happily, then.

Will had loved Ian once, like a brother. As brothers often go, they were as different as night and day. Perhaps that was what had drawn them together in college. Ian always admired the honesty and loyalty his best friend gave so easily, and Will wished that some of Ian's polish would rub off on him. Ian's life had always been filled with total freedom and the responsibilities of his choosing. Ian unashamedly described himself as selfish, but honest and made his modus-operandi known, to even those he'd said he loved. Rain and Ian were two of a kind. In a meeting of tempers, the exchange was always electrifying. It had drawn the two of them together, like magnets, and with equal force, could repel them, if their goals were different. When things began to go wrong in Palmetto springs, at Ian's, Rain had wanted to believe that Merry was the problem, but in her heart, knew better.

Rain decided to get out of bed. She went to shower. Moist and fresh-faced, she reentered the bedroom toweling her hair. Merry was fussing over the breakfast tray she and Daddy had prepared "specially" for Mommy. After Daddy had finished dressing. Little "miss" had gone out to the garden to pick a morning glory for the vase on the tray. Merry tried so hard to please Rain. Though just a baby, Merry could sense the emptiness in her mother, and tried to fill the void with flowers, hugs, love and kisses. It was almost as though she felt responsible for it all. Sadly, she was not so far from the truth. Rain knew from the moment she'd found herself pregnant, that she did not want a baby.

Will watched Rain silently as she emerged from the bathroom. He had always loved her hair. It was long, soft and shiny. It was fine and curly, too. Light seemed to dance off of it. Surprised by the entourage in her bedroom, she stopped mid-step, frowning at Will. This look was lost on Merry, but not Will. Picking up the baby for a goodbye hug, he announced his departure for work. Merry insisted on walking him to the door. For her, it meant a free ride on his shoulders, and a ticklish ride to the floor. She squealed in delight, as he obliged her secret wishes. Rain stood at the top of the stairs waiting for Will to leave. There really wasn't anything to say.

Knowing Rain all too well, Will waved goodbye to her over his shoulder. He knew they'd talk later. Rain had a way of defeating him without words. He loved her still, but he knew how fragile was their relationship. What he'd never understood was, why she'd had married him in the first place.

Rain watched Will through the stained- glass palladium window over the door.

Whenever she had hurt him, his whole being reflected it, in the drooping of his shoulders and the bow of his head. Today, he was totally and utterly defeated. Rain did not know what she would do next, but one thing was sure. As soon as Will was out of sight, she was going to call Ian.

Three

ill pulled into a parking space outside of Penrose
Regional Medical Center, situated in the center of
the city of Bristol Point. Grabbing a set of fresh scrubs
from the back seat, he headed for his day. After ER shift change
Report and Review, attended by both oncoming day staff and
outgoing night staff, Will headed for the Pediatric Ward, to check
in on his appendectomy patient, Justin Thyme, smiling to himself,
as he remembered the patient's name.

As he stepped off the elevator, Will went directly to the nurse's
station to review his patient's chart. None of the nurses was there.
It was too soon. Surely the oncoming ward staff were still being
briefed in morning report. Will preferred to review charts in the
silence before shift change.

He could see lights on in several rooms. No doubt some patients
were being released today, he thought. The cartoon network was
showing Batman. Will could hear it as he entered Justin's Room.
Picking up the chart, at the foot of the bed to review vitals and night
progress reports, Will looked up briefly at Justin, who was engrossed
in television or slightly glazed from his pain medication. Well Nick",
Will said smiling at the now-attentive patient. Justin attempted a

smile. It was tough to accomplish with the oxygen mask still over his mouth and nose. Will patted his leg in understanding. "Justin Thyme" really is the perfect name for you. That's pretty much how I found you."

Justin nodded his response. "Bet you'd like to change your name sometimes...huh?" Again, the nod. Justin's parents entered the room, smiling over the joke they had heard so many times. Justin's mom, Betty Miller-Thyme had endured worse. Her good-natured acceptance of the constant jokes about her own name, had taught her son to laugh-it-off and not become angry. Even Justin's Dad had to get into the act. After running his hands through his son's hair and unashamedly kissing his ten-year-old's cheek, he said...So Doc, got a little Thyme for me?" They all laughed. Justin blushed a beautiful beet-red while receiving his father's love. "As a matter of fact, I do", Will stated. "The oxygen mask will come off sometime between today and tomorrow. His lungs are clear, but, his temperature keeps spiking. Actually, this is to be expected. The appendix did rupture. He did have quite a bit of infection down there. But, we've got him on some high-speed antibiotics, so he's pretty much out of the woods. He'll probably be here for another three or four days. Then it'll be "thyme" for him to go home." Smiling broadly at each other, they shook hands. Assuring Justin he'd return to check on him later Will winked at the boy and left.

Floor nurse Diana Thomas was coming in to take vitals. The ward was starting to come to life. Food trays were being dispensed. Will waved to his colleague, Dr. Beauregard M. Longmire, "Bo", to his friends. He and Will had developed a friendly professional relationship, but had not spent much off-duty time together. "Thyme", Will mused, to head back to the ER, to see what was going on, smiling once again.

The ER was short two doctors, one internist and another ER physician, so Will volunteered to pull a twenty- four- hour day, if needed. Grabbing snacks in between patients, he'd worked well into his shift before the smoke cleared. Where were they all coming from, he thought, as he moved from viral symptoms to fractures. The ER received a call from the internist scheduled for duty. He was on his way, so Will would not have to stay for an extra shift. Bo Longmire was going to assist in the ER until then. Will needed some time to think about his family. Decision time. He did not like ultimatums. For Merry's sake, he was going to ask Rain to decide her own future, with or without him and their child. By the end of his day though, Will found himself exhausted and starving. Fight or not, going home would still be a blessing.

Four

Ian Adams bounded from his bed, full of energy, ready for this day. What a beautiful day it was, he thought. The sky was an electric blue with clouds like cotton balls floating gently across it. It was one of those rare moments when you think all is well with the universe.

The change in jobs and location had been good to him. Ian's new position at Bosch, Schuyler and Smith-Marshal, had been all that he'd hoped for. Ian loved Palmetto Springs, located near the southern-most border of Colorado. The small city had the feeling of a metropolis and yet was quaint enough to still be charming. On Sean's advice, Ian found a real estate agent, who led him to the most wonderful house sitting right next to a small lake. The house had a huge stone fireplace and was an A-Frame loft, with a wrap-around deck. This house, the lake, his new job and his relationship with Sean, told Ian that he was well on his way and Ian was determined to let nothing, but success get in.

Smiling broadly, Ian looked down at the long and very shapely leg that lay uncovered by the satin sheets. Sean Smith-Marshal. Even her name made its own statement, and she was certainly the kind of bonus Ian Adams had expected to get. The trip he had made to interview with the Law firm of Bosch, Schuyler, and Smith-Marshal, had brought him face to face with her. Sean was an Associate-Attorney in the firm already. Ian reasoned that her father's senior partner status had certainly not hurt her progression. Upon meeting, they had acknowledged each other, but nothing more. Life, Ian decided, had presented him with a bounty and he was sure of two things. His good looks and charm would tame even this tigress, and he would make it his business to do so. Ian wanted the life being laid before him. Never before had he wanted anyone, nor any thing, this much.

Sean didn't have to work that day, so she was sleeping in. The night before, she and Ian had gone swimming in the lake next to his house and eaten fresh Maine lobster, sipped champagne. To the beat of soft music and crickets, spent a sensual evening with the compliments of a very full moon.

Sean liked waking up quietly, slowly and alone. In many ways, she and Ian were exact opposites. Sean was easy, Ian intense. She demanded very little from him and required virtually only what he chose to give. Sean had been born to wealth and privilege. More importantly, she was the embodiment of her mother and father's love for each other. Beautiful, wealthy and secure, she had no need to walk on the wild side. Determined to ground their only child, Sean had been sent to North Carolina, to her maternal grandparents' farm during summer vacations. On the farm, breakfast started with a trip first, to the hen house to gather eggs and next, to the smokehouse for bacon. Digging gently into the ground in Mima's garden, she unearthed the potatoes to be fried, to go along with homemade buttermilk biscuits. It was also Sean's job to make the butter. Sean loved to sit and churn until magically, the butter was ready. "Mima", Sean's grandmother, would check the butter over and again. "Not yet, baby-girl", she would say and gently touch her baby-grand's cheek. Then she would look Sean straight in the eye and remind her that "in God's time, everything is made ready". This pronouncement always made Sean feel connected to something greater than herself.

Even as a child, she understood how to wait, but more importantly, that for some things, she had to wait. In the quiet of these childhood moments, the woman-seed had been awakened. Sean had learned how to listen and wait.

Ian finished his long shower and dressed quickly. That was the way he did most things, effortlessly and well. He was immaculate in his Armani linen suit. Handkerchief in pocket, Rolex in place, eel-skin briefcase, shoes, wallet, belt and key chain to match, he was ready to leave. "Oh, my pen!" he remembered. He'd left it on the nightstand after working on some contracts the night before. It was a beautiful pen, a Mont Blanc, expensive and classy. Ian could hear Sean humming lightly in her sleep. It was time to go. He grasped the unattended leg by its slender ankle and running his hand slowly and gently up the back of the calf, with a squeeze and soft pat, he was off before she could awaken fully.

The phone started ringing as Sean was trying to wake up. Ian's touch had started the rhythmic twitch of her foot, which like an alarm clock awakened her totally. Somewhere in her head, she could hear ringing. Ian, she thought...picking up the phone with a smirk on her face, Sean kissed her good morning into the receiver. "Ian, she said, you could have followed up with a good morning kiss you know?" Dead silence, then "click". Call disconnected, maybe a wrong number, she thought. Probably Ian calling from his car phone. Smiling, she headed for the shower, thinking Ian and his toys".

Sean's parents had always provided her with access to the very best money would provide. More importantly, they had instilled in her, a strong sense of self. Price and Brittain Smith-Marshal, both attorneys when they married, had become Associate Partners in the prestigious law firm Bosch & Schuyler. Sean's mother left the practice when Sean was in her late teens, to become an appellate court justice. Price Marshal, persevered and became senior partner and later, through hard work, talent and dedication, majority stockholder at the law firm, and so was born, Bosch, Schuyler and Smith-Marshal. Sean's father had exceeded even his own wildest dreams. Politics, economics, social issues and the law had been served up with each meal. Sean was reminded with each mealtime prayer, "that to whom much is given, much is required".

Ian basked in the warmth of the sun, Sean and his life. All was as it should have been. Well, everything, but the scene he'd had with Rain before she finally left. In front of Merry, her daughter, Rain had become hysterical when Ian told her the relationship was over. Rain accused Ian of being involved with someone else, suggesting that some of those late nights, supposedly working, had not been spent alone. She had been dangerously close to the truth and Ian knew it. Rain could never know about Sean. Rain was irrational and hurt and possessed in that very moment, the power to alter the plans for his entire future.

What had started out as accepted invitations to dine with Will and Rain, someplace to go and someone with whom to laugh had turned into hidden glances and too soon, stolen moments. Will had been stunned, at first unbelieving of it all, when Rain finally blurted it out, took Merry and left. Ian was Will's best friend, he thought. They had shared an understanding of the pain of survival and the costs of succeeding. Rain, the tears, accusations and tormented face, Merry's bewilderment, in the face of her mother's behavior, made Ian feel every bit, the scoundrel he had been. Merry only understood that Mommy was crying and that somehow her godfather Ian was to blame. Merry stood on the sofa next to her mommy, patting her hair, hugging her and telling her not to cry, as she too had tears streaming down her face.

Ian tensed his jaw, reliving the scene. His face was warm and wet with perspiration. Lost in the terrible memory, he startled to hear the intrusive and angry honk of a car horn. Ian had begun to cross the center median on the road, and didn't realize it. He pulled over to the side of the road, turning off the engine. Slowly, he pulled the rearview mirror around so that he could see himself. Picking up his car phone, he decided to call Sean. Ian needed to hear her voice desperately. The phone rang and rang. No answer. Maybe she could have lunch with him. He'd call back later. Right now, he needed to pull himself together and get to work.

Five

Rain gripped the phone receiver so hard her knuckles changed colors. She was in a moment frozen in time. Her senses had already processed everything her conscious-self wanted to hide away. Some woman had answered the phone. Ian had someone living with him. Rain had just left, only days ago. Who...???

How long??? Why??? Rain knew that taking Merry with her had been a terrible mistake. It had made things more complicated. But now, it was as though she had never existed in Ian's life. He already had someone new. From the way the voice on the other end of the phone had spoken, this relationship was anything but new. Question after unanswered question swirled like a kaleidoscope in Rain's head.

Merry's little hand was tugging at Rain's pants leg. "Mommy, Mommy?", she asked, "now that we're home again can I call Grandma Emma, on my new telephone? I missed her Mommy, didn't you???" Rain tried to keep from fainting. Rain had fully expected Ian to ask her to come back to him. In Rain's heart, as sad as was true, she would have returned, even if it had meant that she had to leave Merry behind. Rain looked down at the large brown eyes staring at her. "Yes, Merry, we can call in just a little bit, I have to take care of something first." Merry's face crumpled in defeat. "I just wanted to call Grandma, that's all…"

Rain felt guilty over the way she neglected Merry sometimes. Merry went to the den to watch television until Mommy could help her call Grandma. Struggling to get up on the sofa, Merry smiled thinking about how her Daddy had played with her earlier that morning.

With fingers trembling, Rain dialed Ian's office number. "Bosch, Schuyler and Smith-Marshal? How may I assist you?" "Ian Adams, please"? Rain inquired. "One moment please", the voice returned. "Suzette, this is Rain, Rain Thorpe, may I speak to Ian please"? Suzette Butler, Ian's paralegal knew the voice only too well and also how cruelly Ian had played her. "I'm sorry Ms. Thorpe, he hasn't come in yet". Suzette wondered if Rain had been told anything about Sean, before she left town. She instantly felt sorry for Rain. Suzette had been there herself with Ian. "I'd be happy to give him a message, Ms. Thorpe. He really has not come in yet". Rain decided to try calling back later.

Ian parked his car and headed for his office, needing to bury himself in his work. Suzette was not at her desk, when he arrived, but her computer was on, so he assumed she'd come in early too. He reached his office just as the phone began to ring, so he picked it up. "Adams." "Hello, Ian???" The sound of her voice brought alive the nightmare he thought was over. "Hello, Rain.." The ensuing silence was and would be their most honest exchange. "Hmm-hmmm-huhmmm..Ian cleared his throat. "How are you." came the flat and annoyed statement, not question.

Rain knew every word she needed to say by heart, but to give birth to them she knew, could bring an end to her hopes of reunion. "Ian… I", she started. Rain, Let me stop you now", Ian stated abruptly. "There is not going to be any easy way to say this, but I must". "There's nothing left to us"…."I'm not sure there ever really was an us." 'I'm sorry, but there's no place… in my.. here for you". Ian wouldn't put it off any longer. "But Ian?"… Rain could not hold back any more tears. "I love you, and I know that if we could just try, we could have a better relationship, and I would leave Merry with her father this time. I know bringing her made it harder for us... just give it another chance... please give us a chance". In one long breath Rain had offered her soul to the devil and even he did not want it. The words spilled out begging and pleading a case she never in a million years had a chance to win. "I'm sorry Rain, it's over".... Click. Inside Rain died a thousand deaths. Through her tears, Rain murmured to no one, "If I can't have you, then I don't want anyone, nor anything"...

Ian sat down on the side of his desk, abruptly as if he had fallen there. His hands were sweaty and his face clammy. Suzette entered the room moving quickly, arms loaded with files. "Mr. Adams, you're here, good morning. I have your mail and those cases you wanted to get to first thing this morn....." Ian was still sitting on his desk, when she arrived. He'd made no effort to greet nor respond to her presence. Then it hit her...Looking up at him finally, she paused open-mouthed. Rain, she thought. She must have reached Ian.

Rain never moved away from the phone. As if something inside had broken, she stared off into space refusing to think, head awash with dark thoughts. Words no longer had any meaning. Her mouth was stuck shut and yet her brain screamed out into the quiet. She wanted to move, but could not. Eyes blank and staring had begun to sting. She blinked. No tears came to soothe them.

Rain had forgotten about Merry. Merry wandered into the kitchen looking for her mother. "Mommy?, can we ple-e-e-ease call Grandma now?????" Rain looked in Merry's direction, but never saw the child. Mistaking her mother's look for some kind of acknowledgment, grinning broadly, Merry tried to hurry up the stairs toward her bedroom to get the new phone..." I'll be right back Mommy, I need my new phone." One-two, one-two, up the stairs she went. This phone had a built-in memory activated by photograph buttons. Whenever she pressed a picture button, it automatically dialed that person's number. Her favorite two pictures were of Daddy and Grandma.

Rain walked as if in a trance up the stairs to her bedroom. She pushed to close the door, but it did not close all of the way. Rain had tried to close the door without even looking at it. She could hear the sounds of Merry dragging her new phone to her mommy, but never spoke to tell Merry that she too was upstairs.

Rain's body involuntarily sucked in an extra breath and pushed it out as quickly. Her breathing began to slow down. Her senses took control from that moment forward. She sat on the side of the bed and reached for her nightstand drawer. Forgetting the special lock, she could not get it open. Reaching around the back of the table, Rain released the lock and pulled it open.

Even though she had left Will, nothing in the drawer had been touched. Rain reached for the 22 caliber pistol Will had insisted she keep for safety reasons. At first, Rain had refused to have it in her home. Will offered to provide lessons, reminding her that he'd chosen this pistol because it was small and the sound of the gun when firing would not frighten her even more. Rain wasn't even sure that she had the nerve to pull the trigger. Rain sat, simply staring at it.

Rain placed the gun on her lap. Even though it was warm in the room, the gun felt cold and small. She looked down at it, eyes still wide, unblinking and focused on only one word...Ian. Her hand curled softly around the gun. She pressed it up against her rib cage and pulled the trigger. The small "pop" sound it had made could be heard by no one else.

Rain's eyes opened in surprise. She gasped.... The pain was sharp and centered. A small circle of red had begun to grow on her shirt. She didn't understand what to feel, or, to do. How do you let yourself die?? It seemed a strange thought to have at that moment. Her stomach was beginning to feel the burning. A calm, absent of fear bathed Rain like a warm bath.. Time had taken on a new dimension, measured in the rhythmic swoosh of the blood in her veins, which was getting slower and slower. The sorrows caused by too many of her yesterdays had to be placed to rest and all set to right. Rain picked up the phone to try to call Will. She scribbled Ian's number on the phone pad and laid it down next to herself. Her fingers felt so stiff as she dialed the phone. "Penrose Regional, may I help you?" the operator pronounced. Rain was beginning to lose her ability to concentrate. She had underestimated the seriousness of her own actions, much the same way she'd misunderstood her own life. The bullet though small in caliber, had entered the soft tissue of her abdomen, deflected off of her rib cage and grazed her heart. Rain had begun to hemorrhage. Almost a whisper fell out... "Dr Thorpe..Dr. Will Thorpe please.. hurry...". "I'm sorry ma'am, the operator stated, but I can't hear you. Would you repeat that"? Rain attempted to clear her throat. She felt so strange. She remembered the possibility of going into shock, so she reached down for the comforter throw she kept at the foot of her bed and covered herself, to preserve body warmth. Rain tried to shout. "Dr Thorpe, ER", though barely audible, the operator heard. One moment please?" "ER?" Someone answered the call. "Dr. Thorpe", once again whispering. Rain was fading. "I'm sorry, the name again please?" "Beau", Rain said simply. Rain had called for her husband using the nickname only she and Will's father ever used. No one at Regional Medical had ever heard Will called by this name. "Oh, he's right here, just one moment. Dr. Beauregard Longmire spoke into the receiver. The pain was unbearable, so Rain rolled onto her side for comfort. "ER", the voice said... Rain could not hear very well at that moment. There was a ringing in her ears and the rhythmic swoosh of her heartbeat and blood pressure drowning out clarity. "Beau", she said faintly. "I'm shot"... "I'm bleeding". Dr. Longmire quickly reached over the counter to turn the ID caller box around in order to see the number. Someone was in trouble. Whoever it was had called him by his nickname "Bo". Motioning frantically to the head nurse, while pointing to the ID caller, he whispered, "police.. address..GSW". "Hold on. Someone is coming". Don't hang up!....." Dr. Longmire knew he had to try to monitor this patient and to keep the caller on the line, but he still did not know who was calling out to him personally for help. Head Nurse Sally Woods picked up the phone to call the police, but stopped, frowning at the number showing on the ID caller. She knew this number. A small sheet of paper taped to the desk next to the phone confirmed her fear. "Oh no!", she whispered loudly to Dr. Longmire. This number belongs to Will Thorpe. This call is coming from his home. Any hospital ER is like a small community. Everybody knows everybody else's business. There had been stories circulating about Dr. Thorpe and his wife and their marital problems. Will had been putting in long hours and doing extra shifts, which only helped to fuel the rumor that they had split. Will was a very private person. So no one really knew for sure.

Nurse Woods immediately paged Will to return to the ER, stat. Will had gone to check on one of his surgery patients, missing this call entirely. The nurse called the police, then said a prayer.

Sirens blaring, the ambulance raced to 1112 Elm Street. Dr. Longmire hurriedly provided Will a running account of what the patient had told him, before Will dashed out to his car. Time was running out and they both knew it. "What about Merry?" "Was the baby safe?" Will demanded frantically. Dr. Longmire knew nothing about the child's condition, but that would explain the sound of random dialing he'd heard while trying to communicate with Rain. First, an open line, but no sound. Will ran to his car, determined to get there in time.

Neither the screaming sirens of the police car he heard, nor the roller-coaster ride through the streets could surpass the magnitude of the grip of fear squeezing Will in the middle of his chest. Dr. Longmire remained on the phone hoping to keep the patient talking and to try to determine her condition. Rain was in shock. Her blood pressure had become dangerously low. She was hemorrhaging internally from the heart. "Beau", the voice had said. "I'm so sorry.... you deserved better.. Merry too. She's a good baby, Beau... my best work....no..our best work....forgive me...tell ... The last word in her mouth was "Ian". No one would ever hear the next words, "We were so wrong." Rain's hand released the cordless phone.

Merry pushed the half-closed door open to her mother's bedroom and went in. Rain appeared to be sleeping. "Mommy, Mommy?, wake up Mommy?" "You said I could call Grandma Emma". The gun and its fatal wound were mercifully hidden under the covers from the baby. Merry picked up the cordless phone and started pushing buttons on her mother's phone, but never picked up the receiver.

Merry and Will had practiced singing rhymes to help her to learn to count. Her favorite was, "one, two, buckle my shoe". Daddy had also shown her his phone. But it didn't have any pictures so she could not use it to recognize memory-coded phone numbers. But he had told her that on his phone, If you pressed number one, it would dial his number at work and that if she pressed number two, it would "matically" as Merry called it, dial Grandma.

Merry sang one, two, buckle my shoe. She tried to dial her daddy, but no one answered. She only heard the musical notes each number performed. "Mommy, Mommy?", once more she cried. I can't call Grandma, and I can't call Daddy, Mommy wake up". Rain didn't move. Merry frustrated and sleepy crawled up into the bed, scooting up behind her mommy for warmth and fell asleep.

Minutes later, the ambulance, police and Will converged simultaneously on the house. Will unlocked the door, running two steps at a time up the stairs, calling out to Rain and Merry. Fear gripped his heart. Looking first in Merry's room, Will could not find her. The run from the child's room to his own bedroom seemed to happen in slow-motion. Will pushed open the door and could feel the specter death with its hollow silence. Will could barely breathe. Rain and Merry lay motionless on his bed. That drawer next to Rain unlocked, could only mean one thing. "Up here", Will shouted. Policemen and paramedics rushed into the room. Someone grabbed Will from behind to steady him. It startled him even more. The paramedic closest to Rain uncovered her body to reveal blood soaked clothing, sheets and the gun. Will could not look away, only cry out. "Merry"….."my baby"….."I've lost them both"… As Will spoke, Merry began to rub her eyes. Looking around the room at all of the strange people, she cried out when she saw her father. The paramedic closest to Merry scooped her up, handed her to Will and instructed the policemen to take them both downstairs. They worked on Rain, whose vitals were nonexistent, then prepared her body to go back to the hospital with sirens wailing. Will had seen Rain's eyes as she was carried past him by the EMTs. Both shook their heads "No" at Will. Having seen Rain for only that brief moment, he knew. Pupils fixed and dilated. Rigor starting to show. Will knew that it was too late.

The sounds of the ambulance siren frightened Merry. Will held her close, hiding his own reddened, tear-stained eyes he knew would frighten her even more. Merry was crying for Rain. "Daddy, Daddy.. I tried to call you on the phone, but I couldn't get you". "Mommy promised to let me call Grandma Emma, but she wouldn't help me. She just went to sleep. Daddy wake her up! Wake Mommy up! I couldn't wake her up". Will faltered on his feet. The strain of it all was finally hitting him. The two policemen looked at each other and nodded. Good cop, bad cop. The husband for the moment, was the prime suspect, until they could determine otherwise. The big cop who had held Will, from behind after he'd discovered Rain and Merry asked Will to sit down. The other cop offered to take Merry to wash her face and visit with her. The doorbell rang.

It seemed odd since the front door was already wide open. No doubt some neighbor wanting to know what's going on.

Officer Williams carried Merry back downstairs while he answered the door. "Will???" Will honey, it's me?" Merry jumped down from the policeman's arms and ran to her Grandma Emma like a bird in flight being pursued. The force of her fear and body weight bumped into Emma, almost causing her to lose balance.

Surprised to see Merry, Emmalyn folded her arms around the child and held her tightly. "Merry, darlin' when did you get back?"

"Grandma, Grandma, I missed you so much. Did you miss me too?" Emmalyn Brown stood only four-feet ten inches tall at best, but she bent down in order to see Merry eye- to- eye. The officer and Emma could see the red eyes and confusion. "Yes my love, said Emma. I did, and so did Rex."

Will and Officer Baxter went to the door. "Will, what's wrong?" I just came in from grocery shopping and saw the ambulance leave and the police car. What is going on here. Where's Rain? When did they come back"? The two officers glanced briefly at one another.

"Officers Wiiliams and Baxter, I'd like to introduce you to Mrs. Emmalyn Brown. She is family. She is Merry's Grandma Emma. "Emma, please come in", Will offered. "Yes Grandma, come in and see us. Did you bring Rex with you?". "No, baby, but I just bet he wants to see you". Emma knew that Will needed her love and support at that moment and so did little Merry. The circumstances Emma could hear later. She knew Will Thorpe and that was enough.

"Emma, Rain is sick, and the ambulance had to take her to the hospital. Frowning, Emma could see his reddened eyes too and knew that much more had happened here. Emmalyn Brown loved Will and Merry. She'd tried to develop a relationship with Rain, but they'd never connected. Emma always pretended not to notice for everyone's sake. "Merry", she said looking down at the troubled face, I think you and I need to go check on Rex". "Will, if it's alright with you, I'd like Merry to spend the night with me and Rex." "Oh Daddy, can I please???" "Thanks Emma." Emma, he knew would always be there, no matter what. Will packed a bag for Merry. Emma reminded him not to worry. She loved to go shopping for Merry and did so at every opportunity. If Merry needed anything, Emma was going to see to it. Will reached down and picking Merry up, told her that these nice policemen were going to give him a ride to the hospital to check on Mommy and that he would see her very soon. "Is Mommy going to be alright, Daddy?" "Maybe now sweetness. Say a prayer for her like we do whenever someone we love is sick or unhappy." "I will, Daddy". "I prayed for Mommy a lot when we were away, because she was unhappy all the time". Will let out a long breath of air. Merry had seen too much in her three, almost four years on earth, and consequently understood much too much. When Emma and Merry left, Officer Baxter radioed the police station for a forensics team to come to the scene of a potential crime. Officer Williams provided Will a ride to the hospital to check on Rain.

Will sat in the back of the police car feeling lost, so very grateful he'd had Emma in his life. His mind played back the memory of his encounter with Emma and Rex. It had been raining that Wednesday morning. Will was preparing to go home from work. Patient load in the ER always seems heavier on rainy days. The weather had been miserable all morning and his own mood, as dark as the day. Will and Rain still had not found a neighborhood they wanted to build a new home in and frankly Rain's temper and mood swings had become unbearable. Going home was becoming more chore than joy. ER Shift over, he changed from his scrubs into jeans and a T-shirt and headed for his car. Low on gas, he'd decided to pull into a gas station near the hospital.

The neighborhood near the hospital was older, but immaculately kept. Manicured lawns, Cape Cods, Tudor and Country French brick homes lined the wide streets. Most impressive were the giant trees that shaded the lawns and streets. Even on this dank and ugly day, there was something comforting and protective about this place.

Will drove slowly down Maple Street and turned left onto Elm Street. As he turned the corner, a wonderful Cape Cod style home came into view. Of course, it was much larger than he could afford, and on a lot about two and one-half acres. Tired and in need of a moment of peace before he went home, Will pulled over to the curb in front of the home. It was still very early and very quiet. He closed his eyes and leaned back on the headrest, sighing. He was startled when he heard short quick yelps coming from the sidewalk near his car. Leaning his head on his left hand, he turned to see a tiny Toy Fox Terrier barking and jumping up and down in front of his car. As he turned to look over his shoulder for the owner, a small elderly woman came into view. The moments came back to Will's memory as though happening only the day before. "Rex...Rex, stop fussing at the nice man. What is wrong with you?" Will sat up and smiled at the small dog carrying such a fierce name. He was tiny, but feisty, and certainly protective.

The woman turned to look at the face with the tired eyes sitting in the car. "Is there something I can do for you, young man?" "I'm Mrs. Brown, this is my home right here." "I'm sorry, said Will, forgive my manners. I'm Will Thorpe and I hope you don't mind. I just stopped to admire the view. This is a very nice neighborhood and you have a lovely home. My wife and I want to build a house. The new subdivisions have chopped down all the beautiful trees though". Mrs. Brown smiled again. "I know what you mean, she sighed, that's what made George and I buy this big lot when we were younger. The trees really are beautiful, aren't they?" "George was.. is.. my late husband. He passed away about a year ago, lips trembling a little as she said it. "Arf, arf", yelped Rex, as he continued to warn Will to be off. "Rex, Rex, stop that, she chided her little dog. George and I, she apologized, were not able to have children, so Rex became our baby. I guess he's a little spoiled, but he's a good dog and we take care of each other now." "Mr. Thorpe?" said Mrs. Brown. "Please Mrs. Brown, it's actually Dr. Thorpe, but I prefer to be called Will". "Then you must call me Emmalyn. I know it sounds a little unusual. Sometimes people try to call me Emily, but I always correct them....I'm sorry, I'm rambling". "Dr.... Will, would you like to come in for a minute? I have some fresh coffee brewing, and my coffee is really pretty good, if I say so myself. George used to love it, she smiled bravely. I made a pineapple upside down cake this morning..?" Will looked into her eyes and saw both loneliness and a softness. He was tired and more than a little hungry. Hungrier, he was thinking for someone to talk to.

As Will stepped out of his car he noticed that the rain had stopped. Smiling now, "I'd like to Mrs. Brown, I'm sorry..Emmalyn". Rex continued to yap at Will, bouncing up and down and nipping at his heels, but this time playfully. Since George had died, the long walks and games with the balls in the garden had stopped. Rex had more stored up energy than he knew what to do with.

Will even remembered that he'd walked a little stiffly toward the soft grey brick house that day with the wonderful red front door whose brass carriage lights stood posted on either side of the door. The memories of that day would never leave him. The trees stirred in the gentle breeze adding even more freshness to the air. The light sprinkle of rain falling from the wet leaves misted Will's sleepy eyes refreshing him like a cool washcloth. As he looked back at the street from the front of the house, he felt safe, peaceful and very, very much like he belonged there. Emmalyn Brown smiled to herself this time, as she unlocked her door and invited Will to enter. When she got to know him better, she decided, then she would share her observations made that very first day. She and George had felt the same good feelings, she knew Will was experiencing for the first time. Emma found Will a sensitive young man. A rare thing. He'd reminded her so much of her George. It was as though George had come back to her. Will wiped his feet carefully, as he prepared to go i inside the house. "Now Rex, chirped, Mrs. Brown, wipe your feet too?" As Will glanced down at the six-pound and surely no more, puppy, he was surprised to see the dog doing an awkward little dance, actually trying to wipe his front paws and hind feet. Will involuntarily let out a hearty laugh, as Mrs. Brown joined in. It felt so good to laugh, they were both thinking. "Well Emmalyn, if you can do this well with Rex, I have a three-year-old daughter I'd love to enroll in your obedience class. They laughed together once more. This time, Emmalyn beamed a little brighter. Not only had she met someone she knew George would approve of, but maybe she would get to know his little one. She and George had both wanted a little girl. Children of their own was the only thing life had denied them.

As they walked through the house toward the kitchen, Will's eyes and senses took in fine furnishings, antiques and collectibles, leather-bound books and a quiet sense of security. Will could feel the love and continuity in this home. They passed the mahogany grandfather clock, keeping note of time and precious moments, as was expected. As Emmalyn pushed open the door to the kitchen, Will was met with a bright softness and cacophony of color, that came neither from the sun, nor paint. Facing the door was a huge bay window, with a window seat. It brought to the table in front of it, nature's splendor. This table needed no centerpiece. The window was the vase and it was filled with nature's ever- changing bounty. In the garden beyond, there was a lovely swinging chair bolted to an Elm tree branch and bounded on each side by miniature rose bushes. Over the sink was another large window with French-lace curtains that tied back, like those at the bay window. The counters were filled with wicker baskets, cook books, porcelain and ceramic sculpture, flower pots and the finest copper cookware collection Will had ever seen, heavy-gauge pieces accented with brass.

As Will sat down at the table, he had to fight the urge to curl his feet under himself on the chair, as the aroma of the warm butter, brown sugar and pineapple wafted toward his nose. The coffee was ready and so was he. Without much coaxing from Emmalyn, he ate two large pieces of cake and downed two cups of her wonderful coffee. He even succumbed to Emmalyn's urging to take some cake home to Rain and Merry. Emmalyn enjoyed fussing over and feeding him. George had been sick for so long before he died, there had been no need to cook the way she loved. Will had spent the better part of two hours listening to Emmalyn share the stories of her life with George. Will too, needed to share his own story. He told Emmalyn of his search for neighborhood in which to build a home, and the frustration of not being able to afford the kind of neighborhood she enjoyed each day.

Emmalyn liked this young man… this Dr. Will Thorpe. The seedling of an idea was taking root and she decided to take a chance. Her own home was on two and one-half acres, much of which she no longer used. Gardening was becoming more a chore than joy and as her hip complained of it often. She had no family to share this wonderful home with and missed having others around. What if, she offered to sell Will one acre of her property. She had a corner lot, and with a variance to allow for the building of an additional structure.... Emmalyn decided to take a chance and presented the idea to Will.

Will had not been financially ready to build a new home, but wanted one. Rain too, needed something to hold onto, anything that could possibly make her happy. Will had just finished his residency in surgery and money was still tight, but maybe....Rain had wanted a small Cape Cod with a bay window with lots of sunshine coming inside and Will, a good neighborhood where people were not afraid to say hello, streets on which they could stroll with Merry in tow and a garden which would offer starry constellations in the evening breeze. Trees, he beamed, fully grown, and beautiful.

He became so excited over her generosity and offer of friendship, he reached down and gave Emmalyn a hug, even before he realized what he'd done. She blushed from her head to her toes. No other man, except George, of course had ever hugged her quite like that. They were both embarrassed and pleased. Will wanted her to meet Rain and Merry, and asked if he could use her phone. He wanted to share the exciting news. Rain, Emmalyn decided, must be a wonderful girl, to have married someone as special as Will, someone as special as her George.

Will, returning to the present nightmare, sat in the back of the police car reliving that former feeling of hope for the future, given to him by this woman who had scarcely known him at the time. A tear rolled down his cheek and unbeknownst to him, that day, a single tear had made the heavens cry.

Six

o Longmire had lost a patient he'd never seen, nor touched.
Rain had uttered her last words almost an hour ago.
Hanging up the phone had been tough for the doctor. The
EMTs had communicated with him by two-way radio until arriving
at Rain's home, and now the phone would be, no longer needed.

Even though presumptive signs of death existed, the paramedics
were required to search for any signs of life. Rain's basic vital signs
had been nonexistent. There had been no response to painful stimuli.
No carotid, femoral, nor other heartbeat or blood pressure, either by
palpation, or auscultation. They could find no breath sounds, nor chest
motion. There was the absence of corneal and deep tendon reflexes;
flat baseline on all ECG leads; rigor mortis had begun to set in and
a definitive coldness of body temperature although she had been
wrapped in a blanket. Dr. Longmire suggested they dispense with
use of the body bag for the sake of the presence of Will and Merry.

Bo Longmire walked slowly out of the ER and into the sunshine.
He wanted to see and hear the sounds of life. When he returned to
the ER, he noticed an influx of additional hospital personnel, of all
levels. It made the room seem busier than it actually was. Groups of
nurses, doctors, aides and even housekeeping staff, whispering and

shaking their heads, were coming into the ER, as though requested. The news had circulated quickly. Their curiosity about the morning events had brought them in like research ants. Picking up blank Emergency Room Treatment Record forms, Dr. Longmire headed for his office. Bo sat quietly recording the event of Rain's call for help and subsequent death. He knew that the circumstances would automatically require an autopsy and coroner's investigation. Death as a certainty could only, in cases like this, be certified at that time. Bo scribbled, "Determined that patient's death occurred between approximately 0900-1000 hours. Preparations made to contact coroner's office for subsequent transport. Final determinations to be confirmed following arrival of DOA/DAR." Bo concluded the notes he'd need to present regarding Rain's death. A heaviness had settled upon him. Knowing who she was made it all the more difficult. Having to share her final words with her husband, his colleague, would drain him.

Rain's body arrived connected to an IV and EKG leads. Trauma Room #1 had been prepared, expected to be used for resuscitative treatment. Dr. Longmire examined Rain for any signs of life. Finding none, as was expected, the body was removed to the morgue, pending transfer to the coroner's office. Incidental to his notes, was a finding of gunpowder markings on the right hand, consistent with possible attempted suicide. ER notes completed by the paramedics confirmed the presence of a weapon, found at the scene and secured by the attendant policemen. Bo wanted to leave the hospital, to go home, to hug his wife and children and to praise the Lord for the blessing of their well-being. Officer Baxter and Will entered the ER together. Will had requested to see Rain once more. This was irregular, as the investigation into the details of her death was underway. Will would be allowed to go to the morgue, escorted by Officer Baxter, but was told that he could not be left alone with her body, nor could he touch her. So far lost in the surreality of it all, Will agreed. He wanted only to look at her. Maybe, just to be able to believe that she was really gone.

The clinical reality of the morgue never bothered Will. But never before, had he to find anyone whom he loved there. By this time, the entire hospital staff was abuzz with the news of Rain Thorpe's death. Will stared vacantly at the many faces approaching him, offering consolation. He was as polite as always, but offered nothing. This great pain, he wanted to share with no one.

Rain, pale and curled almost into the fetal position appeared so much less powerful in death. Her wishes had filled his life, ruled his world and made unhappy most of their days together. He had forgiven it all when she gave him the special gift...Merry. For that much, he would be eternally grateful.

Officer Baxter stood and waited in a corner of the morgue. An orderly had pulled Rain's body out of cold storage and uncovered her face. The policeman nodded for the orderly to leave. He then watched as Will placed his hands up to his own lips, and while tears flowed freely, his broad shoulders heaved in paroxysms of grief. Dr. Longmire appeared. Officer Baxter clenched his jaw and wiping away a tear, nodded permission for him to go to Will. Dr. Longmire put his arms around Dr. Thorpe and held him like a child, as he cried. Officer Baxter could see Dr. Longmire whispering to Dr. Thorpe. Whatever it was, it had made Dr. Thorpe turn away and lean against a wall. Dr. Longmire patted his colleague on the shoulder and walked away. Officer Baxter reminded Dr. Longmire that he would be questioned at a later date by the assigned detective.

Head down, shoulders drooping, Will walked over toward the police officer, ready to go. They headed to the precinct for questioning. Officer Baxter knew that it would be pretty routine though, in this case. It had already been confirmed by at least four other hospital staff members that Will had arrived at work at approximately 0600 hours, and remained on duty, without ever leaving the premises.

Will was released from the police station by about three that afternoon. The detective assigned to the case believed this to be suicide, but had to await the final coroner's report and death certificate. He'd promised to call Will when he knew more.

Will wanted to see Merry. He pulled into his driveway at 1112 Elm Street knowing that nothing would ever be the same again. Leaving the car in the drive, Will walked slowly across the grass to 1111 Elm Street, to Emma's house. Emma had been looking out for him to return home, and met him as he knocked at the door. "Come in, son", she said not needing to look at his face. His rigid silence told all. "Will, sit down, I've made some coffee". Even Rex sensed something of the sadness in Will. Instead of yapping, as he usually did, he walked over, jumped up on Will's lap, looking sorrowfully into Will's eyes and just put his head down. "Merry, poor baby is asleep." "I gave her a bath and put her down about two hours ago. She hasn't budged since". "Will, honey, Rain is not just sick, is she?" "Will dropped his head into his hands, shoulders shaking, and unable to hold the flood of tears within his fingers.

Rex became alarmed and licked Will's hand trying to comfort him. "She's gone, Emma". "She shot herself with that 22, I got her last year". "She never wanted that gun. If I'd never forced her to have it and maybe she would still be alive today....And Merry would still have a mother". Emma put her arms around him and let him cry. Will pulled a handkerchief out of his pocket and wiped his own face, trying to regain control. Emma left Will alone for a moment, knowing that the oncoming deluge of tears was necessary in order to purge the pain. She returned with a warm washcloth.

Will lifted his head and looked into Emma's face. "What am I going to do without her?" "Live on, son". "Merry and I will take good care of you. I suspect Rex will help too", she said, smiling bravely. Rex, hearing his named, yapped in affirmation. ...and finally have a life worth living, Emma was thinking. Rain's name had always seemed so appropriate to her cloudy disposition and nature. She had been incapable and unwilling to bring Will Thorpe or Merry, any lasting peace or happiness, until now, she thought. "Life, she reminded Will, would have other plans for him". George's death had led Emma to this new chapter of her life, which now included the equivalent of a son and granddaughter. The emptiness had at first seemed so senseless and unfair. She'd remembered asking God in a moment of despair, "Where are You?" To which He replied, "How do you think you got this far?" The revelation had made her laugh aloud for the very first time following George's death and funeral. She knew then that somehow everything was going to be alright. She knew that George and God had always loved and protected her and would continue to do no less, and she loved them both. Emma knew too that together, as a family, they would get through this. 'Will, why don't you go and snuggle up with Merry and get some rest. When you wake up, I'll cook for both of you. Will smiled for the first time since Rain died. His parents were gone too. There was no one else to cook for him. Merry lay quietly snoring in the middle of the large bed. She had been scrubbed and combed and loved back to a state of some peace. Will could see Emma's love and goodness all over the child. Taking off his hoes, he bowed down onto his knees, burying his face in his hands, he prayed. "Heavenly Father, in whom I place all of my trust and faith, help me", looking over at Merry, "help us", he restated, "to understand this moment we must endure". "Thank you for the blessing of a mother figure and friend in Emmalyn Brown. Lord, I don't understand why this had to happen. I'm sorry Father, but I'm angry at Rain, and angry at myself. Maybe, if I had handled this all differently, at least Rain might still be alive. At least Merry would still have a mother." Speaking to Rain, for the first time in his prayer, he said, "Rain, why" Why? Why Ian?" The deep hurt that he was feeling was not for Rain, nor Ian, but for himself, for not being enough for Rain, nor worthy enough of Ian's loyalty. God's sigh must have nudged Merry, for in that moment, she rolled over and sighed. Reminding Will that for little Miss Merry Adams Thorpe, the best Rain had to offer him, he would always be more than enough. Will knelt for a long time just staring at his baby. He could finish his prayer now. "Into your hands do I commit my soul and sprit, past, present and future, and confess that I am lost here…but know that to be lost inside the mighty hands of Jesus Christ is to found, indeed". Will stayed on his knees. When he could cry no more, he climbed into bed with Merry and fell fast asleep.

Three hours later, he could feel someone tapping on his face. Merry was now awake, hungry and anxious to know about mommy. Will smiled with his mouth only. Merry reached over to her father and stretched one of his eyeballs open. "Daddy?, she asked, are you awake?" Then she gave his head a hug. Emma heard their voices coming from the guestroom and entered carrying a tray of steaming hot food. Will was looking at her and asking for help with his eyes. "Hi, Grandma", said Merry, sitting next to Will looking crumpled, but rested. "Hello my little darlin", you sure look hungry". "Grandma she said, look, Daddy's here!" "I know, pumpkin", she replied. "And I've brought enough food for both of you".

"Will, she said, if it's alright with you, why don't we all go down to the park and feed the ducks in the pond?" Will looked at her gratefully. "I think that's a great idea Emm, but only if Merry eats all of her food". Bouncing up and down on the bed, she exclaimed, "I will! I will". "And that goes for you too Will. You need to eat son". Now, it was Merry's turn to laugh at him.

Will had been so caught up in the day's events that he'd forgotten to eat. He finished before Merry, and announced that he was going back to their house to shower and change. Emma promised to help Merry get dressed for the excursion. Will needed the escape from reality the shower would offer. Stepping into the steamy shower, he once again let his tears fall. He scrubbed vigorously as though he could wash away the nightmare clinging to him. Reaching for the showerhead to help steady himself, he just stood there letting the water run. Will fought no more. As Will stepped out of the shower, the phone rang. Wrapping the towel around his waist, he picked up the receiver. "Hi, Daddy? Are you almos' ready?" The sound of Merry's voice and love for him, filled the void he was feeling. "Yes, my sweet, he replied. Be there in a few minutes". Will said a silent prayer asking for help in telling Merry the news. Will was sure the phone call had been Emma's idea. She must have been worried about

him. It felt so good to have others around him who cared enough
to miss his presence. So excited about going to the park, Merry had
insisted that she and Grandma meet her daddy in front of the house.
Emma and Will each took a hand and off the three went. Merry was
wearing a raincoat with a hood. Will had not noticed the gray clouds
floating overhead. Merry looked so cute and well-tended. Will was
so grateful to Emma, for so much.

As they walked to the park, Merry gave a running tour of all
of the neighborhood, points of interest, pets, flowers and foliage.
Will could tell that she had missed their discussions" about life. She
opened up like a sieve. Rain had probably not spent much time
talking to her while at Ian's, Will thought sadly.

"Look, Grandma! Look Daddy!" Merry had seen the ducks and
was so excited. Emma handed Merry the small plastic bags of bread
crumbs to share with them. Will sat her down on his lap, lest there
become one more duckling swimming around with the others.
Merry smiled at Will and started throwing the food. The ducks
swam close enough to get the crumbs. Merry was thrilled when they
came toward her. A light sprinkling of rain had begun. Will reached
down and pulled up her hood. The three sat quietly until all of the
crumbs had been dispensed.

"Merry", her Daddy said, as he picked her up and turned her on
his lap, to face him, need to tell you something very, very important."
Her enormous brown eyes gave him undivided attention. "It's about
Mommy, sweetheart". "Is Mommy coming home today? Is she better
now?" Merry interrupted. The tears filling her father's eyes now
were frightening her. "No, my little darling. Mommy's not coming
home any more." "But why Daddy? Did she go away again to see
my godfather Ian"? Emma looked away sharply. So that is what had
happened, she thought. Sighing deeply, she tried Sighing within,
she had to quiet the long, slow breath she needed to release. "No,
baby. Remember when the ambulance came and took Mommy to
the hospital this morning?"

Merry nodded, frowning. "Mommy was very sick and the

doctors tried to help her, but they couldn't. "But Daddy, can't you help her? Can't you go to the hospital and help her?" Merry was becoming frantic and squiggled down from her father's lap. Running to Emma, she cried "I want my Mommy. want my Mommy!" Emma lost her composure for the first time, but quickly regained it. "Merry honey, your Mommy has gone to Heaven to live with God". "But Daddy, she said, you told me that God is your friend. Can't he help us?" she asked in desperation. "Mommy is gone sweetness". Will could think of nothing else to say. The three-year old looked into her father's teary eyes and said "Ohhhh Daddy" and hugged him tightly. Will and Emma knew Merry did not understand. Emma and Will took turns holding her. After a little while, Will told her that Mommy had said to tell her goodbye and that she would always miss her, and would watch over her from heaven. The dark cloud had passed over them. The sun was beginning to shine again. Emma saw a rainbow and said "Merry, look up, baby. See the rainbow in the sky"? Merry nodded, lips downturned. "Every time you see a rainbow, it's your Mommy saying "I love you". You just smile at the rainbow and talk to your mommy, because she'll be right there with you. Your mama Rain's love, all wrapped up with a bow…a Rain bow baby". Merry understood something. "Can I talk to her right now"? "Yes", Emma and Will said simultaneously. "I miss you Mommy,. but Daddy says God will take care of you. Can you come and visit me again soon?" Will answered for Rain. "Mommy said yes darling. You have to listen now to her with your heart, not your ears. In your heart you'll be able to hear her". Merry put her head down on Emma's lap. "Merry, my baby, you will still have Grandma Emma and Daddy to love you. We will have to take care of each other now". Each sat, lost quietly immersed in separate thoughts. In silence they prepared to go home. Emma suggested that Will and Merry stay with her until things became more settled. Will would need the support and agreed thankfully. Merry said nothing.

Seven

etective Joe Gacki had been in the police business fourteen years. He'd seen all manner of human cruelty and tragedy, but suicide still remained the truest mystery of all, for him. He was a good Catholic and believed in his heart, that the one sin God would never forgive was suicide. True or not, he believed. He'd gone down to the morgue to talk to the coroner this morning on the Thorpe case. The autopsy had been completed. IMMEDIATE CAUSE OF DEATH: Acute Hemorrhage. CONDITIONS IF ANY WHICH GAVE RISE TO THE IMMEDIATE CAUSE: Laceration of Heart. STATING THE UNDERLYING CAUSE LAST: Gunshot Wound of the Abdomen. ACCIDENT, SUICIDE, HOMICIDE, UNDETERMINED PENDING INVESTIGATION: Suicide. DESCRIBE HOW INJURY OCCURRED: Discharged 0.22 Caliber Gun into Abdomen. INTERVAL BETWEEN ONSET AND DEATH: About 60 minutes. Detective Gacki finished reviewing the death certificate and asked for copies of both the Certificate and Final Autopsy Report. One last loose end and he could probably wrap the case up by the end of the week. If it all checked out, the body could be released for burial soon.

Detective Gacki went straight to the airport from the Coroner's office. His flight to Palmetto Springs from Bristol Point, would be departing shortly. Boarded and waiting for takeoff, he reached into his jacket pocket and unfolded the note taken from a pad found by policemen at the crime scene, lying next to the victim. "Ian 717 429 3334", had been scribbled on it. Phone company records revealed that the number belonged to the law offices of Bosch, Schuyler and Smith-Marshal. Further investigation revealed "an Ian Adams", employed there.

Detective Gacki arrived in Palmetto Springs in about forty minutes. The weather was gorgeous, with blue skies and puffy white clouds. He took a cab to 444 Tower Plaza. The Law Offices occupied the entire fourth floor of the lavish building. The elevator doors opened effortlessly into a lobby replete with Kentia Palms, marble floors and much leather furniture. One of three receptionists greeted him smiling. "Good Morning, Sir, may I be of assistance to you? Smiling tersely, he replied, Yes please, the office of Ian Adams". "One moment please?", came the almost automated reply. "Suzette, I have a gentleman here to see Mr. Adams. A Mr.???, she smiled reaching for Gacki's business card. A Detective Gacki. Alright, she smiled into the phone. "I'll send him right in". The receptionist pointed a long-nailed finger in the direction of Ian's suite.

Suzette was waiting for him. "I'm sorry Detective, but your name is not listed on Mr. Adams' schedule". Showing his police shield, he stated "I know, Miss I'm here on official police business, but this should not take too long." "Of course, she apologized, I'm Suzette Butler, Mr. Adams' Paralegal and Office Administrator. Frowning slightly, "perhaps I can be of some assistance to you." He's currently with a client. But if you care to wait, he should be available soon." "Not a problem", stated the Detective. "Please, sir, have a seat. May I offer you some coffee or perhaps some tea?" She waved her hand toward a mahogany sideboard placed against a wall in the reception area. Sterling silver coffee and tea service, glistened in the bright sunshine. Covered dishes, he was informed, held a light continental brunch, if he cared to partake. "Don't mind if I do". Detective Gacki went over to help himself. Suzette smiled to herself recalling the jokes she'd heard about policemen, doughnuts and coffee.

Ian appeared after some minutes, smiling and shaking hands with his new client. In his hand, he held a retainer check which he promptly handed over to Suzette. Detective Gacki could not make out the exact amount, as he rose from his seat to meet Ian, but the was pretty sure, it contained more than a few zeroes.

Suzette introduced her boss to the detective and reached for the check which would need to go directly to accounting. Placing the check in a special envelope, she nodded to Ian. He smiled and nodded in return, understanding that she would be away from her desk for a brief time, while she made the deposit with the firm's accounting office. "Suzette, take the phones off the hook please, until you return?" She did so, and left. "Detective, please come in."

Ian's office was not as large as Detective Gacki though it would be, but it was certainly outfitted in the grandest style. It was obvious to the detective that this Ian Adams was very much accustomed to luxury. His phone number lying next to the Thorpe woman would definitely require an explanation. Once again producing the shield, he proceeded with the questioning. "I'm here to try to ascertain your relationship to one deceased, Rain Thorpe" stated the detective. Ian stood up quickly without thinking, recovered, and sat down again. He tried to keep his voice from cracking. "You did say deceased?" Ian looked at the policeman in utter surprise. The detective took out his notepad and took some notes. The news of Rain's death, certainly evoked a response. Ian looked even more nervous. Just then the door opened without a preceding knock. Not immediately noticing that Ian was busy, "Ian darling, what time is dinner tonight and where are we going. I heard the phone ringing this morning".......her voice trailed off. Standing, Ian says, "Detective Gacki, let me introduce to you, my... Sean Smith-Marshal" They shook hands. "Ian, I am so sorry, I didn't knock. Forgive me detective. Ian, call me at home later. Sorry again, Ian? Detective?" Sean left as quickly as she'd breezed in.

"Now, where were we detective? Ian stated, offering no explanation of his relationship to his visitor. Scribbling Sean Smith-Marshal on his pad, He reminded Ian... "Rain Thorpe, I believe". "Yes she passed away yesterday morning. Not intending to reveal any more than absolutely necessary, Ian countered the question. "Tell me detective, how have you come to link my name to hers? Note scribbling again. Answered question with question. Hiding what?, he then wrote.

Ian relaxed and reminded himself that he was a lawyer and that he had done nothing wrong. He decided to just answer the questions, he knew would come. "I'm sorry detective. I do know, .did know Rain Thorpe, and in fact her entire family. Her husband Will and I were best friends in college. I was best man at their wedding and am also godfather, to their daughter Merry Adams Thorpe. The child's middle name is also my last name. But I'm sure you know all of this." Ian stopped himself. He speech had been delivered like a confession. Bating, the detective went on, "Yes I do ". Ian sat back in his chair, spinning around to face the window. Then I'm sure you know about the affair. Again leading Ian, "Yes, I do. Would you care to share your side of the story? Ian stood up crossing his arms in front of his chest. He sighed, offering that "For all concerned it was an unfortunate lapse in judgement. Rain and I just, happened. Will, her husband had been my best friend in college. She...we... When I finally told her it was all over, she went back home to her husband." Turning to face the detective, he said "and that's all there is". "When was the last time you spoke to Rain Thorpe?" "Actually, early this morning. She called me here at work wanting to continue our relationship. I told her no". "Mr. Adams, can you account for your whereabouts for the last two days and nights?" "Yes I can, Suzette, my assistant can confirm my days and hours here at work, and Sean Smith-Marshal and I have been together each of the two nights in question. Without looking up "BINGO!", wrote Detective

Gacki in his pad. Now all the pieces fit. Affair with best friend's wife. New girlfriend, a knockout who also happens to share the name of one of the law firm partners. Detective Gacki stood up and put away his notepad. He reached for Ian's hand. The two shook hands. "I hope you don't mind if I confirm your Whereabouts with both your assistant and your. friend?" "No I don't". Here is a number you can use to reach Sean and Suzette is, of course, at her desk".

Detective Gacki met with Suzette at her desk. She did confirm that Ian had worked each day and late on both days. For reaction, he decided to inform Suzette that he was looking into the circumstances surrounding the death of a Mrs. Rain Thorpe. Suzette looked shocked. That said enough. The detective decided to call Sean from the airport. Rain had committed suicide. No one else had a hand in the act. Now he was sure he understood the entire scenario. As a detective, he was satisfied. Case closed, he wrote in his notebook. He called Sean at the number Ian had given him. She validated everything Ian had said, but told a little more. Sean had been seeing Ian for several months. Rain had only left a day ago. Ian had been two-timing both of them. Detective Gacki could not blame Ian for the choice between the two, after all, Sean was drop-dead gorgeous. Her father's ownership of the law firm certainly didn't poison the pill either. It was clear that Ian was ambitious and reckless, but not homicidal. Joe Gacki had seen too many men like Ian, on and off the job. Men like him wore neon signs that spelled "dangerous curves ahead". Well-lighted signs that attracted all kinds of women, like insects to a bug light. The outcome was always the same and too often lives were lost in the entanglement. By comparison, thought Detective Gacki, his own life was dull and predictable. At least all elements of it were truly his own.

Grateful to have landed safely, back home in Bristol Point, Detective Gacki headed back to his office to finish his report. Office Baxter's notes had made reference to a Dr. Longmire. Upon questioning the doctor by phone, the detective learned of Rain's last words. Not surprised by their content, he added the details to his report. Her words provided the multi-layered texture to his report of which only truth is capable.

Detective Gacki placed a call to the Coroner. The two discussed their parallel Investigations, which left both men satisfied of the finding of death, by suicide, self-inflicted gunshot wound. The Coroner's office would release the body for burial, without autopsy.

Eight

ill continued to go to work at the hospital despite the stares and whispers. Bo Longmire offered his condolences and friendship to Will. It seemed strange to Will, to be surrounded by the same people day after day and never really know one another, until something good or bad happens. Rain's death had provided more conversations with colleagues and co-workers than he'd ever had. Will knew they meant well, but it was at times overwhelming. Will worked instead of staying at home because he needed routine and continuity. Rain's death reconfigured his entire life and future. A fact he did not wish to agonize over just yet. She had not even been buried. Merry was safely tucked away at Grandma Emma's house. At least a few times each day, she would ask for her mommy, then cry when told that she could not see her. Emma's heart was breaking over the circumstances life presented this young child. She was going to make sure that Merry was loved back to a sense of security. Will split his time between the two homes at 1111 and 1112 Elm. Emma's home provided a refuge for them, while his own home a reality check. For now, Will needed to straddle the two for sanity sake.

Will was sitting alone in the hospital cafeteria when his pager went off. He headed back to the ER. Medical clerk Van Helkins handed him a written message to call the coroner's office. Will walked slowly back to his office. Leaning on the edge of his chair, he rocked back and forth a few times before calling. Then he dialed. "Dr. Thorpe returning the coroner's call", he said. The coroner was preparing for an autopsy so his assistant answered the call. "Dr. Thorpe, this is Dr. Nguyen. I am the Assistant Coroner. The Coroner wishes to express his condolences to you, and to inform you that the autopsy on your wife, would not be needed. The Death Certificate has been signed. Your wife's death has been ruled a suicide. The police have been notified of this. The body of the deceased can now be released for funeral arrangements. Have you the name of a mortuary yet?" Will was trying to take it all in, but his brain refused to move forward. "Uh, I'm sorry Dr. Nguyen, I…No, not yet, but I will make the necessary arrangements immediately. Thank you for the call". Will hung up the phone not knowing why he had thanked the man.

Reality now stood face to face with Will. He called Emma with the news. She and Merry were baking cookies. Later they were going outside to pick flowers from the garden. "Will honey, if you don't mind, I could take care of the arrangements for you. The Morgan Funeral Home did such a marvelous job with my George and they are such nice people. That is… she stammered, unless you want to do this yourself?" "Will, Merry wants to say hello". "Hi Daddy, we made cookies!"

"Alright sweetie, save some for me, please?" "Bye Daddy" and off she went. "Emma, I don't want to burden you. You've been so wonderful to us already…" "Will honey, I want to say something to you. It's important that you know this. When George died, so did my whole world. Since finding you and little Merry my life is full again. George and I were blessed with a love that only soulmates ever know. I must be honest and say that I never really understood Rain. But I did pray that she would someday come to understand the blessings that surrounded her, and now there is nothing else I can do for her. I would be grateful if you would let me make this last gesture." Will was moved beyond words and said only, "Thanks Emm". Emma understood what he was feeling.

Will decided to take the afternoon off. He could no longer concentrate. Forest Wethers, the Chief of Surgery agreed immediately to the request, insisting that Will consider an extended leave until after the funeral. Will agreed. He spent the next hour checking patient charts that needed updating. Leaving them on his desk for the Medical Records Clerk, to pick up later, he departed.

Will went directly to Emma's house to pick up Merry. He wanted to take her out for a picnic. It was a beautiful day and he wanted to spend time alone with her. When he arrived, Merry was sitting on the floor playing with her dolls. Emma was on the phone. Motioning to him to come sit down with them, Emma concluded her phone conversation. "Thank you so much. I knew you would handle everything as well as you had for my George. Yes, Dr. Thorpe will come in tomorrow to sign the necessary papers, goodbye".

"Will, I have just spoken to the Morgan Funeral Home. They would be happy to handle the arrangements. You can go tomorrow to sign the papers so they can pick up Rain and prepare her. I will take care of the other arrangements. Will glanced quickly down at Merry, who was playing mommy. She was totally oblivious to the meaning of their words. "Emm, I've decided to take some time off, so I can help in any way we need. Right now, I'd like to take Merry out for a picnic". Emma read his thoughts. "I understand. In fact, while you two are gone, I will go down to Morgan's and look at caskets. I'll bring back brochures so that you can make a final selection. I think it might be easier for you, this way. If you don't mind, I would like to shop for a suit for Rain and one for Merry". "Emm, that is very generous of you. I don't know anything about selecting women's clothing. But I had not decided about taking Merry to the funeral". Merry heard her name this time. "Taking me where Daddy?" "On a picnic my sweet. Now go get ready". "Can I bring my dolls?" "May I bring them, Will corrected". Merry laughed and said "May I Please?" "Go into the guestroom Merry and get your shoes", Emma encouraged, and don't forget your jacket, it's on the bed". Emma had dressed her in a pink denim jean and jacket outfit. Merry loved pink and so had Rain. Looking over at Emma he smiled and said only, "Rain and Merry both love pink". Emma stood up and gave Will a hug. Merry came running in to ask for help with getting her shoes on and tied. The crumpled jacket in her arms was dragging the floor. Finally, she was ready to go. "Will, here are a set of keys for the house". Come and go as you please. We are family now." Will closed his eyes softly and nodded. Merry was excited and ready to run.

Emma watched the two of them from the window. Will wanted to protect the baby. She'd understood that, but the funeral and saying goodbye to her mother even if she would not yet understand, was a necessary fact of life. Emma was actually more concerned about Will, than Merry. Children have an amazing resiliency. Emma would dress mother and child alike, and both would be pretty, in pink. The next days flew. So much to do. Too soon came the time to say goodbye to mother and wife. The newspaper obituary for Rain had been brief. Rain had not made any friends in their neighborhood. So Emma and Will decided that the small memorial chapel would provide ample seating. Interment would take place at the Pinelawn Cemetery, just outside town.

Will chose to go see Rain early in the morning, alone, to say his own goodbye to his wife. A soft light glowed in the room above the casket. It had been opened in preparation. Will entered and stood at the casket, watching Rain. She looked as though she were only sleeping. Emma had selected a beautiful ice pink colored dress. It swirled softly in ruffles at her neck. Her hands were folded across her chest as the gentle folds of the ruffles on the sleeves caressed them. Rain's hair lay in waves around her shoulders. Will reached out to touch her hair. He had always loved it. Bending over, he kissed it for the last time. Taking off his wedding band, he tucked it underneath her hands. Her reign was over and yet in spite of everything, she would still forever own a place in his heart.

Later Will, Emma and Merry returned together before the service would begin so that Merry could see her mother. They both had tried to explain to the child that she was going to see Rain, but hat Mommy could not wake up. Merry did not understand. Once more Rain seemed to neglect her only child, and forevermore seemed destined to hurt the child over, and again. Will held Merry in his arms. When she heard the piped funeral music begin, she looked around for its source. This was a place Merry had not ever seen before. Her head turned in every direction as she tried to take it all in. They entered the chapel where Rain lay and stood, both adults quietly watching Merry. They whispered to her as if to cue her. "Daddy, she whispered also saying to him, "I want to see Mommy". Will took a deep breath and walked slowly toward the casket. "Mommy!" Merry nearly shouted". Will hugged her close and whispered into her ear. "Mommy cannot wake up baby, but she can hear you". "Daddy can I kiss Mommy?" Tears filling his eyes, he said "Yes, I think Mommy would like that very much." As Will leaned over to hold Merry for the kiss, one of his own tears fell into the corner of Rain's left eye. When he stood up again and looked at Rain, she appeared to be crying too. Emma took Rain from her father's arms and sat down with her. Will knelt down in front of the casket, praying and crying. Will hated for Merry to see him this way, but today he couldn't help, even himself. Will's parents had long since passed away, first his father of a stroke, then his mother, the next year, of a broken heart, he'd suspected. He had no siblings nor other family ties. Even though Emma helped to fill so much of the void, he still felt so alone, in that moment. It would have been some help if Rain's family could have been present, but she had no one Rain had been an orphan. The emptiness of her inner core reflected in her restless and unhappy spirit. Will had accepted this fact as an explanation of so much of her behavior.

One by one, his colleagues came in to pay last respects. Will could not hear the words spoken in eulogy. His eyes only witnessed the many wreaths of flowers and lips moving offering condolences. Out of helplessness, he permitted the funeral home director to lead him like a frightened child in a school play, through the service and the limousine ride to Pinelawn for the burial. At the cemetery Merry asked only once where was Mommy. "In heaven with God now", came the quiet reply. She didn't ask again.

Detective Gacki hated funerals. He did not want to intrude on Will's sadness, but he at least owed Dr. Thorpe official closure to the police investigation. He waited at the cemetery for the burial services to be completed. Will maintained control of his emotions as Detective Gacki repeated the words of the Assistant Coroner.

$\mathcal{N}ine$

Will never worried about the outcome. He had committed no crime. The day Rain decided to die, she took with herself, a total of three lives. None ever to be the same again.

Will moved blindly through the next weeks. Emma had taken on full-time care of Merry while he worked. Father and daughter had moved back into their house at 1112 Elm. Merry started having nightmares, always involving her mother.

She now spent as much time in her father's bedroom as she used to, happily playing in her own. Will's night sweats following the funeral, awakened him more than once. All of his dreams involved not Rain's, but Merry's death. He could not bear the thought of losing the child. Merry gave freely, the love and devotion Rain could never. Merry was for Will, the better side of Rain, and probably, the only reason their continued marriage made any sense. Merry's very existence bestowed upon Rain's life, some meaning.

Will's boss, and Chief of Surgery, Dr. Forest Wethers watched as he threw himself into work. He was worried about Will and wanted to help. A medical conference on Medical-Legal Ethics was coming up and Dr. Wethers was scheduled to attend. He had been looking forward to going. This year's conference was being held in Hawaii. Dr. Wethers had made plans for his family to join him on the trip to Honolulu. His wife was also excited about the trip. The hospital was providing his funding. Forest knew that Will would decline his offer, but he had every intention of sending Will, in his place, no matter what.

"Dr. Thorpe, please report to Dr. Wether's office", announced the hospital operator. "Dr. Thorpe"... and once again. Hearing his name, this time, Will finished the prescription for Ibuprofen 800 mg, and Flexeril, he'd just written for an ER patient involved earlier that morning in a minor fender-bender, who was complaining of back spasms. Will suggested that the patient follow-up with his regular physician should his complaint continue. He went to see the Chief of Surgery.

Will knocked on Dr. Wether's office door. "Come in", said the voice behind the door. "Good Morning, Will. Please come in and sit down", invited his boss. "Will, I have a favor to ask of you". Now I know, that with your recent family tragedy, this may not be the best time to ask, but I need for you to go out of town to a conference, in my place". There's been a rush put on budget projection reports, so it's going to throw my plans completely out of the window. Now before you say no, I realize that you are a single parent now, but my accommodations included a suite of rooms. Since I was planning to take my family along, the invitation for you to do the same, is open. I'll bet your little one would just love playing on the beach". "Will, he said smiling, this year's conference is going to be held in Hawaii". If you can find someone to go along to care for your daughter, then you won't be away worrying about her. Truthfully Will, you'd be doing me a favor. After all you are the best man to go in my place. As your friend, I'd like to see you go, just because". Will smiled at him. "Forest, I know what you're doing and I appreciate it. In fact I am going to say yes to this, and thank you". Will decided that it was time to say yes to life, once again. Will knew that his marriage had preceded Rain in death. When he'd told Emma and Merry, all Merry heard were "beach" and airplane.

Emma had not been to Hawaii since she and George honeymooned there. She was as excited as Merry. They packed lightly, as everyone had decided to make this an excuse for a shopping spree, too. Will was beginning to breathe again. Emmalyn firmly established as mother-figure of this new family, was happier than she'd been since George's passing.

Will and his family were picked up by limousine for the ride to the airport. Will was grateful for the fact that this limo had been white and not black. Merry did not seem to mind riding in it, and seemed not to remember her first limousine ride. Emma had fussed over the details of preparation. She too, needed a vacation and the airline tickets were for first-class. Will, Emma and Merry reveled in all the luxuries first-class afforded, as Hawaii met them with its legendary brilliant blue skies, sunshine, unending white beaches, and of course, complimentary welcome leis. Their hotel suite was on the twenty-first floor. The panoramic view from the suite afforded an oceanfront view of the and of Diamond Head. Room service, and a nap were ordered by Grandma Emma for Merry, with the promise of an ocean frolic later, if she cooperated. Merry ate lunch and fell asleep easily with the wind from the ocean blowing softly across her face. Emma decided to take a bath and rest also. "Will, she suggested, why don't you go down for a swim? Take some time for yourself, for a change?" Emma always knew what Will needed. Smiling, he said, Emm, I think I'm gonna' keep you". Emma blushed and grinned back at him. "Go on, then, get out of here!", she laughed.

Will unpacked his swimming trunks, grabbed a towel from the bathroom, sunglasses and headed for the ocean. The hotel sat on the beach, separated by cabanas and an Olympic-sized swimming pool. Will never understood the need for a pool, right next to the ocean. Who was he to complain. The best of everything was coming his way, it seemed, and it was time.

Will finished his swim and stretched out on the beach to relax.

His body had been so tight. He'd lived the last six months under constant tension. His muscles responded happily to this renewed exercise. When he returned to the room, little Miss was up, dressed adorably in an orange, yellow and pink swimsuit with sun umbrella to match and bucket and shovel, ready to take on Hawaii's best beach. This happy day, she played and swam until exhausted. Later, the three ate dinner, courtesy of room service, by candlelight on the balcony of their suite. Each had been lightly toasted by the sun and was shining brightly from head to toe.

Will and Merry snuggled up together after dinner to watch one of Merry's movie choices, in their room, while Emma settled in with a good book, in her own. Will's conference would begin in the morning and he needed rest. Tomorrow, Merry and Emma had plans to go shopping at the Ala Moana Mall, one of the largest in the world. Merry fell asleep in about twenty minutes. Will covered her up, turned off the light along with the television and said a prayer thanking God, for carrying them so far forward.

Will dressed quietly for the conference, not wanting to awaken Merry, nor Emma. The abundant fresh air and sunshine had breathed new life into all of them, he thought as he picked up his room key card from the dresser. Slipping out on tiptoe, he blew a kiss to a lightly-snoring Merry. He checked to make sure the note he'd left Emma with his itinerary could be easily found, in case Emma needed or just wanted, to find him. The swim he taken the day before, left him with an enormous appetite. He headed for the hotel restaurant "Chez Moi", to eat. A bountiful spread of fruit dishes lay before him. He could smell fresh pineapple and feel his stomach begin to rumble. Covered dishes revealed light steam and delectable aromas, only some of which Will could identify. He picked up a plate and filled it with much early morning temptation. As he looked around for a table, he noticed only one other guest seated so early. A beautiful woman, perhaps in her mid-fifties sat reading from a stack of newspapers spread out on her table. She was dressed in impeccable style. Her dark hair was swept up into a French twist revealing a long slender neck. Her head held an aristocratic tilt, as it rested ever so lightly on her right hand. She must be here for the conference too, Will thought, as he dove into the feast before him. Will ordered a Parisian café-au-lait, to finish the delicious meal. The oversized cup of hot milk with tea poured in, warmed his hands as he sipped slowly, allowing this latest good fortune to overtake him. Some minutes later, the room began to fill with the sounds of hungry guests. Will checked his watch. The conference would begin in about an hour, so he decided to wander around and check out the agenda, programs and schedule.

The female patron who had sat reading the papers had already left, he noticed, as he prepared to leave. Following the greeting signs, Will headed for the main Conference Room. Small groups of conversations could be heard as he passed by. The doctors and lawyers were already debating the issue of euthanasia. Dr. Kevorkian's historic attempt to force the state of Michigan to charge him with murder, in order to bring the issue of assisted-suicide closer to legal consideration, would no doubt be discussed at length. Will believed in the rights of the individual to self-determination and endorsed the possible legalization of assisted suicide, with, of course strict medical and legislative controls. The program listed a number of well-known Doctors, Attorneys, Law Professors, and members of the Clergy. He picked up as many brochures and literature provided, for later reading.

The room was beginning to fill. Will wanted a seat somewhere in the middle of the room and decided to go sit down. Checking his watch, he noticed only about fifteen minutes remaining before the start of the conference. As he looked toward the podium, he saw the attractive woman he'd seen at breakfast earlier, reviewing some note cards she held. He wondered who she was.

The bright lights went out as hardwood floor-reflected halogen lights came on. The podium light gave a soft glow to the speaker, saying "Good Morning and introducing herself as Appellate Court Justice Brittain Smith-Marshal. Will raised an eyebrow and nodded

slightly. So, the woman he'd seen at breakfast was an attorney and a
judge. She certainly looked the part. She had a masterful speaking-
style full of confidence and a generous sense of humor. Will had
always admired women like this, but had never known any personally.
She spoke at length on the necessity for a multifaceted approach to
the possibility of legalization of doctor-assisted suicide, which she
believed, would, in time would coexist with now-legalized living
wills. She spoke about current laws regarding the right to refuse
resuscitative efforts, through use of DNR (Do Not Resuscitate), as
the cornerstone to the right of self-determined euthanasia and thus
doctor-assisted suicide as its logical and natural extension. She stated
her personal admiration for the courage and amazing foresight of
Dr. Kevorkian's quest, while reminding the audience, that for the
present, as an Officer –of-the-Court, she would however continue
to support current legal precedent, as she must, but also speak to her
own true beliefs. Her speech met with thunderous applause. It was
quite chilling to watch and listen. She had straddled the fine line
between Ethics and Law, like a cat on a fence. The rest of the day was
equally stimulating. Will was beginning to miss his family though,
and wondered what they were doing.

Emma and Merry had eaten breakfast in their room after Will
left. The two sat admiring the view. Fruit and hot cereal sent curls
of steam up Merry's nose, while Emma ate rolls and drank freshly
ground gourmet coffee. They had just finished putting their heads
together to plan their first day of shopping. Merry wanted to see
everything. Emma wanted to get a few things for both of them to
wear. Merry loved shopping with Grandma, because Emma took the
time to talk to the child and to listen. Emma asked Merry's opinion
all of the time. Emma loved having someone with whom to talk.
She had been lonely too. Merry made her laugh much of the time
because of her straight-forward child's logic. "Grandma, she'd said
at breakfast, Daddy's says God still loves us even when we are bad.
Daddy says bad people don't go to Heaven. Why can't everybody go
to Heaven?. It's not very nice to tell the bad people, they can't go to

Heaven". Emma was floored and laughed aloud. She had no answer the child would understand yet.

Bathed, dressed, and flying breezily down Ala Moana Boulevard, headed for the Mall, in a taxi, the two had begun their day. Merry had asked about Daddy, and Emma reminded her that Daddy had to do some work and that she would see him later. She accepted this. It was, after all, too sunny and beautiful to feel unhappy about anything.

Emma and Merry returned to the hotel later, arms loaded with bags. Some of the bags were as large as the child. The doorman carried most of them. Emma smiled and tipped him generously as he put their purchases down at the front desk. Emma checked for messages before going upstairs. A guest clerk handed Emma the note cards. The veterinarian had called to let her know that Rex was fine.

He had spent the first night crying, but had recovered. A message from Will reminded them that he wanted to have dinner with them at six o'clock. The last had been a note intended for another guest. It read "Hi Mom, miss you. I Can get away to join you, for a day or two. Be in tonight. Love Sean. Confused, Emma looked at the name on the front of the card. "For Brittain Smith-Marshal". Emma's face broke out into a huge smile. The message was not for her. Put into the wrong box by fate, she suspected. Brittain Smith-Marshal was an old friend of the family. She'd met Britt when George worked for the law firm of Bosch and Schuyler. "Excuse me, said Emma, you've given me a message belonging to another guest". "Oh, I apologize", said the Guest Clerk. She was a young woman, Hawaiian, judging by her olive skin and beautiful gleaming black hair. "Her room number ends with the same last two digits as yours."

"No harm done, sweetie. In fact, Judge Smith-Marshal is an old friend of mine. May I leave a message for her. It's luck actually that I found the note. Thank you, my dear". The pretty young woman smiled, showing relief. A lapse in the security of guest information and room numbers, especially during a major conference event could have cost her job.

"Well Merry", said Emma looking down at the sleepy face peering out from under the sun bonnet. "We'd better head upstairs to take a nap". "Daddy is going to meet us at six o'clock for dinner". Merry nodded sleepily. "Miss if you would, please have my bags brought up to my room?" "Of course, said the Desk Clerk smiling, "Get some rest. We'll take care of this for you". Brittain Smith-Marshall, former District Attorney, Circuit Court Judge and now Appellate Court Justice, married to the senior partner of Bosch, Schuyler and Smith- Marshal, was blessed with beauty, brains and a love of Truth, Fairness and Justice. Brittain also had presence. Quiet in demeanor, she could enter a room without speaking and command the attention of most of the men in the room and pique the curiosity of the women present as well. Class had been conferred on her at birth. Regal in carriage, yet natural and possessing a common touch, Britt fit in anywhere. In her courtroom, she was formidable and sometimes intimidating, but strived always to be fair. This world she understood. Her roots in rural North Carolina had provided her a front-row view of the lives and values of real folks. Her experience in the District Attorney's Office, served up humanity, too often at its worst. The court challenged her daily to hear complex truths and provide simple justice, and this she did, and did very well.

Brittain had finished her lecture on Euthanasia and Doctor-Assisted Suicide and could now spend some time relaxing. Sean was due in around dinner time. Brittain missed Sean and looked forward to having her daughter, all to herself for a few days. Sean spent most of her days in the law office working with her father, Price. Brittain was so proud of their only child. She had grown up to be quite beautiful inside and out, and was becoming an exceptional lawyer, which came as no surprise to either parent. Britain was happy that her daughter had postponed having any serious relationships until now. Even though her father was senior partner and CEO of Bosch et al, Sean had to work hard. She would someday run the entire firm, but it would never be simply handed over. Sean knew this.

Brittain stopped at the front desk to get her messages. Smiling, she read Sean's note. She would be in later for sure. Brittain planned dinner and a slumber party so the two could talk until the early morning hours. Brittain expected a full update of her daughter's life. She especially wanted to hear more about this Ian Adams, Sean's new friend. Price was determined to leave those details for his daughter to share with her mother. Price Smith-Marshal had learned when Sean was only a little girl, how to extricate himself from the mother-daughter entanglements, Sean wanted him to referee, but Brittain would have none of this. Brittain stopped mid-step when she read Emma's note. Brittain had not seen Emma since George's funeral, and was surprised to know that Emma was staying in the same hotel. Brittain headed for her room to call Emma.

"Operator, she said, would you please connect me to Emmalyn Brown's room?"

"Of course, one moment please?" The phone rang only once. "Hallo-o-o-o, the child's voice said. This is Merry. Is this my Daddy?" "No, darling", said Brittain, confused. "May I speak to Emma?? Brittain tried again. "Grandma-a-a-, said the little voice. "It's for you!" "Hello, this is Emma?" Brittain laughed aloud and said "Emm, are you going to need a lawyer? Have you kidnapped yourself a baby?" Emma recognized the voice immediately. "Well, if I do, at least I know a good attorney who can help!" Britt, how are you?" said Emma, smiling from ear to ear. "I have missed you, my dear". Britt sat down on the bed, leaning back on the pillow and put her feet up. "I'm really fine now, said Brittain. My baby girl will be here shortly, and we get to see you Emm. Believe me, no business trip has ever been this good to me before!

Emma, who is that adorable child to whom I just spoke? Brittain continued." "Britt, Emma said, let's meet for dinner downstairs at seven o'clock. I have so much to tell you. There's someone else along with my little one, I'd like for you to meet." "Great! said Britt. Sean will be in by then. We can all eat together. I'll call downstairs and make sure we have reservations for a good table, Brittain offered." "Good, said Emma. We'll see you then. It will be wonderful to see you." "You too!" Brittain decided to go downstairs for a facial and massage and maybe shop for a new dress for dinner. Something elegant, but more casual than her suits.

Emma put the receiver down and called Merry over to sit on her lap. Merry climbed up and gave her grandma a hug. "Well thank you, my baby! Here's one for you. Sweetie, grandma wants you to take a little nap because later we're going to get all dressed up in that new dress I bought for you today, and go have dinner with Daddy and some friends of mine. Would you like that"? "Yes, Grandma, but, can I wear my new shoes too? …and my "pockabook?" Merry insisted. "You certainly may. I think your Daddy is going to be so surprised when he sees you." Emma said. "But we must get our beauty rest, so we can be pretty tonight. Come my little love, let's tuck in for a nap. It'll be time to get dressed before we know it!" Merry was so excited about dressing up, it took her a while to fall asleep. Emma watched Merry as she slept. She loved this child so much. Merry owned Emma and Emma was a very happy pet. Emma fell off to sleep remembering how cute Sean had been at three.

Will returned to the suite after the last lecture of the day. Calling out and hearing no response, he assumed the girls were still out shopping. So he decided to do a little shopping of his own. A new suit, Armani maybe and some Bally shoes. Will had not splurged on himself in a very long time. The idea of it felt good. He headed for the specialty shops in downtown Honolulu feeling refreshed by the sun, the tropical breezes and the freedom he felt.

Emma woke up before Merry. Poor baby, she thought smiling, that shopping trip wore her out. Emma had finished bathing just as Merry woke up. Robed and glowing, she picked Merry up, and headed back to the bathroom to pamper her too. Emma put ribbons in Merry's long dark hair. She let the curls bounce freely around the ribbons. Merry's new dress was a crinoline wonder. Pink chiffon ruffles around the hem, showed off her matching lace tights. Once Emma put the shoes on and handed little miss her purse, Merry was ready to go. Emma sat Merry on the big bed in her room and asked the baby to sit still while she finished dressing herself. Merry was engrossed in the opening and closing of her new purse. Emma finished dressing and quickly scribbled a note to Will. "Dinner at seven. Meet us downstairs at Chez Moi. Some friends of mine are here. I want you and Merry to meet them. See you then". Emma helped Merry draw a big heart on the bottom of the note with a big "M" in the middle. La dame and la 'demoiselle were off to dine.

Will glanced at his watch, as he stepped out of the cab. Six–fifteen. Tipping the driver generously for a speedy return, he hurried to his suite to shower and dress. He felt annoyed with himself for spending so much time shopping. Merry must be starving, he thought. Will rushed into the room calling out to Merry and Emma. No answer. This time, he decided to knock on Emma's door, in case they were napping. No answer, still. Will nudged the door open a little. Seeing that the room was empty, he looked around the suite for a note. Emma had left one on his dressing table. Saying "good" to himself, he blew out a short breath. He did not have to meet them until seven, and would still have forty-five minutes to shower and change. Thank goodness, he'd taken the sales clerk's advice and gotten a haircut. Will had never gone to a stylist before. Real men, he'd laughed to himself, went to barber shops. This new cut looked great though. Will dressed quickly in his taupe Armani light wool, single-breasted suit with vest. His shirt was a pale yellow striped silk with white collar. The salesman had helped him select a silk tie that was taupe, with a splash of bright red and the faintest hint of pale yellow. His shoes were the exact shade of taupe, as his suit. Tucking in his matching silk handkerchief, Will stepped back and inspected. Will had surprised himself. He had never owned clothing as elegant before. He felt elegant. Key card in hand and tucking his wallet in the suit jacket, he headed for the restaurant downstairs. Sean went down to the baggage claim area to get her bags. She was glad she'd taken a nap on the plane. She knew that she and her mother would spend half the night talking and catching up. Sean and her mother both had hectic work schedules and, consequently had limited time to spend together. Sean saw her Dad daily and usually sent messages to Brittain, so that her mother would not worry. Sean had been very happy when her father had offered to finish her briefs on the Walford file, so that she could share a few days in the sun with her mother. Almost seven, Sean noticed on the clock on the wall in the baggage section. Handing her claim checks to a porter, she headed to find the limousine her mother had arranged. Its driver stood in the lobby holding a sign reading "Smith-Marshal". Sean smiled at him and nodded. The driver blushed and opened the door for her immediately. Sean was incredibly beautiful, captivating everyone with that brilliant smile. She rolled the privacy window down for the porter to be able to see her. He saw her. The driver put the bags into the trunk while Sean tipped the porter. He smiled at her and bowed as he backed away from the car. Sean had been told so often of her beauty that compliments rarely affected her any longer. She had also been reminded by her mother daily "beauty is as beauty does". This lesson took hold. Sean felt attractive, but never used it as a weapon. She arrived at the hotel about seven-thirty. Her mother's note read "Dress and meet me for dinner at hotel restaurant". Sean showered quickly and dressed.

Will walked into the restaurant and Merry saw him first. "Daddy!" she called to him. As he headed for the table, he noticed a woman sitting next to Merry and Emma As he got closer, Merry declared "Ooh Daddy, you look so pretty!" Will blushed. He did look grand and Emma echoed Merry's sentiment. Will turned to look at the woman sitting next to Emma, and with surprise, saw Judge Smith-Marshal. Will, Emma, said, I'd like to introduce to you, my good friend Brittain Smith-Marshal".. Will extended his hand to Brittain, blushing unmercifully. "Judge Smith-Marshal provided a most stimulating lecture on Medical Ethics at the Conference I attended this afternoon.

Judge, it is a pleasure to make your acquaintance." Please, she said, call me Brittain." "Will is a Surgeon Britt, Emma interrupted and this pretty little one, is my Merry, my grandbaby. Will frowned, embarrassed and not knowing just how much Emma had shared. "Well you all certainly make a beautiful family", Brittain offered. "Emma has been the true blessing for my daughter and myself", Will said softly. Brittain watched as Emma beamed. Emma had already shared enough of the details with Britt. The child had lost her mother and the young man his wife.

Will wanted to change the subject. Judge, excuse me, Brittain, I was fascinated by your lecture this morning. I too, feel the time is at hand to discuss doctor-assisted suicide. I am especially interested from a medical perspective. With stringent guidelines, we could continue to honor the right of the individual to self-determination, while providing merciful assistance to a patient who is terminal or facing an increasingly debilitating, fatal disease... Brittain's gaze moved so slightly away from Will as he spoke, and he noticed it. Will followed her gaze as it settled upon the most beautiful young woman he had ever seen. Her totally unblemished and shining skin reflected the soft light as she glided gracefully across the room, headed in their direction. The little black silk dress she wore, ruffled softly in the breeze created by her movement. Her curly black hair was cut very short revealing a slender neck and beautiful shoulders. Her scent arrived just moments before she stopped, and once again when she stood before the table, smiling at its occupants.

Looking down at Brittain and Emma, the stunning face with perfect teeth smiled. Will stood up lost in her gaze as she smiled at him next. Brittain and Emma had witnessed this scene many times before, and understood exactly what Will was going through. "Dr. Thorpe, may I introduce my daughter Sean-Smith Marshal?" Will stood offering his hand. Sean looked up into his face and into his eyes and held him there for a moment. Will could barely think, let alone speak. Good manners helped him remember to offer his chair and to pull it out for her. As he held her chair, she whispered thank you softly to him. As he leaned forward to push her in, the softness of the whispered politesse landed on his neck, just below his earlobe. Will felt like the wind had been knocked out of him, by a feather.

Emma came to his rescue. She regaled him with stories about Sean as a little girl. She spoke of the career George had retired from at Bosch and Schuyler. George had taken the young Brittain Smith and Price Marshall under his wing when they were only new associates at the firm. Will had not known until then, much about George's life's work. Sean had graciously held her questions regarding the nature of Aunt Emma's relationship with Will and Merry. She knew her mother would explain later. Merry had grown very quiet during the conversation. She had always been a shy child. Sean looked over at Merry and winked. The child smiled, grateful to feel included once again. Merry looked Sean straight in the eye and across Emma's conversation simply stated, "My mommy's in Heaven". Emma stopped talking and Will looked so embarrassed. Brittain felt the sadness in the child's words and looked over at Sean. Sean stood up and walked around the table and stopped in front of Merry. She held out both hands to the baby. Merry searched Sean's face and eyes for a long moment before responding. Then she reached her little arms up to Sean, permitting Sean to pick her up. Looking at the group with an evident sadness in her own face, Sean told them all that she and Merry were going to the Ladies Room and would be back. Will stood up, his long thick dark lashes drooping, closed softly as the pain he felt traveled the distance of his face. As he raised his lashes again, only a millisecond later, he saw himself reflected in Sean's eyes. Brittain not only loved and respected her only child, but she liked her too. She had been so proud of her daughter in this moment. Brittain also decided that she liked very much, this sad young doctor, with the very sad child.

Emma and Brittain made plans to spend time together the next day while they waited for Sean and Merry to return. Britt offered Will her condolences on the death of his wife. Will thanked her and became quiet. Emma wanted to help, but couldn't just then. Merry and Sean returned smiling. Sean had sprayed a little of her perfume on Merry's neck. Merry loved it. "Look Daddy, smell me", she insisted. Will dutifully obeyed. Sean's scent filled his nostrils, his mind and soul until it reached his loins. Will had not thought of his needs until that moment. He gently kissed the spot on Merry's neck. Sean missed none of this. Emma and Brittain professing fatigue, left with Merry. Sean promised to take Merry to t the beach tomorrow. Then Sean invited Will to have dinner and to take a walk on the beach. Will did not know how to say no, when every fiber of his being screamed, please. Sean was everything Rain could never be. She was the kind of woman Ian would possess, not him. Could she care for someone like him? The kindness she had shown Merry had been so sweet and natural. Had he seen something in her eyes when they met. Or was it just his hopeful imagination?

After dinner, walking toward the beach, they took off their shoes and headed toward the moon. Neither spoke. Her response to Merry had touched him in the place in his heart he'd kept only for Merry. The sound of the ocean gently teasing the shore and playfully hitting the rocks reminded Will of children at play. Sean stopped and turning to face Will with tears in her eyes, took a step closer and put her head on his chest. Slowly and gently Will enclosed this tiny and precious angel inside his big arms and let out a long and low sigh. So close were they, their souls touched. Will could barely breathe. Nor could he move. Sean reached up and gently guided his head toward her own. In the moonlight, she saw herself reflected in his eyes. Together, the two floated off into the softness of a kiss to a secret place. Will's heart opened, just a little, and wrapped itself completely around Sean's.

Ten

rittain lay quietly in the bed as she listened to Sean enter the room. Britt was prepared to listen if Sean needed it. Sean undressed quietly. Slipping on a t-shirt, like she did as a child, she climbed into her mother's bed instead of her own. Thinking her mother asleep, the child kissed her mother's forehead and said "thank you Mom" softly. Brittain could see the tears run down the side of Sean's face and understood. Brittain fell asleep with two names in the back of her mind, Will Thorpe and Ian Adams.

Merry was the first to awaken the next morning, excited about her trip to the beach with Sean. Emma heard the little feet moving busily about the room. She opened her eyes and saw Merry packing her beach bag. "And where are you going my baby?", she asked. Merry ran to the bed and gave Grandma Emma a good morning kiss. Grandma, I'm going to the beach with Sean, 'member?" Yes, darlin', I remember, but first you need a bath and some breakfast". "OK?" "OK, but can we call her on the phone first?", Merry insisted. "I don't know if she's up yet honey. But we can try." Merry ran over to the phone and handed the receiver to Emma. Emma dialed Sean's room while Merry jumped up and down, clapping her hands. Will knocked softly on the door to Emma's room saying "Good morning, may I come in?" "Yes Will, please do", Emma said. Merry ran to her Daddy who scooped her up for a belly kiss. "What is all the excitement about?" Merry squirmed and giggled. "Daddy, I am going to the beach with Sean and Grandma. Can you come too?", Merry insisted. "Sorry pumpkin, but I must go to do some work today." "But Daddy, please????", she begged. Emma interrupted and called Merry to the phone. Sean wanted to speak to her. Will watched as Merry nodded at the phone and said, "uh-huh", about a dozen times. She looked so happy at that moment. Will had not seen her look that way in a very long time. "OK, Bye", said Merry, "Grandma, she wants to talk to you", said a satisfied Merry. Emma was watching Will and he knew it. Will was not ready to think about last night or Sean. As he gave Merry a sloppy kiss, Sean's perfume made him remember last night. "I'll see you two later, gotta run".

Will threw Emma a wave and left. Will deliberately sent no message to Sean through Emma. Last night had been an aberration, he decided. Sean probably just felt sorry for him, and the kiss just happened.

Sean got out of bed and stretched. She walked over to catch some of the fresh air and sunshine inviting its way into the room. Her mother had left already. Sean was glad. She knew her mother would want to hear about last night. She wasn't sure what to tell her mother, or herself, for that matter. Will Thorpe was attractive and quite nice. He seemed a very caring and loving father. Given the death of his wife, the sadness his eyes held was understandable. Sean had kissed him last night, but had not been prepared for the feelings that one kiss would impart. It seemed right at that moment. Sean dismissed thoughts about Will when the phone rang.

"Hey good lookin', said Ian". "Miss me?" Sean smiled. "I just left you yesterday", she said teasing him. "What shall I bring back", said Sean. "Just You", Ian countered. "You are a cheap date, my sweet, Sean teased. I'll be back tomorrow night. Don't make any plans. I'm a little tired and I know I'll need some extra sleep." "If I didn't know better, I'd think you met someone else", Ian teased. As a matter of fact, I did. My Aunt Emma is here vacationing with her family. Her grandbaby is the cutest little thing. Sean was babbling and it wasn't like her. "So, said Ian, I don't have anything to worry about?" "Yes, you do, as a matter of fact. The child's father is a very handsome and dashing doctor...." Sean teased some more. "I'm sure the doctor's wife would agree with you..." Ian reminded her. "Look babe, gotta run. See you tomorrow. Love you." Ian rushed off to work.

Sean hung up the phone. She crossed her legs and closed her eyes trying not to think about the wife. Instead, Will's face filled her mind. Better get dressed she thought. Standing in the shower, she made up in her mind that she'd kissed him because she'd felt sorry for him. Nothing more. She also convinced herself too, that Ian would understand her actions, if he knew more about Will Thorpe and his family problems. Sean was determined to avoid having to explain Will or Ian to Brittain or Emma. She had no ready answers about her relationship with either man.

Merry and Emma met Sean in the lobby loaded down with all the beach paraphernalia they could possibly need Merry ran over to Sean and took her by the hand. "Look Sean, we have a pic-a-nic basket!" "I called the restaurant and had a lunch and some beverages packed in this cooler. I hope you don't mind?", said Emma. "No, said Sean, it just means we can play in the water longer, right Merry?" "Yep!" volunteered the excited child. Emma had promised herself not to ask Sean about last night. Will had offered nothing. Sean seemed to busy herself with the child. So Emma took the hint and decided to simply let Merry enjoy the day with her new friend.

Emma watched as Merry and Sean played in the ocean and built sandcastles. She could not help thinking what a wonderful pair Sean and Will could make. Sean, exhausted from play brought Merry, sand bucket and shovel closer to where Emma lay under the beach umbrella. Merry waved at her Grandma Emma, then sat down to play alone. Sean joined Emma under the large umbrella. "Aunt Emm, I'm worn out. I'll bet Merry could go on and on playing in the water." "And right you are sweetie. She is starving for attention and affection. Her Father gives her all that he can, but he's hurting too." Sean hesitated, then asked, "How did his wife die?" Emma took a deep breath and lowered her voice. "Suicide" was her only reply. Sean sat looking over at Merry, her heart filled with sympathy. As if to answer her thoughts, Emma added, "the child was the only one at home when Rain, that was her mother's name, shot herself. The baby went looking for her mother and found her in bed. Merry tried to wake her up, but couldn't. So she climbed into the bed with her mother's body and fell asleep. That is how Will and the police found both of them". "But why?, countered Sean. Why would she do such a thing?. She had a wonderful husband and a beautiful baby?" Emma smiled softly at Sean. Sean's life had been a love-filled triad of mother, father and child. For her, the circle of love had never been broken. "Sean honey, apparently, there had been another man. Rain loved someone else, who apparently did not feel the same way about her.

She had left Will and taken Merry several times over the past year and returned home each time something went wrong with her new relationship. God Bless him, Will took her back every time. He'd loved his wife, but couldn't understand er. She had hurt him deeply and wounded his pride more than once. All done in front of the child. Merry has been wounded too. The stability she should have been able to count on wasn't there, had never been there. Her father's love was without question, but you know for yourself, without motherlove something happens to you, even if, you are only three years old". Sean saw Merry and Will with new eyes from that moment on, and Emma knew it.

Sean called Merry over to sit with them under the umbrella. She wiped Merry's Face with a cool moist towelette, and replaced her sunscreen. Pulling the child closer to herself, she laid Merry on her lap, inviting the child to take a nap and rocked her back and forth until she fell asleep. Laying her down on the blanket and covering her with another one, Sean gently stroked the wisps of hair that had blown across the child's face. Sean was falling in love…. with the child. Emma smiled, closed her eyes and said a silent prayer.

Eleven

Brittain searched the restaurant for a table. The room was pretty full. Then she saw Will sitting alone and decided to join him. He noticed her just as he looked up to signal a waiter. Will stood up to shake hands with Brittain. Then he invited her to share his table. The waiter took their orders which left them some time to chat. "I am so sorry to hear about your wife's passing", said Brittain, carefully. I can see the sadness it has brought to you and Merry. You have done well with her." "Actually, Will offered hesitantly, Emma has been the one source of a woman's love that Merry has come to count on. I don't know what I would have done without her". "I know what you mean, said Brittain. Emma's husband George mentored my husband and myself, out of the goodness of his heart. Emma likes to say she's only guilty of "s'mothering". I can see how well you two have benefited from her skills.

The drinks arrived. Brittain offered a toast and changed subjects. "To Emma", she said "and may I add, To Sean", said Will as he blushed. Your daughter was very kind and understanding with Merry last night". "and to you, also??" Brittain baited. Will looked away and blushed deeply. So, thought Brittain, something had indeed happened between the two last night. "My daughter has some good instincts Dr. Thorpe. I trust them too. I am fortunate also as a mother to be able to say I like my child. She is a very fine young woman, respected lawyer and our very favorite, only child. Will smiled. Warning understood.

Will seemed to relax a little. Lunch took on less of a formal feeling, as the two debated the conference issues that had been presented. Brittain got what she needed from Will. Brittain had been afraid that Will wanted only the ten million dollars George had left Emma. This young man needed a mother for himself and a grandmother for his daughter, and Emma needed both of them. Three kind and lost souls. She knew very clearly that this young man's presence in her child's life would not end there in Hawaii.

Roasted to a well-done, and rested well, Emma, Sean and Merry decided to return to the hotel. Sean had to prepare to leave. Merry extracted the promise of a phone call from Sean, who gave it freely. Emma thanked Sean for spending so much time with them and encouraged her to call. Merry insisted that Grandma Emma help her scribble the phone number for Sean. Sean winked at Emma and made a big fuss over the promise not to lose it. Sean already had Aunt Emma's number. Merry stood watching Sean leave. The quiet that surrounded Merry touched Sean. As she stood waiting for the elevator doors to open, Merry stared deep into Sean's eyes with the kind of wonder only a child or a pet could. Merry waved only once. Sean returned the courtesy, but could look no more.

Brittain opened the door to her suite and called out to Sean. "In here Mom!" Sean answered. "Honey, you're packed already?" "Sorry Mom, I know we didn't get to spend much time together. I promise we'll steal away for a weekend, soon, okay?" Sean begged. Brittain could hear her child trying to escape the questions she knew her mother would have. Brittain moved forward anyway. "And this Ian Adams? When will I get to meet him? "He's just a friend. Tell you what, I'll bring him to dinner soon, and you can scrutinize him for yourself!" Sean smiled, knowing they'd both won. Sean would not have to explain where Will Thorpe fit in, and mother had extracted a promise to be presented the mystery man. The two lawyers shook hands and hugged laughing. "Shall I go with you to the airport, baby? Britt asked. "No thanks Mom, you know we both hate saying goodbye. I'll leave you instead knowing Aunt Emm is here. Isn't she amazing Mom? She really loves Merry and Will. They really are like a little family." Sean realized she'd just opened Pandora's box and checked her watch in defense. "I've got to run Mom, don't want to check in late." Checkmate. Brittain and Sean had played this mother-daughter cat and mouse game since Sean could babble. Britt called downstairs for a bellhop to take Sean's bags to the limo. They kissed goodbye in the suite.

Sean stepped out of the elevator not watching where she was going and bumped into a guest. Apologizing, she looked up and into Will's face, and felt his big hands take hold to steady her. "Hello there", said Will raising his brow. And where are you rushing off to in such a hurry?", he asked. "I'm on my way to the airport to catch my plane home. "I only came to spend a few days with my mom". Will looked stunned. "I'm sorry we took up so much of your time. I didn't know you were leaving so soon". May I accompany you to the airport? "To see you off safely, of course…" he hesitated. "….Sure, yes that would be nice", Sean returned. "My limo is waiting outside. Shall we go?" Will tried to find the words to lighten the moment. "A limo…well, well, well. Then, I'll do my best to make this a pleasant limo ride". Sean laughed, feeling relieved and said "Good, then you can pour me a drink and we can say goodbye properly". "Deal".

Will and Sean stepped out of the limousine at the airport. Sean gave the driver instructions to take Will back to the hotel when he was ready. Once again, she tipped the driver generously. Will took her bags from the driver and carried them to Baggage Check In. Will found himself wondering who was the lucky man that would meet this beauty on the other side. Surely there must be someone. He decided to take a chance. "If you're ever in our neck of the woods, please feel free to stop in. Merry and I live right next door to Emma. Easy to find", he grinned. "I may have to take you up on that!"

"Merry is an absolute delight and just a wonderful baby. We had such a good time this morning. I'll miss her for sure." said Sean. "… And I'll miss you…Will braved. Sean was caught off-guard. Moving closer to her, he touched her chin and brought his lips fully and softly and determinedly down on hers. The kiss spun a momentary cocoon around them. Neither pulled away. Both pressed lips with the unspoken promise they dared not utter. Will tried to apologize. Sean placed her fingers across his lips to quiet them. She walked away from him, not trusting herself to look back.

Will headed for his suite to change clothes and take Merry for a walk on the beach. Emma was tired from the morning frolic. Will took over the child's care and offered Emma respite. Merry was excited about their walk on the beach. Will had promised to help her find seashells to give as presents.

A light sprinkle of rain started to fall in the midst of the sunny day. "Hey, said Will, a sunshower!" Merry laughed and looked up at the sky and opened her mouth to catch some rain water. "Open your mouth Daddy! The rain will fall inside". So Will and his baby girl spun around in circles on the beach in Hawaii, with their mouths wide open, catching raindrops. Will had not ever been so happy. "Look Daddy, Look" shouted Merry. "A Rainbow! It's Mommy! Mommy is saying I love you!". Will stopped turning and looked up. The rain had stopped. A soft cool breeze had taken its place. Will felt peace and love inside himself. The doubts and unhappiness he could not rid himself of and the aching pain and sadness had been replaced by something else. "Yes, my sweetheart, It is your Mommy and I do believe she is saying I love you". Rain had finally managed to give the child the gift of a mother's love.

Twelve

Ian was not going to have a good day. Suzette, his office administrator and paralegal had called in sick early this morning because her son had the flu, and needed to be taken to a doctor. Ian had not known that she had a child. Ian had dated Suzette a few years ago, while clerking the summer following first year law. She had no children then. It was harmless fun and frolic.

No one got hurt. This is the way Ian saw it. He knew that a serious relationship with her was never going to materialize. She was working reception when they'd met that summer. Ian figured their paths would probably not cross again, so he had nothing to lose. Women like her, Ian had thought, knew the rules of the game, simple enough, every man or woman for self. When he stopped asking her out, she never asked why. The end of the summer marked the end of their romance. Fate and being hired out of law school by Bosch and Schuyler meant he'd have to see Suzette again. At first Ian worried about it. But Suzette had been frosty enough when he interviewed to let him know, he was off the hook. Suzette had since then been promoted to senior paralegal, then temporarily transferred to Ian as his Personal Office Administrator. Neither seemed adversely affected by the new relationship. In fact, neither had ever broached the subject of their short-lived romantic liaison.

Then of course, there was Sean. Sean's beauty and position in the firm beckoned him like a red flag to a bull. He had made no secret of his feelings for her and rather pointedly pursued and captured, at least her attention. Price Smith-Marshal took great pains to remind his daughter that a romantic relationship in the workplace was a recipe for disaster. In this case could present legal problems for him should the young lawyer's presence ever become a hindrance to the firm, in any way. Sean had assured her father that she would take his opinions under advisement and laughed while reminding her father that his own relationship with Brittain Smith had blossomed under then, Bosch and Schuyler umbrella with absolutely no problems. Price had forgotten that the baby girl to whom he offered advice, was now an accomplished attorney.

Suzette had taken an important file home to work on and Ian needed it immediately. He was supposed to meet and discuss the contract proposal with the very same client. Ian tried to phone Suzette, but there was no answer. So he left a message on her machine, then called the client to reschedule their meeting. Actually, it had worked out well because Sean was coming in from Hawaii and Ian wanted to meet her at the airport. Ian buzzed Price and briefed him on the status of the Wolfgang Account and told him that he would be leaving early to pick up Sean. Ian knew that Price would not object, after all, she was his own daughter. Sean was tired and ready to go to her own home to get some rest. She was glad she'd told Ian not to expect to see her right away. Will's entry into her life had complicated things and Sean had no answers for anyone yet. Sean definitely needed sleep and to sort out her feelings. A porter brought her bags to the lobby. Sean was ready to take a cab home when she looked up to see Ian strutting confidently toward her. She frowned and put on her sunglasses not wanting him to read, or misread anything her eyes may reveal.

"Hello, gorgeous", Ian conferred on her, as he automatically kissed her face. "You didn't have to come down here Ian. I really want to just go home and catch up on my rest. Hawaii was wonderful, but I've had an exhausting two days", Sean apologized. "Well I certainly must say that Hawaii looks good on you. You've got a glow going on", Ian complimented. Sean relaxed a little.

Same old Ian, she thought. It would never occur to him that perhaps she had met someone who could offer him competition. "Thanks Ian, and thank you for coming anyway. Listen, if you don't mind, just a ride home and we'll talk tomorrow and maybe have dinner". "Deal", Ian said. The way he'd said it reminded her of Will and the ride to the airport they'd shared only a few hours ago. Ian's conversation was lost on Sean, as she relived the moments shared with Will and Merry. "Sean...Sean, I asked you what you thought of the Wolfgang proposal??? Hey sweets, you must be tired. I don't think you've heard a word I said", Ian accused, sounding wounded. "I'm sorry". I promise to make it up to you", Sean apologized realizing that she had in fact heard none. Ian reached over to stroke Sean's left leg and as he touched her, she jumped. Ian frowned at himself in the rearview mirror, but said nothing. Sean reached out for his hand, as if to assure them both that everything was still the way it used to be. But nothing would ever be the same again, for either.

Suzette was worried about her son Tristan. He was only three and hated being sick and having to take medication. Tristan had slowly developed some breathing problems along with the new strain of influenza he'd caught, at the day care center. Suzette had tried medicating him, but he was not getting better and needed to see a physician. She could tell that she was going to have to take some time off and knew that Ian would not be happy.

Tristan was the joy of his mother's life. Suzette had lost her mother the year before to breast cancer. Suzette grew up seeing her mother Anne Butler, working several jobs to take care of the two of them. Suzette had never known her father and Anne seemed determined to keep his identity, a secret she would take to her grave. Suzette had always wanted to know, but refused to sacrifice her mother's feelings in exchange for that knowledge. Suzette grew up missing having a father, but not missing him personally. She had known nothing about him.

Anne Butler tried hard to make up for the loss, by being her daughter's greatest cheerleader. Anne encouraged her child through undergraduate studies and had been so proud when Suzette graduated summa cum laude. Suzette's dream was to become an attorney. But insisted that her mother stop working now that she had graduated. Suzette had landed a job at Bosch and Schuyler as a receptionist. At first Anne felt disappointed for her daughter, until Suzette explained that her plan was to work hard and move from reception to office clerical and become a paralegal, while attending law school at night. Suzette knew it would not be easy, but was determined to succeed. When Suzette told her mother that she was pregnant, in her first year of law school, Anne supported her and did not criticize. Suzette knew that the birth of the child would delay completion of law school. Anne cherished the idea of a grandchild and would help care for the baby. Tristan was the love of Anne's life and brought to Suzette an even greater reason to work hard and succeed. When Anne died, Suzette realized that the untimely pregnancy had actually been a gift from God. Anne lived long enough to meet and love on her grandchild. "God doesn't create accidents" her mother used to remind her. Tristan was all Suzette had left when Anne died, but it was also all she needed.

Suzette had almost completed law school and was already the senior paralegal at Bosch and Schuyler and could write briefs as well as any of the associate lawyers. Price Smith-Marshal had paid for her law school expenses including books because he saw her potential. She'd reminded him of himself, once a young and struggling law student, given a hand up by George Brown. Price required his staff to do "pro bono" work on a regular basis.

He reminded them religiously that "to those whom much is

given, much is required". By the age of ten Sean could mimic the mantra in a sing-song fashion whenever one of her parents felt she needed reminding. Suzette secretly hoped to apply for a position at Bosch, Schuyler and Smith-Marshal after passing the bar exam. Only Price and the Accounting Department knew of her law school attendance and Suzette wanted it to stay that way. She was stubborn and proud, and Price admired her for it.

Suzette carried the sleeping three-year-old into the house. He was getting so big. With all of the bumping around to open the door and carry his baby bag, he should have awakened, but didn't. Thank goodness, thought Suzette, he needs to sleep. His doctor had given him a booster dosage of cough syrup, decongestant and Tylenol while they were in his office. His lungs sounded clear to the pediatrician. It was a virus and all he needed was to be cared for. Suzette was just going to have to stay home with him and pump him full of fluids and let him rest. This sounded simple enough, but she also had a job.

Suzette checked her messages and found one from Ian. She knew he'd need the Wolfgang proposal and had completed it the night before. Suzette's ability to juggle her life's challenges came from watching her mother. Single parenthood was a tough job but she had been trained by the best. At the end of each day, Suzette's own battle to survive, reminded her of all the sacrifices her mother had made.

Suzette peeked in on Tristan. He had curled up in a little ball, but was sleeping peacefully. Suzette called the office looking for Ian. The main reception desk answered. Ian had left early for the day to pick up Sean from the airport. Suzette instructed reception to send a courier to her home to pick up the Wolfgang File for Ian. She then placed a call to Tabitha Stone, her best paralegal. Tabitha would have to fill in her for the whole week. Suzette would still be available for phone conferencing if needed. Price Smith-Marshal had called and left a message for her also. Suzette reached him on his car phone. She briefed him on the status of the file she had completed and would give back to Ian, and Tabitha's assignment to fill in as her assistant for the week. Price assured her that he would make sure everything would be fine and told her to take good care of her son. Price found himself thinking of the vast difference in the lives of his daughter Sean and his senior paralegal Suzette Butler. They were only a few years apart in age, but Suzette seemed so much older and mature, law school at night, burying her only living relative, a young child and her job. Price had every intention of offering Suzette a position at the firm as soon as she was ready. He believed Suzette could just about run that entire firm, if she set her mind to it. Price Smith-Marshal was not about to let her get away.

Sean was taking no chances with Ian. She hopped out of the car and signaled her doorman to get her bags. She knew that if Ian walked to her door, she'd never be able to get rid of him. Ian protested, but Sean persisted and prevailed. Ian gave up. He told her that he'd phone later and to get some rest.

Ian decided to swing by and pick up the file from Suzette and take it home to work on. He knocked on her door and heard the sound of footsteps rushing to answer. Suzette unlocked one lock and left the chain link connected on the top, as she spoke to Ian through the remaining small opening in the door. Suzette could hear movement coming from Tristan's room and feared that the knocks on the door had awakened the sick child. Tristan had indeed awakened and walked toward his mom crying and rubbing his eyes. "Hold on honey, I'll be right there!" Suzette assured him. "Oh, Ia, Mr. Adams, hold on a moment.

Suzette opened the door after a few minutes and handed the file to Ian. "Sorry about making you wait. Here is the file you need. I've already requested courier pick up, so I'll contact the messenger and cancel. If you have any questions, feel free to call. Tabitha Jones, Mr. Marshal's paralegal, will fill in for me this week. I've already cleared this with Price. Any questions?" Suzette finished her spiel as though it had been rehearsed. "Uh, no. I'll read your notes and call if I do", Ian assured. "Alright then, goodbye", said an unemotional Suzette and closed the door.

Ian stepped back away from the door, his ego a little bruised from Suzette's coolness toward him. She hadn't even invited him in. He smiled for a moment remembering that she'd almost called him by his first name, one deliberated barrier in a maze of many. When he'd returned to work for the firm, as an attorney, after completing law school, he had seen hurt, anger and something more. Never again did Suzette call him by his first name. Ian reasoned that the affair they'd had a few years ago would keep them forever in this state of limbo. Personally, he had no problem with it. Suzette did her job extremely well and since this was all he needed from her, it was okay. But Ian had another reason for tiptoeing carefully around Suzette, Rain Thorpe. Only Ian and Suzette knew of the affair he'd had with Rain and her subsequent suicide. Ian's lack of judgment and ethics, he knew, could make him a liability to the firm and maybe cost him everything he'd worked so hard for. No, Ian would not ever chance shifting the delicate balance of his house of cards. Suzette had apparently chosen not to share any of the truth with Sean. Sean had never brought it up and he was certainly not going to. Picking up his cell phone, he called Tabitha to confirm the cancellation of the courier run. Now what?, he thought. He'd taken the afternoon off hoping to stretch it into a night of passion with Sean. Since Sean would certainly phone her dad, he decided he'd better return to work. Ian had a vested interest in making sure Price Smith-Marshal was going to like him. "Must keep "Dad" in my corner", Ian was thinking as he turned around and headed back to work.

Suzette went back into Tristan's room to check on him once more. She watched him as he slept. He looks so much like his father, she thought as she shook her head as if to say "no", over and over. Tristan had Ian's chiseled good looks, but his grandmother's sweetness and good nature. Through the child Suzette could see all of the wasted potential in the man. Suzette did not hate Ian Adams. In fact, quite the opposite was true. Only Anne Butler had known this for a fact. Suzette missed her mother so much. Anne Butler had challenged Suzette's decision not to tell Ian about the birth of his son. Anne felt not only was it his responsibility to help care for the baby, but his right to know. Anne's opinions convinced Suzette that her mother may have been sorry about the nonexistent connection between Suzette and her own father. Suzette wanted neither the reminder that Ian had never truly cared for her, nor the possibility of his rejecting Tristan. Just before Anne died, she told Suzette that she was so very sorry for not revealing the identity of her own father. Anne's very last words were…"but the letter"… Suzette expected to find some letter in her mother's things explaining everything. But she never did. She'd assumed her mother had meant that she had intended to write a letter. Anne had taken care of Suzette completely on her own and Suzette vowed to her mother and to God to do the same for her only child, and without any help from Ian Adams.

Thirteen

In the Hawaiian sunshine and rain, Will, Emma and Merry had become a real family. They had danced the life fandango and completed some pretty complicated maneuvers, together, and each had done some healing in the process. Will no longer felt alone, nor weighed down in fear over raising Merry alone, and discovered to his own surprise that his heart was still beating. Emma had a new family that needed not only what she could give, but just her. Will had never been told about Emma's fortune, nor the future financial plans that would undoubtedly include her new little family. Emma knew in her heart that the love Will expressed was real. The child denied in her youth, had been waiting patiently to meet her, in her tomorrow, and with Will, came the bounty Merry. Emma believed that Merry would still be able to recover from her mother's near fatal emotional wounding.

Father and Grandmother would evermore wrap her in the bands of love, and as sure as Love IS the face of God, all is truly possible. Brittain left Hawaii before the conference ended, but not before sending to Merry a huge stuffed puppy with a collar that read "Merry's Pup". The card was signed "with much love, Aunt Britt".

Will was touched by the gesture and decided to call Palmetto Springs to thank her the next week.

Emmalyn had started humming each day. Merry was delighted by this practice and tried to hum along. Merry had a sweet little voice and together they sounded so happy. Merry would insist at nap and bedtime that Emmalyn hum her to sleep. Emmalyn was more than delighted to do so. It made a fitting end to their vacation. Each member of this new family carried back so many special memories. Family ties are the ties that bind and family is wherever lucky enough to find them.

Rex was so happy to see Emmalyn, that he jumped up and down nonstop, wearing out his little six-pound body. He napped in his basket for several hour, as though he needed to remark his territory. Merry wanted to go home immediately to check on her "babies". Will entered their home carrying Merry, just happy to be there. The house no longer held only painful memories. Will had forgiven Rain for everything. Instead, eh found peace and love in the home she had left to them. It was a part of herself she'd not been able to express in her short life.

Will and his family had come home renewed, tanned and glowing from the inside. He Was grateful that he still had the weekend to recover before returning to the hospital. Will gave Emmalyn the weekend off, to recover, as he laughingly put it. She deserved It. At first, she fussed, but stopped only when Will insisted that on Sunday, he be allowed he be allowed to barbecue for the family. Even Rex was invited.

Sean walked around her apartment opening windows and turning on lights. She had been spending more and more time at Ian's, and neglecting her own. This home had once been her pride and joy. It was her very first grown-up purchase. She had received the first of her trust endowments when she graduated from law school. Her parents had chosen to bestow upon her a living inheritance. At any milestone achieved in Sean's life, and agreed upon by her parents, she could receive portions of her inheritance.

In this way, they could share in her joy while still alive and provide advice, but only if she asked for it. They had no veto power in her decisions to utilize these funds. The gifts were meant to be after all, her inheritance. Her parents had been extremely proud of her first investment.

Fourteen

Sean was too tired to unpack completely. She grabbed her flight bag and emptied it out on the bed. She reached into the side pocket and found a small, but bulky envelope. There were no markings on the envelope. She opened it and found a note from Merry which simply said "I LOVE YOU", and attached to the center of the page was a wallet-sized photo of her with her Dad. Merry had signed it with a heart around the letter "M". The picture must have been the one Will carried in his own wallet. In it, they were rolling around in the leaves and obviously loving every moment. It was a great shot of Merry covered in leaves and laying on her dad's head. Will looked so very happy and handsome in that photo. Sean had met a much quieter and sadder version of this man. Rain, she thought, must have taken this picture, and Will must have put it in her flight bag, secretly when they were in the limo. Sean carried the photo into the bathroom and set it on the table next to the tub. She ran the bathtub full of white magnolia scented bubble bath. She then lighted a few of the many candles she kept around the bathroom.

Pouring herself a glass of sherry and turning on some soft music, she entered the water. Resting her head on the bath pillow, she sighed. Sean picked up the picture looking at her and simply closed her eyes. The warmth of the sherry and the water relaxed her as she waded through mixed feelings.

Sean had not been looking for a permanent relationship with anyone. She wanted to enjoy her life and work hard on her career. Ian was fun to be with, but he was not "the one" for her either. Sean was not even sure, if there was "the right one", or if she would know him when she saw him.

Sean's parents were soul-mates, a rare occurrence. Sean turned the picture sideways, so she could get a better look at Will's face alone. She had to admit that the night they met, she'd felt something. She'd seen the long, very long legs and thighs represented admirably through his slacks. Her eyes had continued up to the beautiful and broad shoulders hugging his suit jacket, then towards the gleaming white teeth and finally those beautiful big, sad brown eyes, draped fully by the thickest and longest lashes, she'd ever seen on a man. Sean smiled wickedly. No man ever had need of lashes like that. They were a weapon for sure. Sean remembered how he'd slowly closed those eyes after Merry announced plainly to everyone that her mother was in heaven. Before those lashes could conceal it, she had witnessed his pain and seen it reflected by the candlelight on the table. Something happened to her heart that night. And when she saw herself in his eyes, she committed herself to denial.

Will had finally put Merry to sleep in her own room. In Hawaii, he'd found her a very special shell. The mother of pearl coloring reminded the child of a rainbow. Will had taken it to one of the many beach craft stands, and finding small chimes, had them connected by wire to the shell, making for his child a dreamcatcher. Merry loved it. Just before she fell off to sleep, Merry would touch it. The sweet small clanging sound was comforting. She'd fallen asleep quickly. Will sat on her window seat watching her breathe. The full moon reminded him that someplace else there was a piece of his heart that he needed to reclaim. Will leaned back against the pillows and indulged in his memories of Sean. Her natural beauty made it impossible to forget anything about her, and her inner beauty outshined even that. Maybe the tropical surroundings forced the illusion that she'd felt something for him. Maybe he was just lonely and nothing had happened between them, only to him. If he could only hear her voice one more time, he'd know for sure. Will went downstairs to the den and picked up the phone. Emmalyn had given him Sean's number wishing him good luck. Emmalyn's butterfly was about to try his new wings.

Sean dried her hair with the towel and put on a short nightie. The phone rang. "Hello? she yawned into the phone. "Hi, baby, it's Mom. I'm back. I tried calling you at Ian's, but he said you went straight to your home from the airport. Are you alright, love?" "Yes Mommy." Sean only called Britt Mommy when she had something on her mind. "Want to talk about it? Britt pressed gently. "No…but thanks. "When I figure it out maybe, said Sean honestly. "Alright, my little bird, get some rest. I did enjoy seeing you in Hawaii. I love you Sean". "Me too, 'night night". Sean hung up.

Brittain rolled over to Price and picked up his arm and tucked herself in under it. He patted her hair and kissed her head. Britt knew that she had been right. Dr. Thorpe had made more of an impression on her baby girl than perhaps he'd even realized. Britt smiled and said softly Ian Adams "Love", Dr. Thorpe "15". Price responded to what he thought he'd heard and said "I love you too, baby. Now go to sleep".

Britt hugged him and rolled over to go to sleep, smiling even more. The phone rang again. Sean did not want to speak to Ian and decided to let her answering machine pick it up. But it was Will's voice that made her reach for the receiver. "Hi? he said. I thought you were out. I was just going to leave you a message". Will could hear the recording still speaking. "Sorry, said Sean. It'll stop in a moment". "I apologize first for calling you so late, and hope you won't mind that I got your number from Emmalyn", Will spilled out. "No, it's alright, she said. "It's funny that you called. I found the picture you put in my bag and I've actually been thinking about you…both. You and Merry". Sean admitted shyly, stumbling over her own words. "You guys look like you were having a lot of fun that day". "Merry and I always have a great time together" Will stated matter-of-factly. "And with Rain, too"? Sean ventured, then apologized immediately. "I had no right", she said. Will was quiet for a long moment. "It's okay, Sean". "In the beginning, sometimes. Look, I may as well tell you, before you hear anything else. Rain... my wife left me, in fact, several times, for another man. He was my best friend and Merry's Godfather. So, I lost two times over. I forgave her each time she came home and we tried again each time. The last time she returned, I was going to tell her that she couldn't do it anymore. I was not going to let her take Merry away from me again, nor was I going to let her put us all through the same drama one more time. But she committed suicide before we'd had a chance to talk". Will grew quiet again and once more Sean could feel his hurt. "I'm so sorry", she offered quietly. "Thanks Sean. Listen, I'm going to let you get some sleep. I just wanted to make sure you got home safely and I guess I just wanted to hear your voice once more". Will hung up. Sean hugged the phone to her chest, next to her heart and fell asleep with tears once again, running down her beautiful face.

Ian read through the Wolfgang File, adding some post-it notes before putting it down. Suzette had, as usual done a superb job of designing the contract. Ian wondered often how she'd acquired such skill. He knew that his boss Price Smith-Marshal held Suzette in high regard. She was the only paralegal with permission to call him by his first name. The office rumor mill floated hints of an affair between them. But no one really believed it. Brittain Smith-Marshal was an awesome catch for any man and Price Smith Marshal cherished the very ground she walked on. Enough so to have changed his own last name from Marshal to Smith-Marshall, all for Brittain Smith. No one at the firm dared joke about the new Smith-Marshal moniker when it first appeared. Besides, everyone knew that between Suzette's job and son Ian, Suzette had no life.

Ian was annoyed by Sean's need for separation from him after the short vacation trip. But he knew that he had to cultivate this relationship at her speed and not his own. Ian wanted this one and for once paid attention to his partner's needs. Her aloofness during the ride home confused him completely. Ian had never experienced any kind of rejection from a woman before, and didn't know at all how to take it, but swallow his pride he did. For the future... he kept reminding himself. Ian dialed Sean's number and got a busy signal. Sean had never taken the phone off the hook before. She'd gone home to her own apartment, but usually only to pick up clothes or mail. In the car, when he'd touched her leg, Sean had actually jumped. So for the first time in his life, Ian felt the insecurity of a relationship that could be in trouble. Tomorrow, he promised himself they would talk.

Fifteen

Will reported to work on Monday morning dressed in a
new suit. He felt the need for a change. It had already
begun within and it had a name, Sean Smith-Marshal.
This new world held new possibilities and Will had every intention
of helping himself, this time.

Bo Longmire and Dr. Wethers were standing at the nurse's
station in the ER. Bo let out a long whistle and Dr. Wethers held
out a hand to the prodigal doctor. Will's entire rhythm and aura
had changed. He was dressed to the nines and looked great. They
kidded him about his new haircut. Dr. Wethers asked if he'd found
any time for the conference, or had he only fought off the women
the entire time. Will grinned and shared in this new camaraderie. It
felt good, like he had suddenly stepped out of the shadows and into
the sunshine. Nurse Diana Thomas was doing temporary duty in
the ER, down from the Surgical Ward. She definitely liked this new
Dr. Thorpe. She had never seen him look so good. The new haircut
gave him just enough style. Diana had been tempted to ask Will out
to dinner after his wife died, but thought it was too soon. But this
new and improved Will Thorpe was going to quickly become the
talk of the hospital. She decided to consider asking him out later

in the day. "Will", she said smiling at him, "welcome back!" "You are looking wonderful!" A couple of days in Hawaii and you have certainly blossomed. Maybe we should go back together?" Will blushed to his toes. He'd always liked Diana, but she had never spoken to him like that before. The rest of his day was spent dodging the compliments. After lunch, a huge bouquet of yellow roses arrived for Dr. Thorpe. The note read simply "Sean". "Yellow roses" Nurse Thomas reminded him, "were a sign of friendship". But two dozen yellow roses, meant something altogether different. Will could have jumped over the moon so easily in that moment. But he managed to hold back. He may be dressed differently, but he was still the same private person. Diana Thomas knew then, that her opportunity was gone. Someone else was already staking a claim.

Suzette was finally seeing a break in Tristan's cold. He had slept quietly through the night and his fevers had ceased. A runny nose and a little cough were all that remained. Suzette had let him sleep with her. Whenever he was sick, she did this. Suzette felt better knowing she could put her finger on him in an instant. When Tristan was about twenty-two months old, Suzette had awakened in a cold sweat. She jumped up for no reason and ran to Tristan's crib. He was stiff and felt cold. She'd tried to rouse him from his sleep and couldn't. Finally, after a few moments, he awakened. Two more times that same, Suzette had awakened for no apparent reason, again, only to discover each time, that Tristan was not breathing properly. God had awakened a mother with a child in danger. Suzette's faith in God had always been strong. Anne Butler praised HIM every day and taught her only child to do the same. Anne used to say "I am not just a believer. I know showing that her faith she'd taken one step beyond. Suzette did not attend services regularly, but was a good and fair person. She also had a powerful singing voice, another gift from the Maker. Whenever she could, Suzette performed for the church, backed up by the choir.

Suzette decided to stay home one more day, just to be safe. She called Ian to tell him. She found him in the office, much too early, and already in not too good a mood. "Mr. Adams, I am going to need one more day off. My son is much better, but I need an extra day to make sure the cold doesn't come back". "Are you sure you'll return tomorrow?" Ian asked irritated. Suzette took a deep breath. Some-times he could be such a pain. Suzette simply answered "Yes". "Good!" said Ian. We'll need to finalize the Wolfgang contract. I've made a few changes". Suzette smiled, but said nothing. She knew that contract was well-done and airtight. "Of course, Mr. Adams. See you tomorrow". Suzette hung up the phone and went to make breakfast for her son.

Sean awakened feeling rested, but apprehensive about seeing Ian. She found him in his office when she arrived. Sean carried two cups of steaming hot gourmet coffee. One was for him, intended as a peace offering. Leaning over his desk, Ian kissed her good morning and she let him. "I tried to call you last night but the line stayed busy" Ian pried. "I know, Mom called to tell me she was back. So we talked a little while. Sean shifted position in her seat. She had not told the whole truth. "I guess at some point I fell asleep without hanging up properly. "Sorry" she offered. "It's alright babe. The good news is that you're home and all mine again". Sean buried her face in the cup of java, saying nothing.

Ian, of course, missed the subtle message. He babbled on happily reporting the events of his life that she'd missed in the last two remarkable days. "How about dinner tonight? Some place special?" Ian proposed. "Fine, said Sean, but I'm going to have to go home a little early tonight, and alone. I've got some work to catch up on". Ian got up and moved around the desk and stood directly in front of Sean. "I'll just come home with you and spend the night". Smiling at her as she shook her head "no", Ian continued "Don't worry. I'll let you work. I promise not to disturb you". "Ian, you obviously forget to whom you are speaking. I've only been gone for two days love, not two light years. You, don't know the meaning of not tonight honey!" Ian pretended that she had wounded him mortally, but laughed. "All right, all right!", he offered. "Dinner, only! But you owe me, young lady and rest assured, I will come collecting!". Ian kissed the top of Sean's head and walked her to the door. "Now off with you. Suzette has been out with her sick child, and I have some catching up to do. By the way, did you know that she had a son?" Ian asked casually. "As a matter of fact, I did. He should be about three, almost four years old by now. I've seen him. He's a beautiful little boy and so smart! "Ian closed the door behind Sean and walked toward his desk doing mental math. No, he thought, dismissing the possibility. He reasoned that she would have told Him if he had fathered the child. Ian felt uneasy though.

Price went to his daughter's office to welcome her back. Sean gave him the Million-dollar smile that dazzled even her dad. "Hi Daddy!", she said as she arose from her desk to give him a hug. Price could see a sparkle in her eyes, he not seen before. "So, my pet, you did enjoy yourself in Hawaii". You look wonderful!!!". "Thanks Dad. It was fun. I have missed spending time with Mommy. It was not long enough though". "Your mother tells me that you two ran into Emmalyn Brown and her new family?", he asked raising a brow. Sean tried to laugh it off, not knowing how much Brittain had shared. "She's sort of adopted a young doctor, who is a widower and his Baby daughter, Merry" Sean volunteered, a tad too defensively. Price looked directly into his daughter's eyes and saw her nervousness. Men had never made her nervous before. This one had to be someone special. "And does this young doctor have, a name said Father?". "Yes, Daddy, he does". Sean glowed softly when she spoke his name "Will Thorpe". "Well now", he said, "and just where will this place our resident-and-currently-smitten-by-you young associate attorney, Ian Adams, Esquire?" Sean turned away from her father, embarrassed. "Dad", Sean only called him Dad when she was serious, Ian and I are…have an understanding. We're not engaged". Price however, was concerned about this situation.

Price understood as a man that Ian, as ambitious as he was, Ian had probably mapped out an entire life plan, which again probably included Sean AND the firm. Price was afraid that Sean took much too lightly the possible consequences they might all have to face, if she ended their relationship, whatever the status actually was. Instead of lecturing, he kissed her forehead and said only "Honey, your mother and I only want to see you happy. Promise ME, that if you find yourself in any difficulty in trying to work this out, that you will come to us immediately". "Oh Daddy, I'll be okay, I promise". "Sean, I am sure that YOU will be alright. Sweetie, you are holding all of the cards. Even though "you" haven't discussed any future plans with Ian, that does not mean he won't have made some. I just want you to be prepared for anything. Unintended lecture of an adult child, over. Do I have your promise though?" Sean stopped skirting the real issue and promised to be careful and to think smart. Price knew that Sean had chosen between the two. He called Brittain as soon as he returned to his office. He was going to need an update on their vacation. He also scribbled a note to talk to Emmalyn. Who was this Dr. Thorpe, and how had he, in only two days, managed to steal his baby's heart. Price had work to do. It took all of his restraint not to utilize his own staff private investigator.

Emmalyn called Brittain hoping to invite her to lunch. Judge Smith-Marshal, as she had been told, was still away on a business trip. Apparently, Britt had scheduled some additional personal days following the conference. "Good!", thought Emma, "hopefully we can get together soon". Emma tried Brittain at her home. Her housekeeper Ellie answered the phone. The Judge, as she put it had gone out early to her Day Spa for a facial, manicure and pedicure. Ellie was surprised to hear Emmalyn's voice.

Ellie had been the Marshal's housekeeper since Sean was a pre-teen. George and Emmalyn had been extended family members of the Marshals, and often shared family and holiday occasions. Emmalyn left word with Ellie that she wanted to invite Britt to lunch. Ellie promised to phone the day spa and leave a message for the Judge.

Will decided to send a bouquet to Sean to say thanks again. He phoned Merry's favorite party store to order a special balloon bouquet. He wanted a stuffed papa bear holding a little baby girl bear. No substitutions. Will knew that Robina Grayson, owner of "Fantasy Bouquets", would exceed his expectations. Will instructed Robina to sign the card with a heart and inside the heart write two letters "W" on the top and "M" on the bottom and nothing else. Will gave Robina the address and asked that the order be rushed, for delivery later that same afternoon. Robina assured Dr. Thorpe that she knew of an exquisite gift shop in Palmetto Springs that would provide the kind of bouquet he wanted. Will reminded her to spare no expense. He wanted sweet, funny, thank you, but most of all unforgettable. Dr. Thorpe had officially entered the race for Sean Smith-Marshal's heart.

Brittain lay relaxed on the table having finished her European facial. The facial also included massage of her neck, shoulders, arms, hands and feet as well. Britt was listening to the sounds of soft music and the ocean rushing to the shore when there was a knock on the door. Her Esthetician Charly, apologized for disturbing her, but the judge had received a phone call. It was Ellie, her housekeeper. Britt sat up alarmed. "Judge, Ellie started, everyone is fine, everything is alright. I hated to phone you now, but Emmalyn Brown called and I thought it might be important, so I decided not to wait until you got home". "Thanks Ellie", Brittain shared. It's alright. I'm glad you let me know. There is a matter of importance that I must speak to Emmalyn about. I'll phone her now".

Emmalyn and Merry had just come inside from the garden after cutting fresh flowers. Merry was making a bouquet for her father's desk at work. Emmalyn heard the phone ring and asked Merry to play with the flowers while she answered the call. Emma sat down at the kitchen table in front of the big bay window she loved.

"Hello Emma?" Britt asked. "Yes dear, how are you? said Emma. Thank you for returning my call so quickly. Ellie told me you had gone to the spa". "Yes Emm I'm still at the salon. I was worried about you though, so I decided to call from here. Are you alright?" "I'm fine Britt, thank you. I called because I was hoping to invite you to lunch today. There are some things I want to talk over with you" Emmalyn revealed. "I'm glad because I want to talk to you also about Will and Sean"

Brittain said. "Emm, you haven't been to the house for a while. Why don't you come for lunch today? Britt invited. I know Ellie would love to see you too". "Honey I am taking care of Merry while Will is working." "Wonderful! said Britt, I would love to see her again. I therefore cordially invite the two of you to lunch. Let's say about one o'clock? I'll send a limo for you both, so you won't have to make the long drive, yourself." "We'll be there Britt and thanks again." "No problem, in fact I'll bet we both want to talk about the same thing." "I think you're right Britt. See you then." "Merry, Emma said, picking up the baby. Let's go and pick some special flowers for Aunt Britt. Do you remember Aunt Britt from our vacation? She is Sean's mommy. She is the one that sent you the beautiful stuffed puppy while we were on vacation." "Okay Grandma, will you help me?" Merry asked happily. Back out to the garden they went. "We are going to Aunt Britt's house today for lunch, so you can give her the flowers yourself". "Can I wear one of my new dresses, Grandma?" "Of course you may!" said Grandma, hugging the child.

Deborah Diggsby, owner of Panache Day Spa, checked in on Brittain, as she finished her pedicure ritual. Judge Smith-Marshal was an old and valued customer. Over the years they had become friends. "How is Sean doing these days Brittain? She hasn't been in for a while?" said Deborah. "Fine Deborah, you know Sean though, always busy. But I have a feeling you just might be seeing her soon though", Brittain shared. "New boyfriend?" Deborah asked. "Between you and I, maybe... This one could definitely be "the one"! "I want an invitation to the grand affair when the wedding bells ring, Britt". "Now you know Deborah, that Sean would be the first one to ask you to handle the task of making her beautiful!" smiled Brittain. "As though your child needs any help" said Deborah. They both laughed and parted.

Sixteen

ean wooed Ian by inviting him to lunch. Suzette's promise to
return to work the next day seemed to lift Ian's spirits a little,
as well. As far as Sean could tell, Ian and Suzette had a decent
working relationship, but shared no office camaraderie. It seemed
strange, but Sean never questioned it. Suzette was the best paralegal
in the firm. Sean liked her. Suzette was a very private person though.
Price Smith- Marshal seemed to know her better than anyone else.
But he'd never talked about Suzette with Sean.

Sean seemed warmer towards Ian, than he'd noticed in a few
days. He'd put his arm around her during the ride back to work,
and she hadn't rebuffed him. Ian decided that Sean must have been
preoccupied with something over the last week and whatever it had
been, had passed. Feeling relieved, he didn't press about her plans
for later. Ian walked Sean to her office. A quick peck on the cheek
as he opened her office door brought him face to face with the most
elaborate balloon bouquet he had ever seen. There were about a
dozen balloons in varying shapes, filled with potpourri and scented
with the fragrance of Sean's favorite perfume. Moire, satin and silk
bows streamed everywhere.

Two bears, one father and one daughter, held bows that read

"thank you". Ian could see the card, which showed a hand-drawn heart inside which were only the letters "W" on top and "M" on the bottom. Sean was overwhelmed by the gift and beamed when she read the card. She said only "Of course", when she read it. Ian was definitely disturbed by this event. "Who in the world would send you such a thing?" Ian tried to inquire without sounding as angry as he felt. Sean had forgotten his presence for a moment. She turned to look at him and immediately stopped smiling. "It's from you know the little girl who is my Aunt Emma's granddaughter. You remember…the one I met in Hawaii, when I went to see Mother!" Sean hadn't told Ian everything. "Well, it seems this child must be the dowager princess, to be able to afford such a gift for you!" Ian stated, obviously livid. "How old is this child? Ian insisted, determined to get to the truth. "She is about three or four" Sean defended knowing exactly where he was headed. "I'm sure her father arranged this for her," Sean admitted not looking into Ian's face. "And might her father be the handsome doctor you spoke of… a widower, I believe you said." Ian had hit bullseye and judging by the look of shock on Sean's face, something he had never seen before. There was obviously much more going on here. Ian silently turned and left Sean's office. Sean was sorry to see Ian hurt that way, but she also felt relieved. The truth was demanding to be told, and Sean no longer wanted to hide from it.

Price passed a devastated Ian Adams outside Sean's office, apparently so upset, he even neglected to speak to his boss. When Price saw the balloon bouquet he understood. "It's time baby girl", he told his daughter. Go ahead and do it now. I'll be in my office, if you need me. I know this may seem like the wrong place to let him down, but at least here, I know you are safe". It made good sense to her. It also made her feel safer, in case Ian lost his temper. Sean had never seen it, but she could not afford to be mistaken either. "Alright Dad. I'll go now".

"Sean, he said as he was leaving the office, I need for you to come to my office as soon as you are done, and I am speaking right now as your father. I will need to know for myself, that he has not harmed you in any way. Promise????". "Alright Dad... I'll be there as soon as I finish". "Thanks". Price Smith-Marshal asked his secretary to call the head of security immediately. Dan Montague instructed by his boss, stationed himself just outside of Ian's office, just in case. He nodded at Sean as she went inside and put his thumb up to let her know that he would be there asap, if she needed him.

Ian stood up behind his desk with his back to the door, staring blankly out of the window. Like one of those balloons popping, his whole world had exploded, right before his eyes. He had read all of the signs, but refused to listen to his own senses. Ian had never before been on the receiving end of this sad scenario. He heard the knock at his door and knew Sean was waiting. He could not find the words to even tell her to enter. Sean opened the door slowly, closed it gently and sat down. "Ian, I'm so sorry. I haven't been completely honest, with you... or myself, for that matter. The gift is from the doctor I met in Hawaii. I didn't go to Hawaii expecting to fall in love", Sean pleaded. Ian whirled around, his face a mask of tears and anger. "How do you meet someone and fall in love, in less than a week??? Explain it to me Sean...Make me understand!!"

"You and I have been together for months, and I honestly hoped that we".....he continued to beg. "Ian please stop. We have never talked about the future, about a future together" she reminded him. "But that did not mean I never thought about it Sean!" Ian sat down in an easy chair and bending over, covered his face with his hands. "You are all that I want., all I ever needed girl. Couldn't you see that, Sean??? I made no secret about the way I felt about you. I let the whole world know that you were my future. How is it that everyone else could see this, but not you". Ian's heart was bleeding. Bleeding like he'd made Rain's as she lay dying.

Bleeding like Suzette's continued to. "I must ask you to forgive me Ian. I never meant to hurt you this way. But our relationship is over. I'm not really sure there ever really was an us", Sean admitted carefully. The very words that killed Rain Thorpe, had come back

Like the Grimm Reaper to claim him, heart and soul and Ian missed none of the irony. "You know he said, finally facing her, my father used to tell me "that even snake- charmers get bit sometimes too". Dropping his head, once again, he said only. "I guess he was right. Listen Sean, you don't have to worry about me. I'll be alright". Hands in the air, Sean reached for him and offered a hug. Ian waved his hand "no" and walked back to the window. He called Tabitha, to let her know that he was leaving early. Ian told Tabitha that he didn't feel very well and truth was, he didn't.

Emmalyn and Merry enjoyed the long ride in the limousine to Britt's house, dressed up like Cinderella heading for the ball. When they arrived, Emma and Ellie hugged like long lost friends. The two were about the same age. Ellie was introduced to Miss Merry Adams Thorpe. Ellie took charge of Merry and invited the child to eat with her, promising to show her Brittain's elegant Japanese gardens and ponds.

Emmalyn was grateful to Ellie. She had so much to tell Britt. They dined on Caesar Salad, grilled Salmon and Kiwi Souffle. Emma looked a little pale and sickly to Britt, since seeing her in Hawaii and inquired about it. "Emma are you really alright? You look more tired than I've ever seen". "That is one of the reasons I needed to see you Britt. "I am not well", Emma revealed. "I've been more than a little tired lately, so I went to see Dr. Robinson. Britt, the news isn't good, but it's alright". I have Cancer" Emmalyn stated too matter-of-factly. "Emm, No! It can't be! Are you going to undergo chemo?" Britt asked frightened for her old friend. "No Britt" she responded flatly. Dr. Robinson says, it has metastasized from my colon to my right lung and honestly, I don't want to put myself through it. Britt, I've had a good life. Will and Merry have given me the joy of having a child and grandchild. George was the love of my life, and I am at peace with whatever is mine to accept. Please understand that I'm not giving up. I am simply giving myself permission to move on to the next natural phase of my existence. Emmalyn had thought out everything. "Britt I need your help though". "Emmalyn, anything.

You know that" Britt expressed with glazed eyes. My Will is in love with Sean but he is so shy and has been hurt so deeply, I'm afraid he'll let her get away. I don't know how much longer I'll have, but I think those two belong together". Brittain reached across the table and covered Emmalyn's hand with her own. "I know Emmalyn. I think Sean is falling in love with him too". Call it mother's intuition. But I know I'm right" said Britt. "Well then, I won't worry about it any longer. Luck, you know, is in the Lord, Britt and now I can see that God's hands have been busily preparing our children to share a future. Those two were meant to be together, like George and I and you and Price. I was worried about how Sean would feel about his having a child to care for. Sean is still a baby herself". "I know Emm, but you know, I remember how she responded to Merry when the child explained that her mother was in heaven. I truly believe that Sean and Merry have already bonded, and that Love will take care of the rest". "There is one other matter Britt" said Emma. "I have changed my will. I want Merry and Will to inherit my estate. Will has no idea of these plans. Nor does he know how vast my holdings are. I want to ask you to become the executor of my estate. It would mean so much to me. Will is going to need the advice of someone he trusts and respects". Brittain bit her lip to keep from breaking down. "Of course, Emm. I would be honored". "Well now, that business is taken care of, come and let's walk through your garden. It's so lovely this year again", Emma complimented. Emmalyn, Ellie and Britt strolled, while Merry ran happily ahead.

Suzette called for Ian, but the call was transferred automatically to Tabitha. Ian had gone home early, sick. That sounded strange to Suzette. Ian never got sick and even when he didn't feel 100%, he worked anyway. Tabitha had heard a rumor and was more than anxious to pass it on to Suzette. It seems that Sean had received a huge and extraordinary bouquet of some sort and Ian had become angry over it. It was from another man. Even the head of Security had been called by Mr. Smith-Marshal, in case things got ugly. It appears that Ian and Sean are history as a couple. Suzette was shocked. Even though she hated indulging in gossip and rumor, most often what was told, was either true or had some semblance of truth to it. If at all true, Ian was going to be tough to work around. Suzette knew that he was not used to being the "dumpee". Oddly, she just felt sorry for him, but all she could think of was, "welcome to the real world". Not all that long ago, Ian had done the very same thing to her.

Sean knocked on her father's office door and silently blew him a kiss. "Dad, I'm going home to see Mom, and if you don't mind, I'm going to spend the night in my old room". Price just nodded. "See you later Sean, and be careful on the road. We can talk later if you feel like it". Sean forced a little smile. Price let out a deep breath of air. At least she was alright. Tabitha had called and told him that Ian decided to leave early too. He'd said something about not feeling well. Price also knew that tomorrow the office would be a beehive of talk and innuendo.

Brittain sat on the terrace drinking iced tea and thinking about Emmalyn. The limousine ride back, she knew was going to be a quiet one. Merry had walked herself out in the garden and eaten a hearty lunch as Ellie reported. The child was probably already asleep. Brittain smiled remembering the small bouquet of flowers Merry had given her. Emmalyn herself, would have much to think about. Emmalyn's estate was worth well in excess of ten million dollars. Will and Merry would inherit the bulk of it, minus charitable endowments and taxes. Britt had been touched that Emmalyn had asked her to be executor. Brittain liked Emm's new family and was happy to know they would be so blessed. She knew too, that on a day too soon, she would have to bury someone she cared so much about.

Britttain was lost in her own thoughts, and failed to hear Sean walk up behind her. Sean reached down and hugged her mother from behind. Britt was surprised to see her daughter and startled by the look on Sean's face. "Is there something wrong with your father, she insisted as she sat bolt upright???" "No, Mommy! He's fine. I am sorry to have frightened you. I just needed to come home. I broke off my relationship with Ian Adams". Sean looked tortured. "And are you going to be okay, baby? Britt asked. "Yes Mommy. Actually, he took it really hard. Truthfully, he exploded when he saw the bouquet that Dr. Thorpe had sent to my office. I couldn't hide my feelings any longer and didn't want to, so I told Ian that I had fallen in love with someone else". Sean looked at her mother directly, hoping she had not disappointed her. "Sweetie, I saw it coming when we were in Hawaii. Something clicked between you and Will, from the moment you met. You just didn't know it. Britt smiled at her child. Seeing that her daughter was on overload, Brittain backed off the conversation. "Listen sweetie, why don't you stay and have dinner with your aging parents tonight and sleep in your old room. I'm sure your Dad would love to spend time outside of the office with you" Brittain announced. "Thanks Mom, I was hoping you'd say that". "I'll tell Ellie to freshen your room and make your favorite Eggplant Parmigiana for dinner tonight. It will be like old times". Brittain smiled at her child and opened her arms for a hug. It was obvious to her that Sean needed the love of her parents to restore her. Sean headed for her room, and Brittain to give Ellie instructions for a change in dinner plans. She also needed to call Price.

Price went home earlier than usual. Sean's situation had distracted him. He finished working on the review of the firm's cases, leaving some dictation to be finished in his study at home. Brittain had called to assure him that Sean had made it home safely, and to come as early as he could, because there were other matters she wanted to share with him.

Ellie took Price's brief case, suit jacket and tie from him as soon as he entered the house. She had not witnessed as much traffic in that home, in one ordinary day, in a long time, with Emmalyn and her Merry visiting, Sean spending the night and then her father home earlier than seven o'clock in the evening. Something was definitely going on. Ellie never questioned the family. They were comfortable around her and shared their conversations without hesitation, in her presence. Ellie could be trusted and they knew it.

Brittain waited until dessert was served to her otherwise quiet family to reveal that Emma was dying of Cancer. Sean and Price expressed absolute surprise. Price had expected the dinner conversation to revolve around their daughter's dilemma. So much seemed to be going on. "Does Will know Mom??" Sean asked. "No, honey. Emmalyn just found out herself. I think she needs more time to deal with it before she tells anyone else. She has asked me to become her executor. Sean, we are going to need to be there for your Aunt Emmalyn and also for Will and Merry too. They are her family now and love her as much as we do. I'm sure of this" Brittain told her family. Sean blushed at the sound of his name. Neither Brittain, nor Price missed this. Sean only said "Of course". Even though the family occasion had unfortunate underpinnings, Price was happy to see his family all under the same roof once more. After dinner, each seemed preoccupied by their own thoughts and everyone decided to retire early. Sean showered and wrapped herself in her favorite terrycloth robe. Opening the French doors leading to her veranda, she stepped out into the cool night breeze and sat down. Brittain knocked softly on Sean's door and entered the room, joining Sean on the balcony. They sat close together on the loveseat, quietly listening to the crickets and the night noises. "I love him Mommy" Sean said only. "I know baby", her mother replied. And the child Sean...what about Merry? They are a package deal". Sean smiled softly. "Yes, Mommy I know. Merry needs me as much as her father does. Maybe even more. Every child has a right to know that a mother could love unconditionally. You have given me that a million times over and I am so grateful for it. Mommy I want them both, but I'm not sure if it's not too soon. I'm not even sure Will feels the same way?" Sean said in a dejected voice. Brittain knew better. But she could not help with this one. Will and Sean had to find each other. "Sweetheart, this time, just trust in God. Remember how my mother Mima, used to say "In God's time everything is made ready. You just pray about it". "By the way", reaching into her pocket, she pulled out a slip of paper with Will's phone number scribbled in

Emmalyn's handwriting. "Here", she said to Sean. Brittain kissed her womanchild and said goodnight, knowing in her heart, that everything was going to be as it should.

"Hello???" The sound of Will's voice reached deep into Sean's heart. "Hi…It's me" she said. Will breathed deeply. Sean could hear it. "Hello, Me. How are you?" Will was trying to keep it light. "Thank you for the most wonderful bouquet, I have ever received. You didn't have to do that" she said. "Oh, but I did, Will admitted. "How else are you going to know how I feel about you….????" Will could hear Sean's smile. So, he smiled too. Goodnight, my love, she said and kissed the phone.

Will walked outside into his garden and shouted in silence at the stars shining brightly just for him. He'd broken out of his shell, and though frightened that he wouldn't be ready for that leap, he now believed that he was going to be alright. In God's own time and according to His wisdom, Love had been offered to Will. With open, greedy and hungry arms, Will was going to grab all that he could possibly hold and hold the most beautiful woman he'd ever seen, in his arms and in his life.

Price asked Brittain to take a walk in the garden. Britt knew that he was worried about Sean. They compared the details each knew, of her breakup with Ian. Brittain and Price held hands as they walked silently past the lily pond and listened to the trickling sound of the small stream running across from it. Price hugged his wife, feeling so grateful just to have such remarkable women in his life.

Seventeen

Ian stopped at a liquor store on his way home and picked up a bottle of Crown Royal Scotch Whiskey. His plan was simple. He was going to drown his sorrows. He could not believe that in a matter of only days, his whole life had fallen apart. A gentle rain started to fall as he reached his house on the lake, the very house, he was thinking, Sean had helped him pick out. The smell of her was in every room. Ian went outside hoping to escape it.

Ian walked down to the lake with only the bottle of whiskey to keep him company. Sitting down on a rock, he opened the bottle and drank from it. Ian was not a big drinker, so the first few gulps made him choke and cough, but the buzz he needed came quickly. Leaning his head against a tree, he let the tears flow freely. Ian wasn't angry with anyone else. Sean had only done what he'd always given himself permission to do, to live life on his own terms. It was true that they had not committed to each other in words. Ian just assumed that she knew that he wanted her in his future. Now, the only thing Ian Adams knew for sure was that he wanted and needed to get sloppy drunk, as fast as possible. He didn't even care that the rain and wind had both come to join him. The black skies promised that the rain was probably going to last for the night. Ian was getting soaked and he couldn't care less.

Suzette knew that she shouldn't care what happened to Ian, but she did. She tried to call him at home, but no one answered. The answering machine had not even been turned on. This was not like him. Ian prided himself on being the consummate professional at all times. Suzette did not want to go out into this rainy night, especially since Tristan was just getting over his cold. But she was afraid for Ian. Suzette had known him long enough to see that his façade was all that mattered to him, and very soon everyone was going to know what happened. She was not sure how he would handle this situation, alone. Against even her own better judgment, Suzette dressed Tristan for the rainfall and headed for Ian's house. Perhaps, now since Truth seemed determined to take center stage, it was time to introduce him to his son.

Suzette pulled into Ian's driveway and honked her car horn. No one came to the door. Frustrated, yet afraid, she picked up Tristan, who had fallen asleep in his car seat and carried him to the door. Knocking loudly, there was still no answer. She tried the doorknob and it turned. Ian had neglected to lock it. Suzette went inside and put the baby on the sofa. She left him in his raingear, so she would not disturb his sleep. Suzette had looked in every room except the kitchen, but found no trace of him. Suddenly, the wind caused the kitchen door to swing open and bump against the door stop. She ran into the room half-expecting to see Ian, but did not. She closed the door then and locked it and went back into the living room, to check on Tristan. Thankfully, the noise had not disturbed the sleeping child. Suzette looked through the picture window in the living room hoping to see some sign of Ian. Squinting to see through the raindrops, she found him. There under a tree he sat. Suzette ran out of the house not sure what she'd find. Her heart was pumping so hard; she could barely breathe. Ian was drenched. His clothing resembled water-soaked leaves left in a pile on the lawn. He wasn't moving. Fearing the worst, she reached for his neck to try to find a pulse. It was slow but thankfully, it was still going. Suzette smelled first the alcohol, then saw the half-empty bottle of liquor. Relieved that he had not tried to harm himself, she tried to wake him. There was no telling how long he'd been outside. Suzette shook him and called his name many times but Ian would not wake up, only mumbling and flailing his arms about. Suzette kneeled down and pulled Ian up. Leaning him against the tree, she managed to get one of his arms around her own neck. The jerky movements awakened him long enough for him to finally see her. Ian offered Suzette a very drunken hello. She begged him to try to at least stumble along and help her to get him inside. He was too heavy for her to manage alone. Half-stumbling, being dragged and leaning on Suzette, Ian reached the dry indoors.

Suzette looked over at the couch at the baby, thankful that Tristan had slept through it all. She dragged Ian into his bedroom. He felt like dead weight with the wet clothes sticking to his body. Suzette undressed him. Naked and exposed, he started to tremble from the cold, so she wrapped him in every blanket that she could find. Suzette rummaged around the bathroom and found a thermometer. Ian's temperature was up. She was hoping the same alcohol that had made him drunk would also help him to sweat out the oncoming fever.

Suzette stopped finally to take off Tristan's coat, hat and boots and covered him with a blanket and placed her sweater under his head for a pillow. Then she started a blazing fire in the fireplace. Going back to the kitchen, she put on a kettle of water for tea. The night was going to be a long one. Suzette borrowed a pair of jeans and a shirt from Ian's well-dressed closet, hanging her own wet clothes over the shower curtain rod in the bathroom to dry.

Suzette awakened Ian many times during the next few hours to feed him the steaming hot Tea with honey. Each time he'd tried to mumble something to her, but she couldn't understand his words. She settled into the armchair located next to the bed. She had just begun to nod off when she heard Ian call her Sean. In an alcoholic stupor, he tried to propose marriage. Even then, Ian could not see who it was that cared for him. Two hours later his temperature had peaked at 102 degrees, then started to slowly drop. Ian had finally stopped fighting in his sleep and remained quiet until the early morning hours. Suzette, exhausted herself, had fallen deeply asleep in her chair.

Tristan sat up, alone, on the sofa, not recognizing anything in the room except his mother's sweater. Frightened, he slid down off the couch and went sleepily in search of his mother. He walked into Ian's bedroom and saw his mother asleep in the chair. Ian was wide awake, but groggy. Tristan, now awake and curious, walked over to the bed and stopped directly in front of Ian. Ian's open eyes settled on the miniature version of himself, in disbelief. He sat up too suddenly and frightened the child. Tristan beelined to his mother's lap. Suzette woke up startled by the hands grabbing at her. She smiled when she saw her little man. When she looked over to check on Ian, he was sitting up in the bed staring at his son.

"How???? Why didn't you ever tell me about him…about my son??" Ian asked ashamed. "Tell you what Ian?" Suzette said as she stood up to leave the room. "Wait. Please", he said. Let's start this…all over, please for me. I realize that you don't owe me an explanation. I treated you badly and left you alone to handle all the responsibility by yourself". I know you may not believe this, but I've done a little growing up since yesterday morning. "You mean, since Sean dum…left you for someone else" Suzette retorted, ashamed of herself. Holding his aching head, Ian said "So, I guess everyone knows all about it, huh?" looking so wounded and embarrassed. Suzette was sorry she'd chosen to strike out at him in that moment. "I'm sorry Ian. You have enough going on". "Suzette how, why are you here?? No. I said that wrong again. Please, I'm sorry. Let me try that again. Ian tried to stand up, but the monster headache left by the scotch, made him sit back down.

"Please, he said, changing the subject and looking at Tristan. "What is my…his name??? he asked, truly wanting to know. Tristan understood that Ian had asked his name. He sat up boldly in his mother's arms and said "TRISTAN ADAMS BUTLER". Suzette waited for Ian's denial of the child, prepared to launch a counter attack. Instead, Ian smiled and asked Tristan to come to him. Tristan looked into his mother's eyes for approval. Suzette nodded yes to him. Guarded and with eyes wide, the child let his father take him from the safety of his mother's arms. Ian slowly took in every detail of the child's face and tiny hands. Ian could feel the slow warmth and tenderness that God bestows as a special gift meant only for new parents. Ian was falling in love with the small copy of himself. The child seemed to possess his father's fearless approach to new experiences. There was nothing timid about him. Ian would have been a fool to deny this one, when everything about him shouted Adams.

Ian took his eyes off Tristan long enough to tell Suzette that he was beautiful and that she had done a wonderful job with him. Suzette was speechless. She had never seen this side of Ian. It was unguarded and unpretentious. "Thank you for giving him the Adams name". Again, Suzette was stunned. She had been convinced that only a paternity suit would make Ian accept this baby. Ian smiled at Tristan and tickled him. Both of them smiled at Suzette. Suzette gave Ian a sad smile and a tearful "thank you" mouthed silently. Father and son belonged together, just as father and daughter had, so long ago. All had suffered from not knowing the other.

Suzette wiped at her eyes and told Ian that she had tried to call him at home, but there had been no answer, nor was the machine turned on and it concerned her. Ian reached for his Rolex watch and put it on Tristan's arm so he could play with it. The child was busily filling it with fingerprints. "So, said Ian, you already knew what had happened when you decided to come over?" "Wait, he said, don't answer. I appreciate what you did, but I don't need you or anyone else feeling sorry for me…" Holding her arms out to Tristan, Suzette just shook her head. Tristan slid down and ran to his mother. Suzette took off the watch and set it on the table next to the bed. "I came because I was concerned about you, that's all! Now I've got to go". In a few hours it will be time to go to work and get Tristan off to preschool" "I'm tired Ian" Suzette slipped. "Sorry, Mr. Adams", she corrected herself. Ian stood directly in front of Suzette as she held Tristan in her arms and looked into her eyes. "May I say thank you and ask you to call me Ian, the way you once did?" Ian asked looking appropriately embarrassed. After all, we do have a son together. Let's not confuse him". A weak smile was all Ian could manage. In just a matter of days, he had begged enough for an entire lifetime. "Alright then Ian it is. I'll see you at the office later...Ian". "Suzette, in case you're wondering, I'll be alright now. Last night was." Ian tried to explain, "...Was last night" Suzette finished for him. "And I will see you at work", Ian assured her. As for you, Master Tristan Adams-Butler, may I come to see you someday soon?" Tristan stuck his index finger in his mouth and smiled at his father, all the while nodding yes.

Eighteen

Judge Smith-Marshal entered her chambers tired, but prepared for her full court docket. Brittain enjoyed the quiet of the morning in her office. The early morning sunlight reminded her that true justice came through God. HE is Truth and Light. It humbled Judge Smith-Marshal to know that in her own way, she could also do His work.

Her meditation was broken by a knock on the door. As she walked over to open the door, she finished her morning prayers. A tall gentleman stood before her holding a briefcase and wearing horn-rimmed metal glasses. His attire told her that he was probably one of the many attorneys she would encounter in her day. "May I help you?" Brittain inquired, as she looked around for her Clerk. Glancing at her watch, she realized it was still too early for the staff to be in. "Yes, Your Honor. I apologize for disturbing you so early, but I have some important documents for you. I am Paris Majors, attorney representing the estate of one deceased Anne Butler. Brittain did not recognize the name. Confused, Brittain said only "Please come in. Have a seat". "Judge Smith- Marshal, I have some documents that I have been instructed to turn over to you, specifically at this time. When you have had an opportunity to review them you will understand better why they have been sent to you. Here is my business card. Please feel free to call, if you have any questions". Brittain thanked the lawyer and placed the thick envelope inside her desk drawer and locked it. She'd have to review it later. She needed to read through her notes on the cases she was scheduled to hear.

Suzette knew that she was going to have to run on raw energy at work. Tristan had awakened in a playful mood. Thankfully, her morning with him had been an easy one. Suzette drove to work remembering the previous night's events. She had seen a very different Ian Adams and wasn't sure how to take him. Tristan was going to have a father in his life. Ian seemed to want it, and Tristan was going to surely need it.

Suzette had left home in the dark of night and returned, herself, a different person. From night to day so much had happened. Tomorrow, she reminded herself, I am graduating from Law School. "Mama, she prayed. I know you can hear me. You were right and I was wrong, but now they have will have each other. I only wish you could be here too". Suzette knew that the day was going to drain her emotionally. Price had asked to be invited to the ceremony and Suzette had hugged him in gratitude because she had no other family with whom to share her next important milestone accomplishment.

Ian entered the office dressed well as usual, but peering out from behind some very red eyes and on this new day, made the coffee and placed the small bouquet of flowers he'd picked up on the way to work in a vase, placing it at the center of Suzette's desk. where she could not possibly miss it. Suzette was surprised to smell the unmistakable aroma of the freshly-brewed coffee. Ian had actually made coffee for her, for a change. The flowers on her desk held a card which read only "Ian". Suzette felt awkward around him the entire day, and Ian probably had as well because he had avoided her too. More importantly was that they had come to a truce and Suzette liked this new Ian Adams.

Ian called Tabitha and scheduled a few minutes with Price before the end of the day. Price was expecting it, but wanted no controversy. Ian entered Price's office quietly. Even Price noticed a difference in him. The arrogant swagger was gone. Ian was no longer center stage, even in his own mind. "Sir, I am sure you are aware of the new developments in my relationship with your daughter". "I am Ian, and let me say first..." "If I may interrupt you, sir, I think you'll want to hear what I am going to say". Looking down at his hands, Ian continued. "I care a great deal about Sean, but she doesn't feel the same way, she tells me. I know that it makes things awkward here at the firm, but I want to assure you, actually both you and Sean, that we can get past this. I made assumptions about the two of us without knowing what Sean wanted. I won't deny that I did have a master plan and "yes", I saw myself marrying your daughter and maybe someday.... Well, now that's history, but I believe that Sean and I can still have a professional relationship at the very least. Mr. Smith-Marshal, I've learned quite a bit about myself in the last few days. It's funny, I always thought I knew exactly who I was and exactly where I was going, too. I was so sure of everything, so very cocky and selfish". Ian rubbed his face and sighed saying "I have hurt some good people whose only guilt was that they had loved me. Maybe, this is what I needed force me to do some growing up. So, in short, I'd like to keep my job and move forward from here".

Any feather could have knocked Price completely out of his chair. He'd never really cared for Ian, but kept it to himself. Price never interfered in his daughter's relationships. He trusted and respected her too much to do so. But he'd been tempted where Ian was concerned. Price had seen too many men like him, arrogant and so sure of everything. Price had known in his heart that Ian's plans probably did include marriage to Sean and eventually taking over the firm. Ian had confirmed as much. Price knew nothing of all that Ian had gone through, but he knew he was looking at someone who was ready to learn from his mistakes. Price liked to look a man in the eye. He stood up and held out his hand to the young attorney. Ian looked up fully into the eyes of wisdom and compassion. "Thank you, Sir.

I won't disappoint you". Ian walked out of the office holding his head a little higher.

Brittain carried the large envelope home. She'd had a long day but was curious to know its contents. Settled in her study with a cup of tea, she sliced open the top with her letter opener. The first document was a letter written directly to her. The handwriting was simple, without flourishes. Brittain finished the first page, incredulous over its contents. Afraid to read it again, but needing some legal confirmation, she thumbed through the pages looking for only one thing. The birth certificate was there in black and white. Irrefutable proof. Brittain was still too shocked to react. She read the second page of the letter, then reread it.

Price arrived home with much to tell Brittain about his conversation with Ian. He'd been convinced that Sean would not have to fear repercussions, and that Ian would be staying on at the firm. Even though Price had not liked him, Ian had potential. Price found Brittain in her study. He knocked softly on the open door and went in. Brittain looked up at him as though she didn't even know who he was. Price had never seen his wife look this way. "Britt, honey are you alright? What's wrong?!

Is it Sean? Is she alright?" Brittain handed him the packet of papers. Price sat down wondering what in the world could leave his wife looking so distraught. Brittain watched him. Price read the first page and the birth certificate in total disbelief. "Brittain, please believe that I have never cheated on you! I knew this woman just before I met you, and certainly before we were married. In fact, I never knew that she had been pregnant. She never told me". "I know honey, she explained it all in the letter. You haven't read it all. Price, darling, we can get through this, together.

Price reached for Brittain. They held onto each other as though together they could will their lives to return to the way they were only a day ago. Suzette Butler, Anne Butler's only child, was also Price Smith-Marshal's daughter. Brittain was hurt because someone else had borne Price's first child. Even though they had not known then, they now held the proof that their precious bundle, Sean had not been his only progeny. But Brittain hurt also for Anne Butler. Even though Price had enough wealth to help her take care of the child, Anne had chosen not to ask. Brittain could not help but to admire the woman. Price was regretful over the lost years with Suzette. Anne had raised a very special young woman. Price realized in that moment, that he was not only the father of another daughter, but a new grandfather as well. Suzette's son should rightfully carry the Smith-Marshal name.

Brittain loved Price Smith Marshal with a protective, but loving fierceness. As though she had read his thoughts, she kissed him and said "Grandfather will look good on you". He knew that his wife was going to support in any way she could. He was so proud of her. "Britt, said Price, Suzette is going to graduate from Law School tomorrow. I promised I would attend". "She had no one else to be there with her". "I know my love", Britt acknowledged. Anne timed the arrival of this letter for this exact day. Before she died, Anne Butler had promised to share the truth with her child, but I guess she didn't get a chance. She wrote the letter hoping I would understand and help. I'd like to go with you tomorrow, if it's alright and help you welcome her into the profession and our family".

Price held his wife and best friend, as tightly as he could.

Nineteen

Will felt his life had filled up so quickly and he was surfing on a mental high.

He headed home intending to ask Emmalyn to keep Merry over the weekend, so he could spend some time alone with Sean. Sean had invited him to come up and stay in her condo. He was excited but, anxious too. He had not made love to a woman for such a long time. Rain took great pains to keep Will away from her, towards the end of their relationship, all the while cheating on him. Will picked up his mail then headed to Emmalyn's. Merry was taking a late Afternoon nap and Emma was stretched out on the sofa. Will walked through the Darkened house looking for his two favorite women and pup. Will had apparently grown on Rex. The two had come to a truce. Now when Will entered the room, Rex barely lifted his head, unless he needed a good scratch behind the ear, or wanted to play in the yard with his ball. Emma listened to Will's footsteps as he entered the house. His once slow step

Now possessed a newly-gained confidence. Emmalyn smiled and prepared to greet him. Will was leaving later to fly to Palmetto Springs for the most important weekend of his life. Sean was going to pick him up, and together they would begin a future. Will patted his pocket, hugging the small black velvet box, lined in white satin which lay next to his heart.

Emmalyn sat up, willing herself to look better than she felt. Will crossed the room frowning at Emma. Even in the darkness he could see that she did not look well. He sat down on an armchair near her and touched her forehead, as much to return the love she'd used to nourish his spirit, as to utilize his medical skills in assessing this special patient. "Emm, I'm worried about you. It is warm in here and yet you feel quite cold." "Will, honey, she pooh-poohed him. You worry too much. I'm probably just coming down with a cold. I promise that while you are gone this weekend, to catch up on my rest". "But Emm, you'll have Merry and you know what a ball of energy she can be", Will reminded her. "Yes, and I have planned for this. I promised to teach her how to knit. She wants to make something for you." "I will keep my plans with Sean, on one condition", Will teased. Emmalyn raised her hands in protest, but Will was adamant. "Rest and Recovery, only, until I get back Sunday night". Emmalyn reached out for Will's hand and held it a few moments without speaking. The two sat studying one another, holding hands securely and memorizing the way love looked to each of them. Emma knew that this young man was every bit the son she was meant to have, and who with Emma's love and patience, had been nurtured into a stronger and happier self. Will reached into the inner breast pocket of his jacket and took out the velvet box. Opening it, he turned it around for Emmalyn to see. Emma did not try to hold back her joy. She hugged him instead.

Sean found herself extremely nervous as she prepared for her weekend with Will. Once more she checked the red velvet box. Her plans were completed. This coming Saturday night, she knew was going to be the most important of her life. Ellie had polished Sean's condo until it was shining. Ellie had brought along Brittain's best silver and linens. Fresh flowers had been ordered and the refrigerator stocked. Sean remembered to pick up some Chateau Neuf-du Pape and called her favorite restaurant, "Tresor" to reconfirm their dinner reservations for Saturday night. She had spent over an hour with the Maitre-d', going over all of the details of the special evening she'd planned. Ellie prepared the guest bedroom for Will. With a little help from Emmalyn, Brittain and Price, Sean had ordered a tuxedo for Will. Her father's advice mirrored his approval of her plans. Now it was all up to her.

Will spent the entire flight staring at the contents of the little black box and hoping. Sean met him at the airport. Brittain had arranged for the limousine to be at their disposal. But Sean would only need it for Saturday evening.

Sean greeted Will with a kiss on the cheek, as he returned the same. The tension between them was palpable. On the way home Sean stopped for ice cream cones, hoping to break the ice. Will could not believe that this lovely creature actually, wanted him, not knowing that Sean had never before been so afraid of rejection herself. The ice cream invited conversation about Merry. Both seemed to relax a little and Sean managed to drive home from the airport without having an accident.

Will had whistled in admiration when she showed him to her Mercedes Sports Coupe. Her condominium brought equal admiration from the young doctor. Will marveled at the marble fireplaces. Sean even had one in the master bedroom.

Hardwood floors, oriental carpets and antiques filled the apartment. Brittain had helped Sean choose the furnishings and accents. Both had been pleased with the results. Sean's favorite salmon-colored palette seemed to flow from room to room. Having long ago learned to make peace with Rain's love of the color mauve, Will felt actually quite at home. They touched accidentally as they departed the elevator which opened directly into her apartment, leaving an electric charge in the air. Will carried his flight bag into the guestroom asking Sean for the opportunity to shower and change. Sean was grateful for a moment to collect herself. They'd agreed to spend Friday night in front of the big screen television watching movies and eating Chinese take-out. The pressure off, they could enjoy the dance of love that takes place long before the touching would begin. Unfulfilled sexual desire and true love are, a highly-flammable combination in the hands of two people, desperately in want, and need of each other. The last movie they watched was a comedy. The laughter helped to release some of the tension they were feeling. Sean and Will were both tired and anxious. Sean shared with Will, the plans for a special dinner at her favorite restaurant and invited him to try on the tuxedo and accessories in the closet in the guestroom. Perfect, thought Will, since he'd planned something special too, for Saturday evening.

Neither could go to sleep right away. Sean lay in her bed holding the red velvet box. Will did the very same holding his black velvet one. Sean's perfume filled her home. Even the sheets offered no respite from her charms. Will lay across the bed wanting so badly to cross the short hallway between their rooms and take her in his arms, and fill her with the raw power of his love. Tomorrow, he thought. Tomorrow, Sean told herself, and she could hold in her own arms the man who held her own heart captive, this man whose very presence made her tremble inside. Tomorrow…was the promise that allowed both of them to finally fall asleep. Sean awakened to the aroma of coffee, bacon and fresh biscuits coming from her kitchen. She put on her robe and headed to the bathroom to freshen up. She could hear the rattle of dishes, as he placed his bounty on the table. He was pouring coffee as she came into the kitchen, nose first. Smiling broadly at her Will pulled out a chair and bowed. Sean tiptoed to kiss his face and said thank you. "So, this is what I can expect??? She baited him. Will was feeling bold. "Yes, ma'am and much, much more" he promised. Sean liked this manly side of him. He had excited her. She could feel the butterflies dancing to the light of the moon, dancing deep down inside of herself. Instead of answering, she filled her mouth with the delicious breakfast. Sean rarely ate breakfast. This food was really good. "Today, my sweet, I have plans for the two of us, but not together", she teased. Will reached across the table for her hands. "I would settle for just the two of us to be together in the same thought Sean". Invoking her name, brought a certain reality to what this day promised to bring to both of them. Will's direct gaze into Sean's eyes, filled with all the love and passion Will felt, filled Sean's senses with a satisfaction like the meal he'd prepared had filled her body. Will took her left hand and kissed the ring finger, then let it go, as Sean did the same to his. Without words they got up from the table and together began to clean up the kitchen, their bodies touching as Will stood behind her at the sink, in anticipated promise. Turning Sean around to face him, Will picked her up, all the while kissing her face and neck and finally, mercifully, her waiting mouth. The kiss, at first soft and pleading, became insistent, possessive, then lustful, as he slowly returned her to the floor, definitively proprietary. Sean's heart was reeling from this sexy and emotion-filled proposition. Tonight... tonight..each heart promised.

Sean handed Will a brochure she'd picked up for him, from her Day Spa, Panache. Will laughed as he read over the selection of treatments for men. Today he would experience pampering formerly-unbeknownst to the hard-working doctor. Sean and Will, both dressed in sweats headed for the Spa to be made ready for the spectacular evening, Saturday's was long-ago covenanted to be.

Brittain had called ahead to Debra Diggsby, owner of the Spa. Brittain wanted Debra of course, to see Sean, but to meet the fabulous doctor who'd stolen her baby girl's heart and soul. Debra had every intention of spoiling both of them. Brittain also shared the news of the red velvet box, and Debra knew only that this visit would be second only to one day soon, designated, the "future".

Will and Sean arrived at the Day spa, full of energy and laughter, ready for anything. Debra watched as they parked. Will out of the car first, went around to open her door and to steal a kiss, which by the way Sean gave willingly and quite publicly. Reaching to take her hand, the handsome doctor and his intended reached the spa door. Smiling and standing with arms opened wide, Debra hugged Sean and reached to shake Will's hand as Sean made introductions.

Lawrence was waiting to guide Will through the next five hours which would include facial, manicure, pedicure, hairstyling, body polishing and massage. Tonight, at dinner, a new man would wear the tuxedo, awaiting. Debra phoned Brittain. The two women shared the joy of knowing that only requited love would, this night take center stage.

Twenty

Will stood in the guest bathroom praying the night would be all he'd hoped. Adjusting the water so the shower would revive him, Will rehearsed the words he wanted to say to Sean later on. Sean ran her bath water and lit some of the candles surrounding her garden tub. She was a lawyer and words were the tool of her trade. Tonight, she would command them to perform a singular magic trick.

An hour later, dressed head-to-toe, in fine and fancy, Will inspected the final product. He was ready. Will entered the living room heading for the balcony to get some air. The stars "twinkled" at him, like some hopeful "thumbs-up" sign. The scent of Sean's perfumed wafted toward him, as he turned around to see her gliding toward him, in a magnificent red silk evening gown. The thin spaghetti straps caressed her shoulders revealing beautiful and softly heaving breasts. The form fit of the fabric hugged her waist and pinched the ample hips and luscious buttocks, no longer hidden by any means. In the one millisecond, it took for him to close his lashes together, Will had scanned from head to toe, the wonder before him and not once in the process, had he taken his eyes off hers. Will patted his breast pocket, reassured by the small box which held his heart's wishes. Sean's compliment to Will was cut short by the sound of the doorbell. The driver had arrived precisely on schedule. Will reached for the red silk drape Sean would wear across her shoulders. Kissing the nape of her neck, he gently put it on as she held her arms out to receive it.

The limousine ride was a quiet one. Neither wanted to break the spell. The Driver opened the door for them and Sean offered her hand, as Will received it gratefully. The restaurant was full of the elegantly dressed. Heads turned as the red silk dress, barely covering the incredible body, graced Sean's splendiferous beautiful face, en route to their table. Will's pace lingered a little, enjoying the looks of admiration and rustle of whispers her presence never failed to elicit. Will was honored to be not only her escort for the evening, but to be the proud bearer of Sean's heart.

Compliments of the Maitre D', the finest champagne arrived. Sean and Will toasted the evening with their glasses and each other with their eyes. Dinner brought light-hearted conversation, but Will had little appetite for it. All that he wished to devour sat before him. Will's entire being longed to hold her in his arms, to claim ownership in that room full of jealous glances at her. Sean nodded yes, as he stood behind her, breathing passion onto her neck, as he pulled out her chair. His chest heaved a sigh. Should this be the moment? His mind raced. No, it was not time yet, he decided. Will took Sean's tiny waist with his left hand and enclosed the right hand in his larger one. Sean rested her head under his chin and held on as though her very life depended on it, as Will kissed, once more, her hair. Sean moved her hips closer to his own. He could feel his manhood swelling in response. Sean raised her lips to his and as they danced across the floor, the kiss bound them together, like "junebugs". They stopped short when they heard polite clapping and looked up to see other guests smiling at them. Embarrassed, but happy and holding hands, the two returned beaming, to their table, as the music ended softly.

Sean nodded to the Maitre D'. He bowed briefly and clapped

his hands, as out came two waiters. One carried a small red-satin covered stool, while the other placed a dining chair in front of it. Will watched the scene with interest, while Sean watched him. The lights in the room grew dimmer, leaving only a spotlight, focused on the chair and stool. The Maitre D', apologized to everyone for the upcoming intrusion into their evening of dining. Pointing next to the orchestra, the sounds of a soft, jazzy love song filled the room. The room grew quiet. The Maitre D' himself pulled out Sean's chair and with gloved hands escorted her to the spotlight. Will was confused. Holding the bottom of her gown, in her hand, Sean turned to ask the orchestra to lower the music. As she gave them that million-dollar smile, they all smiled back. Something was about to happen, but only Sean and the Maitre D' knew what.

"Ladies and Gentlemen", she began, "I apologize for this interruption in your evening, but I am going to need your help, if I may. But first, is there a doctor in the house"? Smiling brilliantly, she held out her hands to Will to join her. I'm just kidding. Everyone laughed. All attention was riveted toward the spotlight and its occupants. First, permit me to introduce myself, and my guest. My name is Sean Smith-Marshal and my companion here, is Dr. Will Thorpe. More laughter as the joke began to make more sense. I brought him up here for a very special reason. But I'm going to need some support and that's where you guys come in. Smiling and opening her arms to everyone in the room, she once again joked "all are welcome…come into the light!!!" This time they applauded. "Dr. Thorpe", she said as she invited him to sit down on the chair. "Lately, I haven't been feeling well. You see I have this ache. At first it was just a little ache, but now I feel it every day. You see…this particular ache", she said as she pulled the satin stool closer to the side of the chair, only seems to go away when "you" are near me". Sean placed one foot on the stool and turned to the side slightly, as she lifted the hem of her dress, to reveal a red satin garter with a little pouch attached to it. Unzipping the pouch, she pulled out a little red velvet box. Lowering her dress, back to the floor, to the groans of the men in the room and applause of the women, Sean once again fed the room that incredible smile. Returning her attention to only Will this time, she knelt down onto the stool. Taking his left hand in her own, she opened the box for him to see. It was a diamond ring...for him. Will's eyes filled with tears, tears he permitted to run down his face. "Now, she said very quietly, Dr. Thorpe, I could be wrong, but I don't think so. I've tried to diagnose my condition. I believe it's terminal, but I think that you could help me through it. You see, Dr. Thorpe...I am in love with you and I want to spend the rest of my life under your care. And if you decide to take my case, Doctor, I promise to be the best patient you've ever had...." Taking the ring and placing it on his finger, Sean simply placed her head down on his lap. Will leaned over and kissed Sean's head. Not to be outdone, Will picked Sean up and placed her in the chair this time. The guests were clapping wildly. Everyone in the room was connected by the electricity of the moment.

Will patted his breast pocket and lifted his hands asking for quiet, once more. "It seems, that I am going to need a really good attorney. Are there any "good" attorneys in this room? Quite a few men and women stood up, ready to acknowledge their presence. Once more, everyone applauded them, as Will invited them to sit back down. "I think", he said "that I know just the attorney I need". Ladies and Gentlemen, I would like to introduce to you ...My Attorney". Sean laughed and waved at the crowded room. "You see, I have a confession to make here tonight. I am guilty counselor... so guilty of love in the first degree. The only appropriate sentence that I can see, is life without, the possibility of parole. I am so.. so ready to pay the penalty, to spend each and every day telling this beautiful, smart, and gutsy woman how much I do love her Kneeling down on the stool, Will took his turn. Holding up the black velvet box amidst thunderous applause, Will smiled through his tears. Sean held out her hand to him, as he placed the diamond ring and kissed the hand. The agony was over and the ecstasy could begin. Sean and Will kissed long and passionately, as everyone in the room cried and whistled and clapped. After thanking the guests and staff and accepting congratulations too many times to count, the newly-engaged couple were ready to go home. Sean slipped off to the powder room, as Will had the driver bring the car around.

They climbed in and snuggled tightly in one corner of the seat. Neither, wanted to let go of the other. Will and Sean stepped off the elevator and were greeted by a huge bouquet of flowers congratulating them on their engagement. The card had been signed for Emmalyn, Brittain, Price, Ellie and Debra Diggsby. Will smiled as he read it. Everyone they loved had given their blessing. The two would tell Merry together. Now, the evening was complete. Will and Sean decided together, to wait to consummate their love on the wedding day they could now plan. Will and Sean fell asleep wrapped in each other's arms, on the sofa, in front of the fire. Will Thorpe would have waited another lifetime for Sean Smith-Marshal.

Twenty-One

Will's flight back to Bristol Point gave him ample time to absorb the events of the weekend. He stared at the beautiful diamond ring Sean had given him. He was returning home to Emma and Merry, but not alone. Sean's sleepy head rested on his shoulder. She wanted to go along, so together they could tell Merry. Sean loved the baby already and only hoped that she would be happy about it as well. Will was returning home sooner than expected. They had been very lucky to catch an early morning flight. It was to be a surprise for Emmalyn and Merry.

They took a cab back to Emmalyn's house. Sean had picked up a big white bear to add to Merry's assorted collection. Will unlocked the door at 1111 Elm, expecting to hear Merry's chatter, but found instead Will found Emmalyn stretched out once again on the sofa in the living room. She had not even dressed. This alarmed Will because this was so unlike her. Emma had initially been frightened when she heard the door being unlocked. Will was not due back until later that evening. "Emm", Will called to her. "I'm here honey". Emma sat up, surprised to see Sean too. "Come here my darling", she said to Sean, and let me hug you. "So", her eyes twinkled, "you two finally did it, and now we have a wedding to plan".

132

"Will and Sean, come sit by me, both of you. I have something to tell you. It's probably for the best that you both are here now. I haven't wanted to burden you, but I can't wait much longer to tell you. I have only shared this with one other person. I guess I had to accept it first, before I could tell others. I have Cancer. Will gasped in shock. Sean had already heard the news from her mother and could only now show her sadness. The cancer has metastasized from my colon to my right breast and lung. It is too late for chemotherapy and surgery is out of the question. My oncologist doesn't know for sure, how much longer I have". "But surely there must be some treatment protocol or surgery.... Perhaps I could Discuss your case, if you will permit me, with your doctor. Which doctor are you seeing?.....Will's voice trailed off as he watched Emmalyn shaking her head "no". "But why not?????" he whispered, like an unhappy and defiant child. Emmalyn understood his reaction. She had given to Will and Merry a new life, love and happiness, and they had come to depend on it. Quite honestly, so had she. Sean sat down next to Will and reached for his hand. Will squeezed hers in thanks.

Leaning forward in his chair while loosening his tie, he tried to absorb what Emmalyn had just told him. Emmalyn watched Will with a sad smile on her face. Looking up again, Will tried to speak, but trembling lips made it impossible. "I know how you feel son. You don't have to say anything. I have come to love you and Merry too. You have become my little family and for that I could never express well enough, what it means to me. I do want to ask you to consider taking care of Rex for me when the time comes". Will nodded silently. "Merry loves him and I know, will take good care of him". "Yes, I think so too" added Will. Will smiled for the first time since arriving, and Emmalyn smiled back. Both were remembering how well Merry and Rex played together. The puppy never complained when Merry tried to dress him up for one of her tea parties. The soft breeze from the open French doors leading to the garden entered the pain-filled room, as no one spoke. Emma leaned back on her pillow to rest. Will excused himself and headed for the guest room to check on Merry. Sean stayed with Emmalyn. Will looked around the house as he walked toward the bedroom, taking in all of the feelings it evoked with its quiet beauty, memorizing it all, for a day coming much too soon, when Emma's nurturing love would no longer live there.

Will sat down softly on the bed next to Merry. She laughed in her sleep and mumbled something he could not make out. Will reached out to touch his baby's hair and smoothed the loose wisps of it from her face. She looked so peaceful lying there. Sadly, she was going to lose this motherlove on which she had come to depend.

At best Will knew, the cancer would only give Emma a few months to live. He wanted to fill whatever remaining time with love and caring. He was so disappointed, especially now that his life was coming together. Ian had somehow made it through his day, grateful for its end. He drove home slowly trying to prepare for the loss of Sean in his life. Ian had grown accustomed to seeing her car parked in front of the lake house, but this, he knew, would never happen again. This time, as Ian approached his once beloved home, he decided to turn around and leave. No words filled with emotion would ever pass between them again. Fighting against this new reality, Ian raced away from the house with the fury of a crazed stallion. Dust swirled all around him as he pulled off the road sharply. Eyes irritated and heart broken, he leaned on the steering wheel and let it all pour out of himself. Like a cranky child fighting sleep, Ian closed his eyes for a moment, drifting into a light sleep. He awakened a little later startled and not knowing for a moment where he was. Starting up the engine, he headed once again for home, physically tired and emotionally drained. All he wanted was a hot shower and sleep.

Ian could feel the difference in the house upon entering. Sean's belongings had all been removed. Ian headed for the shower, refusing to look around for any more telltale signs. Clean and feeling stronger, he headed to the kitchen to find something to eat. Hearing a car pull into the driveway and hoping with all his heart that Sean had changed her mind, Ian rushed toward the front door. The sound of the knock had confused him. Sean still had her key. As he pulled open the door, he looked past the woman standing in front of him, his eyes and heart, searching for Sean.

Suzette watched him look around and understood very well why. Ian looked quickly at Suzette holding a covered dish and apologized. "Why are you here Suzette?? Ian inquired, almost rudely. "I'm sorry Suzette, he said, you don't deserve that…please, come in." She had come alone. "I was worried about you …Ian, and I thought you might need some company, I made this lasagna as a thank you for the beautiful flowers you left me". Ian looked down at Suzette, taking in her nervousness and realized that she was declaring an official truce. "Well", said Ian finally returning to the moment. "That was very kind of you Suzette. Come in please". Taking the casserole out of her hands, he offered to share a bottle of wine and to make a fire. We can eat in the living room in front of it. Suzette raised an eyebrow and smirked. Ian formed his hands into a "T" and offered her a seat on the sofa. Looking into her eyes, he said "thank you for thinking about me Suzette", adding sheepishly and honestly, "I know I don't deserve it."

Ian took the dish to the kitchen, telling Suzette that he would prepare a salad and garlic toast to go with it. Suzette could feel the heat coming from the fireplace and from someplace deep within herself. She watched the flames growing before her and felt herself drawn into the light of the fire. Ian appeared at the living room door to ask her if she'd like a glass of wine before dinner, stopping mid-step to take in the scene before him. Suzette's eyes were closed and her head was leaning on the side of the sofa. The flames flickered leaving her covered in a soft glow. The quiet of the room and her presence filled his home with a peace Ian had never before felt. Suzette looked and felt beautiful to him. Ian covered her with a blanket and went to put the salad into the refrigerator and the lasagna into the oven, to stay warm.

Tiptoeing back and forth until he'd set the table, he poured a glass of wine for himself and sat down in the chair across from her. Before him lay the mother of his child and the only person on earth who cared whether he lived or died. Ian had finally hit that brick wall his parents had warned him about. He had raced through his life accepting no responsibility for his actions and refusing to let consequences affect him, but a Power much greater was offering him another chance to see that road not taken.

Suzette awakened a little later, to the warmth of the fire and Ian. He had fallen asleep holding a half-filled glass of wine. Suzette smiled and took the blanket he'd covered her with, and gently placed it across Ian's chest. Her heart wanted to place a kiss on his forehead. He looked so much like Tristan sitting there. Suzette picked up her car keys and left without disturbing him. He was going to be alright and that was all that was important.

Twenty-Two

Suzette could barely contain her excitement as she jumped out of bed. Tristan was still asleep. It seems little mister had played himself out the night before and went to bed without a fuss, according to Cierra Nelson, his eighteen-year-old babysitter. Cierra adored Tristy and had taken him to his favorite park. When Suzette checked in on him, she gave him three kisses on his forehead, one each, for Mommy, Daddy and Grandma.

Suzette's graduation from Law School was scheduled for one o'clock that afternoon. Price had given her the day off and promised to be there in the audience watching the proud day. Cierra was going to pick Tristan up from preschool and take care of him. Price had insisted they go out for a celebration after the ceremony. Suzette had been so touched by how caring he'd been. After all, she was only an employee. Suzette dropped Tristan off at the daycare center and reminded him that Miss Cierra was going to take care of him later, until she returned home. Tristan could not say Cierra's name. He called her Serra. It was so cute to hear. He seemed to understand, and kissed his mommy back, as she promised to see him later.

Suzette returned home to look at her wardrobe and pick out something to wear. Money was tight, so she'd not bought anything new, but she had several suits that looked good enough. Suzette was still looking through her closet when she heard her doorbell ring. She opened her door to a smiling deliveryman holding a series of large and small boxes. Suzette had not ordered anything and was genuinely confused. The deliveryman assured her that this had been no mistake. Name and address were correct and arrangements made for this special delivery, on this day and at this very hour. Suzette tried to tip him, but he refused it, assuring her that he had already been very, very generously tipped. He carried the numerous boxes inside for her and congratulated her on her graduation from Law School. Suzette was totally confused by then. The only person who knew was Price. Then again, he had always been so generous to her, but never to this extreme. This was different.

Suzette started with the largest box. It was wrapped beautifully complete with satin ribbons. She carefully opened it, wanting to savor every moment of the surprise. Inside she found layers of periwinkle blue tissue paper, covering the most amazing cream-colored suit she'd ever seen. It was a Chanel original. Suzette's finger glided across the silk label inside the suit. It was her size exactly. She hung the suit up on a door and sat down next to the other boxes, just staring. As she opened one after the other, she found herself surrounded by boxes that included matching shoes and purse, silk lingerie, hose, two smaller boxes and an envelope. Not wishing to destroy the fantasy too soon, she opened the remaining two smaller boxes. The first held the most delicate and beautiful strand of Mikimoto pearls, matching bracelet and earrings, she'd ever seen. The last box contained a gold and diamond Piaget watch. It was tiny and breathtakingly exquisite. Suzette stood surrounded by tens of thousands of dollars- worth of jewelry and apparel. She opened the envelope convinced that once again Price Marshal had done the extraordinary in her life. Her mouth dropped open when she read the card. "Suzette, This is your special day, and I want you to feel like the princess you truly are.", signed Brittain Smith-Marshal.

Suzette had met the judge, but had never enjoyed a relationship with her. Of course, this had to be Price's idea, Suzette told herself. Even still, the enormity of the gifts overwhelmed her. Inside the envelope with the note was another card that read "Limo will pick you up at nine-thirty. It will take you to Panache Day Spa. You will receive a facial, pedicure, body polishing and makeover and will take you from there to your Graduation Ceremony. Enjoy". This time it was unsigned, but the handwriting was unmistakably the same.

The reference to time brought Suzette abruptly back to reality. She glanced quickly at her watch and discovered that it was already ten minutes after nine. Excited and nervous, she dressed casually, ready for this magical day to continue to unfold. The driver arrived in an elegant white limousine at exactly nine-thirty. He brought inside with him a set of Louis Vuitton luggage pieces and proceeded to pack the contents of the boxes delivered earlier. He loaded the trunk with her possessions, asked for her keys, and after locking the door to her apartment and returning her keys, held the door to the limousine for her. Suzette was sure Cinderella could have felt no finer than she.

Ian arrived at work hoping to see Suzette to thank her once more for the dinner she'd made. A hungry Ian had inhaled most of the lasagna after waking up. He found out from Reception that Suzette and Price would both be off from work. Office gossip had already created an affair between them. Disappointed but determined, Ian decided he'd stop by to see Suzette and Tristan later in the evening. He was surprised to realize that he was really looking forward to it.

Emmalyn moved slowly to the bathroom after Will and Merry left. She wasn't feeling well. She had a fever and pain in her abdomen pain. The metastasis from the breast cancer left her feeling nauseous and weak. Emmalyn's once sparkling eyes were slowly beginning to show signs of jaundice. She had a scheduled appointment coming up to see her doctor. The need for painkillers was coming faster than she wanted to admit. Emmalyn felt a little better after freshening up. She went back to the sofa to rest a little more, but carried the phone along. She dialed Sean at work and found her in. The two spoke briefly and plans made ready.

Suzette turned slowly looking at herself in the full-length mirror. She was stunning. Brittain's impeccable taste left her in awe. Everything she'd sent worked in perfect concert. Her makeover team applauded and hugged her. Suzette started to cry and her makeup artist quickly pooh-poohed that behavior and touched up her face. It made everyone laugh. Suzette's limousine driver stood and bowed before her, then presented his arm to her. This made Suzette laugh with relief.

Suzette had practiced for this ceremony enough times to feel comfortable, but was still nervous. As she sat with her graduating class, capped and gowned, she turned around looking for Price, but saw first that Brittain was there and had been watching her. She smiled at Suzette and pointed a finger at the stage where the College president and staff, valedictorian, salutatorian and guest speakers were located. Price's eyes were wet with tears and had been watching his baby girl as she searched for him, the same way Sean once did as a child. His heart felt the pain of having missed Suzette's childhood, but the joy of finding her now and an unending pride in the woman she had become, on her own. He clasped his hands together and pointed to her alone. "You" his pointed fingers said. Suzette felt so special, yet so confused. Why was Price onstage she wondered. Britain watched this play unfold before her. She knew all that Price was feeling and felt it too. Even though Suzette was not her own, Brittain possessed enough love to be able to embrace this change in her life. Suzette was Price's child, but had suffered the misfortune of a tough life that could have been made easier. In the child, Brittain recognized the strength and determination she knew to be the stuff of which Price Marshal was made. Brittain wiped at her own eyes and said a prayer to Anne Butler thanking her for her wisdom and for sharing Suzette with them all. Sean would now have a sister. If anything ever happened to Brittain and Price, the two would still have family, in each other.

The speeches presented were all a blur of words to Suzette. There was so much she could not understand. She stood with the other graduates waiting her turn to be conferred. As she moved forward with the group, one by one, to receive their degrees, she saw Price step to the podium. Suzette stood frozen, not knowing at all what to expect. Suzette heard him clear his throat, but everything he said after that was recorded only by her memory. She felt strangely disconnected between her ears and her brain. She'd heard all of his words, but could not process what he was saying. Price Smith-Marshal had just told her and all the world that she was his daughter and only in the last few days came into the knowledge. Suzette walked toward him unable to gain any control over her overloaded emotions. Price held out his arms and the two held on to each other and cried together. Everyone stood and applauded wildy, Brittain included. Judge Smith-Marshal permitted her own tears to flow freely and unashamedly. Price wiped at his baby girl's face and reached up to turn her tassel, while pressing into her hands an envelope tucked inside her degree. Suzette thought her knees would surely fail her. As she departed the stage, Suzette looked at Brittain for reassurance that everything was alright. Brittain broke with ceremony and headed for Suzette, arms opened. She knew that Suzette needed her mother in that moment. Once again, everyone stood and applauded. The two held onto to each other, both giving and taking what any mother and daughter share between them in a moment of joy.

Twenty-Three

Will spent a little less than an hour on the phone making arrangements for a home nurse to be made available to Emma. There would be three nurses. Will wanted her to have around-the-clock care. He also knew that she would fuss, but he was going to insist anyway. Will returned to the living room to tell her his plans. The phone was ringing and he could hear Emma speaking as she picked it up. Whoever it was had made her smile and it lifted Will's spirits to see it. Merry now awake, sat on the floor next to Emma scratching Rex's ear. "Daddy, Daddy" … she jumped up and ran to him. "Daddy! Daddy!" "You're home and Grandma Emma says Sean is here too! Where is she now?" "Is she going to stay here with Grandma? Can we stay too???" Emma grinned at Will. "My Emm" was all that he could say. Emma blushed as only George and Will could make her. "Then it's settled", said Will. Merry and I will head home to get cleaned up" "and" …as he tapped on the bridge of Merry's nose, "pick up Sean. She is at our house right now, my little one. You can see her in two shakes of a lamb's tail". "Emmalyn, Sean is ordering your favorite Chinese takeout. 'll bring it back with us, along with a movie." Emma sat up determined to try to appear healthier than she actually felt, for the family's sake.

Sean's visit would be good for all of them. Emma patted the little lump under the covers. Rex moved closer to her. He had become quieter since she became ill. Dogs and cats somehow seem to know. Price tried to call Sean to ask her to join them at home so he could tell her the news. The day had been everything he wanted. From the restaurant, the three were headed to Suzette's apartment to pick up Tristan. Price wanted to spend time with his new grandson. Sean was not answering any of her phones. Price headed home anyway, believing that Sean would arrive sometime later. Tristan sat in the back of the car with his mother, not speaking a word. He was not used to all of the attention Price was giving him. They pulled onto the grand estate. Suzette had only seen such splendor in magazines, or on television. The garden views were spectacular. There was a tall lighted fountain in front of the enormous house. The sound of the water splashing caught Tristan's attention. Price parked the car in front of the four-car garage. Sean's car had not yet arrived. Price was disappointed. He wanted to share the excitement with her. Price and Brittain had agreed not to reveal the news to Sean until after the graduation. Sean was going to be asked to share her father, her home and her legacy. But they had raised up their child…"in the way she should go" and knew that Sean would be alright.

Ellie greeted them at the door smiling at Tristan, especially. Ellie was a grandmother and adored the little ones. Price introduced Suzette and Tristan to her. Tristan tried to hide behind his mother's legs. They all laughed. Ellie told them that Sean had come home earlier to pack for her trip back to Bristtol Point with Will. Brittain frowned. She'd thought Will would be going home alone. Brittain went to call Sean and returned to the living room with Sean was on the line. Sean wanted to speak with Suzette. "Forgive me Suzette", said Sean. I didn't mean to be rude. I knew Mom and Dad wanted for me to come home tonight, but my mother's old friend Emmalyn Brown is sick. She has Cancer. My…her son was coming home and I wanted to be with him. He didn't know about her illness until now. So, I had to change plans suddenly. Aunt Emmalyn called and asked me to come back to Bristol Point with him. I'm here now. Ellie was going to tell you all, for me later. Congratulations on your graduation from Law School. Mom and Dad told me about it. I'm sorry to have missed the ceremony". Price interrupted, asking Sean to hold on for a moment because he wanted to put the call on the speaker phone. Price asked everyone to sit down. Tristan wanted to sit on Suzette's lap, so she helped him climb up. Price walked over behind Brittain's chair and placed his hand on her shoulder. Brittain reached up and covered his hand with her own. Together they would get through the next moments. Clearing his throat, he began. "A few days ago, Brittain and I received a letter from Anne Butler, Sean. She is, was.. Suzette's mother". Suzette dropped her head and looked down at her hands. The sound of her mother's name was still painful to hear. Suzette missed her so much. Sean could never imagine being without the two most important people in her life. Tristan saw his mother's sadness and leaned back lovingly against her body. Suzette, Price said, as he focused on his eldest daughter, your mother wanted to tell you and intended to, but ran out of time. I am so sorry we both missed knowing before now". Suzette still looked down, but tried to smile bravely. Sean was still confused. "Sean" said Price, now directing his attention to his baby girl, what I did not know until a few days ago was that I fathered a child, born to Anne Butler, before your mother and I even knew each other. Suzette is that child. She is your sister honey". Ellie gasped involuntarily. Brittain's silence told her child that the truth was being told. Sean's emotions were a mixture of happiness and a strange sadness. Sean had wanted a sibling when she was growing up, but learned to accept her fate as an only child. Her mother and father's unconditional love filled her with an immeasurable confidence and gentleness. Sean looked at the eyes staring at her, whose hopeful faces awaited her attention. Will and Merry had returned to get her. Sean's father's voice had a quaver to it that she had never heard before. Sean could see her father's loving, but frightened gaze, in her mind and feel her mother's soft smile, both of which, gave her the strength she needed to sort out her own feelings. But the sadness Sean knew Suzette must feel in that moment, she had witnessed only once before, for herself... when Merry first spoke of her own mother's death. Suzette sat motionless, awaiting final acceptance into the family. Suzette had grown up with few advantages but had persevered. She had raised the beautiful baby boy sitting in her lap, alone without any of Sean's own financial advantages. But more importantly...Suzette was her own sister. Price walked over and and took Tristan from Suzette's arms. The boy did not struggle against his grandfather's love and once again, Sean reached out offering loving kindness to the sister that was her very own.

Brittain went over to Price. Ellie took the child out of his arms as he wept openly, tears of joy. Suzette and Brittain hugged, crying on each other's shoulders. Ellie wiped at her own eyes with her apron, as she took Tristan to the kitchen to find some cookies. Brittain invited Suzette and Tristan to stay overnight, but it was time to be alone and sort out the day's events. Suzette wanted time to talk with her own mother in prayer and to thank the Lord for all of these blessings. Brittain called for the limo to take Suzette and Tristan home. Price asked to ride with them. Father and daughter needed time alone. Tristan was tuckered out and fell asleep in the seat between them, leaning on Grandpa.

"Suzette", said Price carefully as they rode through the night, each toward a new destiny, "I really am happy to know that I have another daughter. I hope we can become friends too". Suzette stroked Tristan's head as he moved over to lean toward her in his car seat "Me too", Suzette said and meant it. "I want all of us to get together once Sean's back" stated Price. "I hope you are not going to be overwhelmed", he said kindly.

The driver carried Suzette's bags into the tiny apartment. The entire place was smaller than Sean's suite of rooms at home. Price needed to see this. Tristan's room, though tiny was filled with as much love as Sean's huge one. This was the only measure of his child that really mattered. The relationship between them would come in time. They hugged at the door. Price promised to call her as soon as he arrived to let her know that he was home safely. This caught Suzette off-guard but Price was doing only what he'd always done. He saw his daughter's surprise and said laughing, "Smith-Marshal rule #1...ALWAYS CHECK IN, SO EVERYONE WOULD KNOW EVERYONE ELSE WAS SAFE". Suzette laughed away some of her tension and hugged him. "Wait", said Suzette, as she scribbled her own phone number forgetting that he already had it programmed in his phones. Suzette stood at the door waving as the limo drove off. "Father" ...she repeated as she went inside and locked the door. Tristan was asleep. Suzette undressed him slowly, careful not to awaken him. She pressed his little body in hug. They were no longer alone. As Suzette laid him down and covered him, the tension she felt released itself. Covering her mouth with both hands, she cried and cried. She missed her mama and wanted to thank her for everything. Suzette wrapped her own arms around herself asking to mercifully receive her mother's spiritual hug and was blessed with the feeling that Anne Butler's love was surrounding her. Suzette did not have to be afraid anymore. She had a family now that wanted her and included a father, a sister, and father for Tristan. Even Brittain seemed to share that wish. Suzette sat in the rocking chair in Tristy's room trying to take it all in. The sound of the phone startled her as she raced toward it, trying not to let it awaken the baby. Suzette smiled when she heard her father say, "Hi! It's your father checking in. I made it home. I'm going to give you all of my phone numbers tomorrow. If you need anything, just call. Goodnight, my little bit". Price had created that name just for her. Sean was his little bird. Suzette was sleepy, but wanted to put her things away first. She picked up her degree. Doctorate of Jurisprudence, she read happily. It had been a long struggle. She could never have made it without her mother's love and support.

As Suzette folded the cover to close it again, the envelope fell out. Addressed to her, reading also "personal and confidential", Suzette opened it. It contained a letter from Price. Suzette recognized his signature at the bottom. In the first paragraph, he informed her of the account opened at his personal bank into which he'd transferred the sum of FIVE MILLION DOLLARS. In trust for his grandson Tristan, were THREE MILLION DOLLARS, put into a separate account, to be released to him upon his twenty-first birthday. Price provided the phone number and address of his personal attorney. His Will had been changed to reflect the changes in his family configuration. In less than twenty-four hours Suzette's life had changed entirely.

Suzette turned off all of the lights in the apartment, checked all of the doors and windows, took one last look at her little man, then climbed into her own bed in the dark. No words would suffice to describe that one day. Suzette hugged her pillow instead and let the tears drop one by one, as her mouth formed only one word, "Mama".

Twenty-Four

Merry could barely contain herself waiting for Sean to finish on the phone. A smiling Sean hung up the phone opening her arms to receive her favorite little one. Will walked slowly toward them, enjoying this scene in his own way. The three of them looked like any family being reunited. Behind the lace drapery Emma and Rex waited for them to return inside the house, completely satisfied that the future was unfolding.

Merry was determinedly happy to share Sean with her father. Sean understood it. She had lived this game many times over, as a little girl, with her own family. One hand holding onto Merry's, Sean tiptoed toward Will's waiting face. As she softly kissed his neck, he turned his head and pressed his lips into hers. As their eyes slowly met, their shared fire consummated the promise of foreverlove. Will reached for Sean's other hand. His big hand wrapped completely, her tiny one and as he squeezed, gently proposing, she returned the squeeze, accepting. Will had never felt so complete. Ian must have walked past Suzette's desk a million times. He knew she was not going to be working that day, but he missed her. He wanted to see Tristan too. Ian called Tabitha and asked her to cover his office. Ian told her that he would be out for the rest of the day.

Without calling first, Ian headed for Suzette's apartment. He rang the doorbell and heard Tristan announce loudly that somebody was at the door. Ian smiled. His son missed nothing. Suzette opened the door, surprised at first, but very much pleased to see Ian. Her emotions were like a loose cannon. The previous day's events had opened her wounded heart to all manner of possibilities. Suzette invited him to come inside.

Ian sat down watching Tristan moving toward him slowly, but methodically, drawn to his father like a magnet. Tristan allowed Ian to pick up him and set him on his lap. Suzette sat across from the two of them feeling so happy. "Ian, she said finally to what do I owe this visit???" Smiling to soften the sound of it, he smiled back at her. "You were not at work yesterday" … Suzette' smile widened to a full grin. "YesI know". Raising an eyebrow, she tortured him a little more….."Did I miss something yesterday???" "No", he said stroking the top of Tristan's head, "But I did". Suzette decided to give him a chance. Ian took the opening. "I was kind of hoping that the two of you could come out to my house and maybe we could share a picnic on the lake. All Tristan heard was go. "Mommy, Mommy, can I go too???" Suzette smiled at her little man. "Of course, you "may" go". Looking very seriously at Ian and asking the unquestioned stated, "I think it would be wonderful for us to spend time really getting to know each other". Ian's joy was apparent when he stood up and tossed his son into the air and much to Tristan's surprise, caught him. Emmalyn appeared at the door waiting for her hug from Sean. "Aunt Emm", Sean exclaimed, "you look wonderful". "No, I don't sweetheart, but thank you for saying it". Emma was trying to help her loved ones accept the truth of her illness. Emma had made some fresh-squeezed lemonade. Will carried Sean's bags into the guestroom and afterward they all headed for the living room to eat and watch the movie. It was late when it finally ended but Merry was given permission to stay up a little longer. They all decided to go outside to the garden. Sean and Merry headed for the swing. Merry turned sideways and placed her head in Sean's lap. Sean tickled her neck while Merry squirmed and giggled Will looked up at the stars above and said a humble thank you. He had arrived at his appointed place in the universe, at a time determined long before he was born. Emmalyn rocked in her chair resting. She'd felt it too. Now she could let go. Will and Merry had Sean, and her George was waiting to be reunited with her. In the night breeze, George kissed her face in affirmation. Emma was at peace.

It was getting late. The evening would have to end. Merry asked to sleep over at Grandma Emma's with Sean. Sean told Merry that they were going to have a slumber party. Merry asked what it was. Sean gave the child an elaborate description, knowing well, that the meaning of slumber is sleep. Winking at Will, Emma took the child inside to get ready for bed and to give Will and Sean two minutes alone. Rex greeted them at the door, with a few disciplinary barks. Merry ran to pick him up. Hand in hand Will and Sean walked back over to the swing and sat down. Sean scrunched up as close to Will as she could. Wrapping his arm around her, he kissed her hair. They rocked back and forth without talking. Finally, letting the swing come to a stop, Will stood up and pulled Sean's body into his own, and holding her head, as though a precious gem, gave her his soul in one look and his heart in one kiss. Ian, Suzette and Tristan stopped on the way to the lake house to pick up some fried chicken, salad, rolls and some ice cream for later. Tristan was so excited when they pulled up to the house and he saw the lake. He had no memory of the rainy night they'd appeared to check on his father. Ian and Tristan went down to the lake to prepare the fishing boat, while Suzette set up lunch under the very same tree, where she'd found Ian drunk and so unhappy. She finished preparing lunch before they were ready to eat and leaned back against the tree counting all of her blessings. Ian and Tristan belonged together. Suzette found herself falling once again for Ian. She wanted to fight it. Financially secure, law school graduate and co-heir to the Smith-Marshal fortune, life had presented her with different options. Tristan needed his father for obvious reasons. But Sean needed nothing else from Ian. What she wanted from him, he had to give for only one reason. Ian had hurt her once already. Tristan was learning how to skip rocks. Tucked into his father's chest, the two laughed and hugged. Still Suzette could hope.

Will checked on Emmalyn, kissing her goodnight. Two more goodnight kisses to complete his circle of three loves and he was off. Merry giggled when she saw her father kiss Sean, but she looked so pleased. Will returned to the darkness of his own home, no longer sad and lonely. Climbing into bed, he could think of nothing more than the feeling of Sean's body so close to his own.

Merry fell asleep quickly. Sean lay next to her thinking about Will. Every fiber of her mind and body wanted to reach out to him. Sean was totally and deeply in love. It had happened so fast. Sean could not move Will from her thoughts. She could hear Aunt Emm moving about in her own bedroom. Tapping lightly on the door, Emma welcomed her in. Rex looked up in disinterest. Sean settled into the chaise next to the bed and in front of the window. Emma reached to turn on the light, but Sean stopped her. The light coming from outside was enough. Sean wanted to talk about Will.

"Aunt Emm", Sean started slowly," I love him". Emma's face relaxed. "I know darling". Needing Advice, Sean waited on Emma. "He loves you too, Sean". My Will is a good man, like my George, like your daddy. "Do you think you're ready for a family?? It's a package deal, baby girl". "I know, Aunt Emm". "But I do think I'm ready. You know I can't even imagine having Will without Merry. They seem to complete each other. Do you know what I mean?" "Yes, my love, I do". Sean sat quietly for a few minutes, taking it all in. "Aunt Emm, I hope you don't think I'm being too forward. "No child, you just follow your heart and let the Lord do the rest". "Aunt Emm, are you in much pain?" "Mommy told me that you had not been feeling well. Is There anything I can do for you? Anything at all?" "Yes, Sean, take care of them for me, please????" Sean got up from the lounge chair and sat down on the side of the bed next to her dying aunt. Sean rested her hands across Emmalyn's quickly thinning ones, saying.."In sickness and in health, for richer or for poorer, and 'til death do we part….. Sean promised. "And what God has joined together, will no man put asunder", ended Emmalyn.

The hungry sailors finally returned to shore. Tristan and Ian ate until they could fit no more food inside. The sunshine, play on the water and the food made for a very sleepy Tristan. Suzette laid him out on the blanket and kissed his cheek. Ian watched them with a pained look on his face. Suzette frowned at Ian when she looked up. "What's wrong Ian?" Ian raised his knee and covered his face with his hands for a moment. Wiping at his eyes, he took Suzette's hands in his own. Looking down at them, he spoke what was in his heart. "I have never been worthy of you Suzette, and am less so now. And Tristan, my son…MY son, is nothing less than a miracle. I look at him and I see such possibilities, not just for him, but for me, and not just in him, but in me too. "And a little child shall lead them…. See, I did listen to a few things my parents tried to tell me. Tristan is a good boy Suzette. You have done a remarkable job with him. I am so…so sorry I was not there for you. You both deserved better. I am sorry that I treated you so badly. All I ask now is for one more chance. I know what I'm saying must sound phony, but I promise you it isn't. I want to be a good father to my son, but more importantly, I want to spend my days taking care of both of you. I don't want to live my life without either of you in it". Raising her chin so their eyes could meet, he vowed…" if only", she'd give him another chance.

Suzette could hear her mother whispering into her ear. "Tristan will have his father. You need now only what your heart needs". Suzette's eyes welled up with tears. Ian was crushed by the sight of it. He had just promised never to hurt her again, and already he had. "Suzette", Ian begged, I am so sorry…I don't know what I did. But whatever it was, please…I'm sorry" …. Suzette placed her lips on his, without kissing him, eyes staring into his, begging to be honored and cared for and let the salty tears flow all over both their faces. Ian closed his eyes and said a prayer. Cupping her face with his hands he kissed Suzette with the promise of a man who possessed a fear of losing something of value.

Twenty-Five

"Sean wake up, wake up! insisted an excited Merry. "Daddy's cooking breakfast. Let's go eat! Sean smiled into the pillow. He even cooks, she smiled again. Normally slow to wake up, Merry's emotional energy had spilled over and into Sean. She got up and headed for the bathroom to freshen up. Will had already said good morning to his munchkin. Merry was an early riser. Will had bathed and dressed her. Emmalyn was still asleep. Will thought it best to let her get more rest.

Sean entered the kitchen looking wonderfully sexy and still sleepy. Merry ran over and grabbed her hand to take her sit down as though she could not find a seat on her own. Will kissed the top of Sean's head and handed her a cup of coffee. He could tell that she was in need of some good java. Will only drank coffee when he was tired and had a heavy patient load. The coffee seemed to get him through anything.

"You make a mean cup of coffee, Will, Sean praised. Will took a bow. He placed an omelet, some toast and bacon in front of her. "So, this really is what I have to look forward to????" Sean teased. "I've already put it into the prenuptial agreement, he volleyed back. Merry was busy trying to put jelly on her toast, rather unsuccessfully.

Sean helped out. Merry picked up the toast slice and licked the jelly, leaving a small lump of it on her nose. "Yuck...teased Sean, wiping at the jelly. Emmalyn came into the kitchen to share the happy sounds. "Oh Emm, Will apologized we didn't mean to wake you".

"I was going to make you some toast and warm milk and bring it in to you. How are you feeling?" Will asked as he kissed her on the cheek. "Actually, much better today. It must be because all my favorite people are right here in my kitchen". Rex came in behind Emma, yawning. Will and Rex had made their peace. Will put a piece of bacon in Rex's food bowl. Rex barked his thanks. "Grandma?" called Merry, Sean made me some jelly toast!" "I can see, my sweet, laughing at Merry's grape-stained happy face.

"Have we plans for today?", Emmalyn asked. "Yep, we're going to barbecue and I will be "Chef De Jour", Will volunteered. "May I ask one small favor today? Emmalyn inquired. "Of course," said Sean and Will simultaneously. "Thank you both", Emmalyn laughed "I would like to visit George today". Emma was prepared for the sad faces. Recovering, but barely able to sustain himself, Will pronounced the next twenty-four hours "Emmalyn's Day". Picking up Merry, he tickled her until she promised to help him make a special day for Grandma Emm. Sean's glazed eyes locked with Will's as Emmalyn watched her brood. "I know, joined in Sean, we'll pack a huge picnic basket and stop for flowers and Merry can help plant them. Sean winked at Will, as Merry wiggled down from her father's arms. She'd heard her name connected to flowers. "I can help", she pronounced. "I used to help Mommy in the garden, didn't I, Daddy?" "Yes, you did my little darling and a good job you always did". In the short span of one sentence, Will found himself surrounded by the specter of death, past and future. Looking into Emmalyn's face, Will saw the compassion of a mother wishing, but unable to save her child from pain. Sean watched them both. She reached out to Emmalyn, and hugged her. Will picked up Merry and joined in the hug. No words were spoken, not even by Merry.

Suzette's heart wanted to speak. Knowing that Tristan and Ian were going to have each other made her feel happy, for them. She had changed so much since her mother's death. She'd grown much, much wiser. Suzette touched Ian's face with the back of her hand. Ian took it and pressed it against his cheek. Suzette smiled and finding the strength, told him what he would need to hear. Suzette never stopped loving Ian. She had for a very long time, even though Ian only wanted Sean. Tristan's birth had been such a blessing for Suzette and Anne Butler as well. It would always be their most precious connection. Suzette wanted Ian in her life, but needed the kind of reassurance only time could provide. Ian was going to have to work to regain her trust. It was more than Ian had the right to hope for. It was a chance for a new beginning. Ian once again softly kissed Suzette's hand. Placing it over his heart, he put his head down in her lap, closed his eyes and breathed long and deeply.

Suzette had so much more to tell him. She'd deliberately held back the news of her relationship with her father. That would be revealed soon enough. Suzette needed to know that Ian's love would be for her alone, rich or poor. Only then could there be time...plenty of time, and God-willing...a lifetime.

Emmalyn sat quietly during the ride to the cemetery to see George. Will worried about Merry's reaction. He wasn't sure she would make the connection to her mother's death and burial. Sean saw the furrow in his brows and gave him a soft smile.

Will relaxed a little. He was worried about Emmalyn too. She wasn't well at all and had refused outright the care he'd arranged with the Nursing Care Services. Lately she'd begun having severe headaches. Will feared that the Cancer was metastasizing to her brain as well. Will decided to take a leave of absence to care for her. His meager savings would just have to do. Emmalyn was trying so hard not to be a burden, but she was beginning to show signs of hypotension, severe nausea, pain and jaundice. Her appetite was all but gone. The pain meds given her, by her oncologist had been started. Will knew that for Emmalyn to have begun taking them, meant she was in much greater pain than she let on. Emmalyn did not like to take anything stronger than aspirin.

They arrived at Bristol Point Cemetery about lunchtime. As Will parked the car, he noticed other families tending to flowers that surrounded their own loved ones. It was a beautiful and well-manicured cemetery, with stone benches and statuary everywhere. Emmalyn awakened realizing immediately where she was. Her right side was hurting, but she was happy to see George. She took a cool face wipe and touched Merry's face lightly. Merry sat upright and yawned. Sean opened her eyes and stretched. Will helped Emmalyn out of the car while Sean assisted Merry. Emmalyn put on her hat to shade her eyes and face. Turning around slowly to get her bearings. She pointed to a small cluster of cherry trees, standing next to a large granite headstone with two swans on top. Sean took Emmalyn's hand and Merry took Sean's other one. They moved slowly toward George's final resting place, which would become Emmalyn's too soon. Will unpacked the flowers and lunch basket.

Emma seemed to grow stronger as she walked nearer to George. She let go of Sean's hand. Sean stepped back holding onto Merry, to give Emma more privacy. Emmalyn reached out for the swans and stroked them gently. Swans mated for life. That is why she chose to have two on the top of the stone. Will moved up behind Sean and stopped. Sean took the blanket from him and spread it down near the bench under the trees. Merry went to see what Grandma Emmalyn was doing. Will and Sean let her go, hoping that somehow her presence would make Emmalyn feel better. Emmalyn bent down and kissed the child's head. As she pointed to the headstone, Merry went closer to touch the swans on top. Emmalyn sat down on the ground, using the stone to lean on. She took out her garden gloves and began to pull weeds. Emmalyn pulled out a smaller pair and put them on Merry's hands. The two sat pulling at the weeds while Emma explained to Merry who her George was. Will and Sean watched, understanding that she needed to be alone with George, and that Merry's presence only helped her to keep one foot in the present.

Sean took Will by the hand and together they strolled the memorial garden, reading headstones. Lifetime partners joined together in death were interred there in great numbers. A peaceful calm graced Bristol Point Cemetery. Will held onto Sean's hand tightly, committed in silence to the same kind of love and future. When they returned Merry and Emmalyn had finished planting flowers and bulbs. Both seemed satisfied with the results. Emma was tired and determined to hide that fact. She had no appetite and nibbled only on some cheese. Merry ate well, having worked in the sunshine and fresh air. Will and Sean only drank some juice. Nodding toward Emmalyn, Will looked at Sean and stood up, pulling out his keys, headed to go get the car. Sean and Merry cleaned up after lunch and repacked the basket. Emmalyn's headache was returning but she had brought along none of her medication. Will loaded the car, then lifted Emm to a standing position. She held onto her painful right side, trying to cover up the pain by smiling. Will half-carried her back to the headstone to say goodbye to her George for the last time. He knew it. Emmalyn had two reasons for visiting George now. She also needed for Will to know where she was to buried and to share some time while alive with him there, so he could feel the attachment. Will realized this. He watched her sadly as she kissed the swan on the left, knowing that she was to become the swan on the right. Will's jaw tightened as he prepared himself for all that was to come. The final chapter in their relationship was being written. The ride home was filled with a palpable, but unspoken range of emotions, with each passenger lost in a different interpretation. Even Merry reacted to the sad day. She leaned on her grandma's hurting right side, as teardrop by teardrop Emmalyn released only a tiny portion of what she was feeling.

Twenty-Six

Will and his little family arrived home just as it was getting dark. Everyone but Will had slept the entire return trip. Merry was still leaning on Emma. Sean sat up first, then Merry. Emmalyn did not move. Will opened her door, prepared to carry her inside, when he realized that something was wrong with her. She was trying to speak to him, but could do no more than move her lips in a twisted fashion. Will realized immediately that Emmalyn had suffered a stroke. Will had worried about that possibility, and now it was a reality. He was not ready to lose her this soon. His prayer was that she could get through this. It was the self-centered prayer of a child not wanting to lose a beloved parent. How severe the stroke was, he could not yet tell. Will placed her as gently as he could, back into the car, trying not to alarm Merry. But Merry wanted to know why they were not going into the house with grandma. It was a blessing that the child did not understand all that she was seeing. Sean was frightened. She changed seats and moved to the backseat next to Emmalyn, placing Merry on her other side. Holding tightly to both, she freed Will to race through the streets to Penrose Regional Medical Center. He arrived at the Emergency Room and ran inside to get help. Bo

Longmire was just preparing to leave as Will ran in yelling for help. Dr. Longmire reached Emmalyn first, with the paramedics, Will and two nurses close behind. They gently lifted Emmalyn out of the car and placed her on a gurney. Merry was frightened and starting calling "Grandma" over and over. Sean tried to calm her, as she hurried Merry into the hospital. CEREBRAL HEMORRHAGE SECONDARY TO METASTATIC CARCINOMA OF THE LUNGS WITH MULTIPLE METASTASES, was the diagnosis Sean heard Will say, as they tried to save her. Bo Longmire asked Will to step back because of his relationship to her. She was family and Will's judgment would surely be affected by it. Will gave the admitting nurse the name of Emmalyn's Oncologist. Dr. Reuben was on staff at Penrose Regional so her medical records were on file. The call was being made to Dr. Reuben's office upstairs. Will could hear the admitting nurse call for Dr. Longmire to look at Emmalyn's records. The computer was beeping. That meant only one thing, but Will's mind refused to accept it. Dr. Longmire was calling Dr. Reuben, and the on-call Neurologist. Will rushed to the computer in slow-motion, so afraid of whatever he might learn. Emmalyn's records showed what he had feared. She had signed a DO NOT ATTEMPT RESUSCITATION (DNAR), WITH AMENDMENT. The amendment included a request to attempt no diagnostic procedures as well. The emergency room staff had automatically begun immediate stabilization protocols. IV, oxygen, EKG, CBC/Chem 24 had all been ordered for the patient. Dr. Longmire hung up the phone. They were being ordered to stop all diagnostic and resuscitative efforts on behalf of the comatose patient. Emmalyn would receive no additional medical care.

The staff could do no more than to make Emmalyn comfortable. Will had to stop himself from hitting a wall. Dr. Reuben finally arrived. Dr. Longmire talked at length with him, as her physician, permitting Will to listen, not to participate. Dr. Reuben took over Emmalyn's care and ordered that she be admitted to the Intensive Care Unit. Will was angry and hurt. Emmalyn had never told him of these wishes. But then she would not have. She would have wanted her passing to be as easy on her loved ones as possible. Across the room the Bo and Will stared in helplessness at each other. Will had always respected his patient's wishes. But this was different. This was his Emm. He did not know how to let go.

Dr. Reuben put his arms around Will's exhausted shoulders and walked him toward an empty treatment room. Will could hear everything the Oncologist was telling him, but could not make his heart believe that Emmalyn was going to die right in front of him, and there was nothing he could do. He was a doctor. His job was to save lives. Certainly, to be allowed to ease the suffering of those he loved. Emmalyn was helping Will to let go the only way she knew. Dr. Reuben left Will alone in the tiny cubicle. He was headed to the to the Intensive Care Unit (ICU), to prepare the nurses for his patient. Dr. Reuben was convinced that Emmalyn's Cancer had, in fact, metastasized to her brain, causing the massive stroke she'd suffered. Dr. Reuben had discussed the possibility of this occurring with her, at length. The intense headaches Emma reported to Will were indicators to Dr. Reuben's preliminary differential diagnosis. Because of the DNAR, only an autopsy could confirm that now. This was not going to be possible. Will felt so alone. He wanted to scream, to cry, to have a child-sized tantrum, all in hopes of making the hurt go away. But he couldn't. Sean and Merry were waiting and they would need him.

Will wiped his face with a towel, blew his nose and headed toward the waiting room. The ER staff turned to watch him as he walked past. They had witnessed a similar scene not that long ago when Rain Thorpe committed suicide. Will had been through so much.

Sean heard something in Will's voice as he came through the ER doors. He picked up Merry and placed her head down on his shoulder. He rocked his baby girl back and forth trying to prepare himself to tell her the news. They had become army of two, comforting one another in each crisis that befell them. Sean could see just how hard their lives had been. Silently, she promised Aunt Emm that she would take good care of her little family. She would provide for all of them, as much love as one person was capable. They had been wounded over and again in life. Two gentle souls who only wanted to love and be loved. Will finally sat down next to Sean and turned Merry around to face her. Merry's eyes grew large as if in preparation for the bad news. Will told her that Grandma was very sick and would have to stay in the hospital. The tears in Will's eyes told Merry and Sean all they really needed to know. Sean tried to hold back her tears. Will's eyes were filled to the brim, but had somehow not spilled over. Sean knew that he was trying to be strong for their sakes. Sean took Merry's face in her hands and kissed the forehead and each cheek. Merry was only a baby, but the language of love is easily translatable regardless of age. The baby reached for Sean and began to cry. It was time for all of them to begin the grieving. Sean rocked Merry until she fell asleep in her lap. Will kissed Sean gently in thanks for being there with him. Sean asked Will to go on ahead to Intensive Care with Merry, so she could call her parents and sister. Will heard Sean say sister, but it made no sense to him. Then again, at that moment, there wasn't much that did. Will took Merry and left Sean in the waiting room. Sean let her body weight fall down onto the sofa as she covered her face with her hands and prayed. She dialed her parent's number on her cell phone to tell them the news. Brittain and Price would arrive within the next hour on the firm's private jet.

Sean stood at the window in front of Emmalyn's room taking in the sadness before her. Will was reading Emmalyn's chart, she knew, hoping to find some miracle. Emma lay quietly, not moving. Merry had been placed on a chair in the corner, with a pillow under her tiny head. Sean took a deep breath and went in. She leaned over Emma and began to whisper to her. Will put down the chart and joined Sean. Sean spoke of the love she felt for her Aunt Emm, and told her that Will and Merry were there too. Sean's eyes begged Will to speak to Emma. Will's long lashes once again closed slowly and opened to release the torrent of hurt he had been holding onto. He thanked Emma for the love she'd shared with all of them. He gave her a gentle hug while remembering how she'd blushed whenever he'd done it in the past. He prayed that George's, would be the face to greet her as she passed over. He told her of the love and devotion he felt for Sean and of his plan to make her his bride. Sean's eyes watered as she fought to maintain composure. Silently she mouthed the words "I love you", to Will. The tightness in Will's chest was unbearable. Standing up to his full six-foot four-inch height, he excused himself. Sean nodded and continued whispering to Emma. Will went to find the hospital chaplain.

Brittain and Price landed safely and were met by a limousine at the airport. Britt was praying they were not too late, as the limo driver sped toward Penrose Regional Medical Center. Price called his daughter from the limo to let her know they had arrived safely and would be there soon. Sean felt a weight lift from within herself. She had never experienced this kind of hurt before and needed support now too. She waited for Will to return. The Chaplain seemed a gentle soul. He stood almost a foot and a half shorter than Will. The difference between them was endearing. The gentle giant seeking the help of this quiet little man. The chaplain went over to Emma to pray for her soul and offer last rights. Sean told Will that her parents had landed and that she was going to wait downstairs for them.

She squeezed Will's hand and left. Merry awakened at the sound of voices speaking. She climbed down from the chair and asked her Daddy to pick her up so she could see Grandma Emmalyn. Emm was resting quietly. Will allowed Merry to touch her Grandma's face. Merry frowned and said "Look Daddy, she's sleeping! Wake her up?" "No sweetness", he replied. "Grandma Emma needs to rest. She is sick". Merry became hysterical, shouting "Wake her up Daddy! Wake her up! "I couldn't wake Mommy up! I tried, but she wouldn't wake-up!. Merry was crying uncontrollably, when Will realized that the child was reliving her mother's death.

Dr. Reuben rushed in thinking Emma's condition had deteriorated. He saw the child writhing in her father's arms. He didn't understand what had just happened until Will reported clinically, "post-traumatic stress s/p suicidal death of her mother". Dr. Reuben remembered the stories he'd heard about the suicide of Rain Thorpe and the fact that the child had been found lying next to her dead mother's body. Dr. Reuben ordered the floor nurse to take the child from Dr. Thorpe and into the next ICU patient room. Will followed Dr. Reuben. Dr. Reuben suggested a mild sedative for Merry. Will gave his permission. He held Merry tightly in his arms, until she calmed down and fell asleep, wondering what kind of parent he'd been. Her life had been so filled with sadness, and now this.

Sean returned with her parents. Brittain hugged Will and Price shook his hand. Britt went immediately to Emmalyn. Sean watched her mother, just happy to have her there. Price had never met Will, but had heard only great things about him, from Brittain. Price respected his wife's judgment. Will asked Price to step outside the room for a moment. The two men stood eye to eye, as Price listened to the young doctor. They shook hands. Then Price hugged Will. Price shared the news of Will's request with Brittain and watched as she smiled and nodded in affirmation.

As she looked at Sean, her heart was full. Will and Sean had sealed their whispered agreement in a kiss. Will then whispered into the chaplain's ear. The chaplain smiled as he looked over at Sean. He then cleared his throat and asked for silence in the room. He asked Will and Sean to position themselves on either side of Emma's bed and to hold hands. Britt stood next to Will and Price next to his daughter. Britt and Price each took hold to one of Emma's hands.

"Dearly beloved, we are gathered here in the sight of God", the chaplain began. Sean was lost somewhere in the depths of Will's gaze. Standing next to his daughter allowed Price to witness the fullness of Will's love and commitment to love and family with Sean. Will's eyes were filled with caring and commitment. Brittain and

Price stood reading each other. Letting go of Emma's hands, they took off their wedding bands, Britt handing hers to Will as the other belonging to her father was placed into Sean's palm. Once more taking hold of Emma's hands, the parents listened as the bride and groom "were joined in holy matrimony". As the chaplain announced "what God has joined together, let no man put asunder", Emmalyn squeezed Brittain and Price's hands and after opened her eyes for the last time. Completely surprised, Brittain and Price watched as a tear ran down the side of Emma's face. Emma had witnessed the wedding ceremony. Then came the sound everyone recognized, but wanted desperately to deny. The EKG monitor registered a flat line. Price held onto Sean, while Will held on rigidly to Brittain. Dr. Reuben asked the stunned group to leave the room. Emma had blessed this new union in her own way, and now she was on her way to be joined once more to her George.

Twenty-Seven

Suzette, Tristan and Ian were spending more and more time together. She'd even allowed Ian to take Tristan to the park, without going along. They returned eating ice cream cones. It had spoiled Tristan's dinner, but Suzette couldn't get angry. They both looked so happy. Ian had stopped trying to force a commitment from her. After he did, Suzette relaxed more around him. Suzette loved Ian Adams and in her own time would tell him so.

Suzette was spending most of her work day with Price. Ian was given a new paralegal and was not thrilled about it. Price had offered no explanation other than to say that he needed Suzette to help with him with a special presentation. Actually, the new assignment provided her with the distance she needed. She found herself missing Ian during the day and enjoying him more when he came to visit his son.

Price had gone out of town because of a family emergency. Sean had called her sister to share the news. Suzette had not met Emmalyn Brown, but sent her prayers. Suzette had chosen not to tell Ian anything yet about her new family. Nor had she told any of the Smith-Marshals about Ian's place in HER life. So much was filled with so much change. Sean called Suzette again to tell her that

Emmalyn Brown had passed away. Price called her next with the same news. Brittain and Sean were going to stay to help arrange the funeral. But Price would be returning in the morning to complete his presentation. He wanted Suzette to attend the funeral with the rest of the family and to bring Tristan but Suzette offered instead to remain behind to run the firm. Price asked if he could come and get Tristan and of course, she agreed.

For the second time that morning Ian heard the rumor that Suzette was Price Smith-Marshal's daughter. It amazed him how easy it was to start and circulate gossip. He gave it no further consideration. After all, he reasoned, if it were really true, Suzette would have said something to him.

Checking his email In-Box, he saw notice of a special meeting of the Board of Directors of Bosch, Schuyler and Smith-Marshal, with addendum requesting the presence of all junior/senior partners and associate attorneys. Ian whistled, big guns, was all he could think. Something important was about to happen. Ian hoped that Price had no ill feelings regarding the circumstances surrounding his breakup with Sean. Blowing out a puff of air, he decided that he was ready to find out, whatever it was. At a quarter 'til ten, Ian straightened his tie, picked up his portfolio, checked for his pen and headed toward the Boardroom. There seemed to be more whispering than Ian had ever heard before any other meeting. Suzette and Price were still absent.

Ian concluded that they were putting the finishing touches on their presentation and sat down. The sound of Price's distinctive voice could be heard before he entered the room. Everyone stopped talking. As Price entered the room, he paused and allowed Suzette to walk ahead of himself. Further confusing everyone, he asked Suzette to sit down in his chair, the seat reserved only for the Chairman of the Board. Ian sat up and tugged at his tie again, nervously. Suzette looked only at Price. Ian could not get her attention. Suzette called the meeting to order, then paused for Price to take speak. "I am sure, he said as he cleared his throat and clasped his hands that some of you may have heard the news regarding Suzette Butler and myself". As Ian looked around the room, he could see the sneers of the rumor-mongers, as though vindicated. Ian leaned forward in his seat frowning. "And for those of you who know nothing of this matter, I want you to hear it from me". But first ladies and gentlemen, I want to introduce you to the person I am grooming to fill my shoes whenever I must be absent, and somewhere in the future, a permanent replacement. I trust that you will ALL conduct business as usual. Any decision reached you can rest assured will be COMPLETELY supported upon my return. Without further delay, I give you all, our newest associate attorney, my daughter, Suzette Butler Smith-Marshal. This time Suzette turned to look at Ian. At first stunned and unbelieving, but accepting, Ian stood and started the round of applause that followed. Suzette and Price both smiled in gratitude. The rest of the meeting involved a review of corporate business, as usual, with one difference. Suzette conducted the entire meeting, with Price augmenting as he needed only. Price had groomed her well in what must have been a very short period of time. But Ian had always known how sharp Suzette was. He'd had no idea though, that she'd been attending law school. There was so much more he would come to learn. Price finished the meeting with his own personal news. He told those in attendance of the passing of one of his oldest friends, Emmalyn Brown, who had also been the wife of former partner and board member, George Brown. Price would be leaving later that day to help with funeral arrangements and would be taking along his grandson Tristan Butler Smith-Marshal, Suzette had generously offered to stay behind to oversee the firm's business, Price reported. The meeting was adjourned in a flurry of small conversations.

Price and Suzette left the meeting in the company of Price's personal attorney. Major changes were taking place, and Ian needed time to absorb it all. Everyone had been dismissed and encouraged to go home early and spend some time with their families. Ian had no family to go home to, so he just went home. Tristan was going away with his grandfather, leaving Ian, inadvertently a very lonely and unknown member of the family, a fact he realized that no one else, but Suzette knew. Suzette was going to be very busy too, he was sure. Ian had always thought he had it all. The emptiness he was feeling told him otherwise.

Ian drove home finding himself looking into the windows of the cars all around him, only to see children and parents, laughing and just being together. He entered his house and decided to light a fire. He found one of Tristan's toys lying on the floor. He picked it up and smiled. His son. HIS SON. Just thinking about him, began to fill some of the void. Ian ate dinner by the light of the fire, alone and lonely. When he finished his gourmet meal of a sandwich and hot coca, he started taking inventory of his life. He didn't like what he saw and remembered the childhood warnings. His father's words came to him so clearly, even a snake charmer gets bit sometimes son" …

Ian had been shot and killed and didn't know that he'd died long ago. Ian was interrupted in thought by a knock at the door. He opened the door to Suzette. Looking down automatically for Tristan, he then remembered that the boy had gone away with Price. "I know" said Suzette, I miss him too. May I come in?" Ian's emotions were completely naked. The bravado was gone. They sat down and Ian offered Suzette some of the cocoa he was drinking. She laughed at him instead. Ian was drinking out of the special mug that he had given Tristan. This Ian was so different that Suzette was feeling awkward too. Even when they dated, she did not really feel as though she knew him.

Ian had been all flash, but tonight he was someone she wanted to know better. "Ian", she began quietly, "I am sorry that I did not get a chance to tell you about my father, before you had to hear it at the board meeting. But to be honest, I was overwhelmed by it all myself. In the days that I've had to get used to it, I came to realize that the only thing that actually changed was my last name. I am still Suzette Butler, born to, and raised by Anne Butler. All the love and support that she gave me, even when I became pregnant with your... with Tristan, reminded me that she would always love me no matter what and that by the Grace of the Lord, we would be alright. I made it through law school at night while Mama took care of Tristan for me. Money was tight, but somehow that did not matter as much as you might think. You see, I knew that ONE thing that makes me whole...and that is that I am loved and will always be. My mama's love was an extension of the love they preach about in Sunday school. ...And because I love GOD, I can forgive you, myself, and even Price for not being there, being the father, I know I deserved to have. The love my mother taught me filled me up, Ian. I have always been whole because of it. No amount of money that Price could share could ever give me that, and for that matter, give YOU that. You see, I've always understood who you were and wished often that YOU could just find YOU. When I look at Tristan I see who you could have been, could still be, too. Even in your relationship, especially in the one with...Sean...my sister now, I knew that it would not last. Sean has always been a "whole" person, not because of her parents' money, rather in spite of it. It was their LOVE that made it so. And now what I really want you to know", Suzette said as she moved closer to Ian, "is that LOVE can make you whole. I know you know how to TAKE it, Ian. A sad smile played around the corner of her mouth as she touched his lips with her fingers, but the real question is...do you think you're ready to GIVE it?" Ian was full. He could only nod and say "yes, please", through the fog of tears he did not even try to hold back.

Twenty-Eight

Merry kept asking for her Grandma Emmalyn. It was time to tell her. Will asked Sean to go along. He was taking them to Emma and Merry's favorite pond to feed the ducks. Brittain had gone to make the arrangements for the funeral. Price would be back later that evening with Tristan. Will felt like Emma had given him another family, in the Smith-Marshals. Sean could only take Will's lead and just be there, for both of them. Will suspected that Merry understood much more than she could tell him. She fed the ducks diligently, but without her usual excitement. Merry grew tired of throwing the bread crumbs. Once more she asked for her Grandma Emmalyn. Sean asked Merry to sit on her lap, facing her father. His face, a picture of his own misery looked down tenderly on his munchkin, hating to tell her that once more in her short life, she'd lost yet another someone she'd loved. Will picked up Merry's little foot, at first not knowing WHAT to say. "Remember, sweetheart, when Grandma took you shopping to buy these pretty shoes you're wearing?" Merry nodded up and down. "She wanted to give you the special things she bought that day because she loved you so very, very much … and each time you look at all the presents, it makes you feel happy inside because your Grandma gave them to you, right?" Merry wiggled the foot her father held and smiled. She truly loved those shoes and the grandmother who'd given them. "Merry, Grandma got sick in the car, remember?" Once again, the nod. Her eyes had begun to release her tears. "..and we took her to the hospital where you work, Daddy", she finished for him. "Yes, my little sweetheart, we did". Sean smiled at Will through her own hurt. "Grandma Emmalyn didn't get better, baby. She has gone to Heaven to live with GOD... But I want you to always remember that the best gift Grandma Emma gave you, that can never disappear is LOVE. She loved you so much. Merry looked at her father thoughtfully, and said "is she with Mommy?" This time it was Will's turn to nod. "... and Grandma and Mommy will be together, Daddy?" "Yes, love". "...Daddy? ...when Mommy makes me rainbows, will Grandma Emma be there too?" Sean could hold back no longer. Will reached out to her. Sean moved closer to Will and Merry and held onto them both. Life seemed so unfair in that, the tiniest of moments. Merry saw Sean's tears and tried to wipe them away. "It's ok Sean", don't cry, she said. "Mommy and Grandma are in Heaven with Daddy's friend GOD. HE will take care of them...." stated the little child leading them.

Sean then told Merry that she loved her too and wanted to know if she could marry her father and become her new mother. The baby grabbed Sean around the neck and hugged her. Sean looked at Will. "So, it's settled then. I will marry your daddy and we will all live together and take care of each other". Merry nodded, never letting go.

The funeral service was beautiful. Emmalyn looked so peaceful. Price's grandson Tristan bonded with Merry at once. The two held hands as their worlds changed before them. Will was devastated, but confused too because each time he looked at the little boy, he was reminded of the friend and brother he once had.

The ride to Bristol Point Cemetery was even harder for Will because they'd been there only recently. He could still see Emma kissing the swan on top of the headstone. That Emma and George were together, never again to be separated freed Will to try to go on with his life. He tried hard to hold onto that even through the burial. When everyone except family had departed, Will went back to the headstone alone. This time, he gently kissed the swan on the right.

Sean asked Will to return to Palmetto Springs and stay with her family for a little while. He agreed and together they closed the houses at 1111 and 1112 Elm Street. Ellie had prepared the guest suite for Will and Merry. Tristan came daily to play with Merry. They both loved the fountain and always played near it. Will decided to resign from Penrose Regional Medical Center. Bo Longmire hated to see him go, but understood and reminded Will that a job would certainly be his, if ever he wanted it. Brittain and Price wanted to give Sean and Will a huge wedding but understood that they would all need to wait. Instead Sean asked her mother to marry them in a small family ceremony, for Merry's sake, so they could move forward with their lives. The informal ceremony at the hospital had been held for Emma. The civil ceremony Brittain would perform would make them husband and wife legally before the world. Merry stood between them as they took the vows before Judge Smith-Marshal. Suzette was a witness. Tristan was there in his grandfather's arms. Suzette still did not mention Ian. Sean promised her parents that at a happier time, they would be allowed to give her the kind of wedding the three of them had always dreamed. Will loved Sean even more, for this selfless gift. Judge Smith-Marshal gave Will his copy of Emma's Last Will and Testament following the ceremony. Emma had bequeathed to him all of her worldly-possessions including Rex and her ten million- dollar estate. Will was stunned. He'd had no idea Emmalyn was that wealthy. They'd never talked about money issues. Will was humbled by her love and kindness. Determined to do something that would honor Emma, Will decided to open his own clinic. He would offer Family Practice and Surgery Specialties. In honor of Emma and George whose money would pay for the new clinic, he would name it The Brown Memorial Clinic. Palmetto Springs seemed like a nice place and for Sean's sake, it seemed the logical plan. Brittain offered to take care of the sale of the two homes he now owned on Elm Street. Will was grateful. There were so many memories there, both good and bad. Rex had been placed under the care of his Veterinarian. The loss of Emma had left the toy Fox Terrier, physically ill and completely uninterested in eating or drinking water, for weeks after her death. Merry and Will missed him too, and as soon as he began to take nourishment again, together they went to get him. Rex, at first sniffed them and ran round in circles looking for Emma. When he couldn't find her, he stopped, jumping up and put his head down on Will's lap and let out a low and lonely moan. Will rubbed and patted the dog's head, hoping in time, the dog too would recover.

The new Thorpe family moved into Sean's condominium. It was too small, but would do temporarily. Will wanted the construction on his new clinic to be completed before they went house hunting. He accepted a job in the Emergency Room at Palmetto Springs General Hospital to establish privileges in conjunction with his clinic. Merry was being nurtured by her new mother. Price offered Sean a six-month paid leave of absence for Merry's sake. They spent a great deal of time in the company of Suzette and Tristan. The relationship between the sisters grew naturally and deeply. Sean learned much about being a mother from her big sister. Now the grandparents of one each granddaughter and grandson, Brittain and Price, threw themselves completely into the role. The children blossomed like flowers in the sunshine of the love that surrounded them. But still, Suzette never shared the identity of Tristan's father and no one pressed the issue.

Twenty-Nine

S uzette buckled Tristan in his car seat and headed for the Northshire Mall to pick up some new clothes for the weekend outing at the beach. Brittain, Sean and Suzette had planned three days of fun in the sun and relaxation for the family. Will was getting off work early in order to go too. His clinic was coming along, just a little behind schedule, but he was happy. Architecturally, it was a beautiful structure whose large windows and atrium would provide a happy and bright setting for his patients. Suzette pulled onto the two-lane highway whose speed limit topped off at sixty-five miles per hour. Even though she'd inherited a great deal of money, Suzette had not bought a new car. She liked her little sedan. Just big enough for her little clan, she used to think. Anne Butler had given Suzette the car when she no longer needed it. That was the real reason Suzette had chosen to keep it. Tristan was happily pointing to all of the cars he could see flying by. Suzette was deep in thought when she noticed a Sport Utility Vehicle weaving out of control and headed in her direction. Suzette looked up into her rearview mirror, frozen in fear. The last thing she saw was her happy little boy playing in his car seat, totally oblivious to the tragic accident coming at the two of them and in excess of 65 mph. Suzette saw herself colliding with the SUV. She could hear the unforgettable sound of metal being crushed and glass splintering. In a surreal slow-motion, she could see, hear and feel the air bags deploy, the driver's bag, with such force, it hit her squarely in the face. Suzette thought her nose had broken. Momentum and centrifugal forces were loose in the car. Tristan was crying for his mother. "Mommy! Mommy????" the petrified baby reached his arms out for Suzette. The blow to her face left her dizzy and semi-conscious, as the rear end of the sedan lifted up into the air and dropped with such force and finality that Suzette passed out. The car's mechanical and structural integrity had been sorely compromised, throwing Tristan forward and out of his car seat. His little body flew forward as his chest hit the corner of the front passenger headrest. The presence of that headrest had actually been a blessing in disguise, because it was the only thing that had prevented Tristan's entire body from hitting the dashboard and windshield.

Horns were blowing nonstop as drivers jumped out of their vehicles to help the injured. Cell phones all over the highway were being used to report the catastrophe. Three ambulances and an army of police and highway patrol vehicles showed up, sirens blaring. The driver of the SUV was mangled so badly, his body could not be readily removed from the truck without the jaws of life. Suzette tried to speak, but her mouth would not form the words stuck in her heart. "TRISTAN...where is my baby" was all she could think. The baby was lying on the floor in the backseat of the sedan. His face was cut badly from the splintering of the tempered-glass side windows.

Two ambulances belonging to Palmetto Springs General Transported Suzette and Tristan to the Emergency Room. Will had heard the report of the awful accident, on the two-way and decided to stay to help out, but even he was not prepared for the fact that it involved his own family members. The child's condition was reported as the most serious. The driver, presumed to be the child's mother had sustained fractures to both of her ankles and right patellar fracture from the force that propelled her legs forward and pushed her knees forward along with them. She also sustained lacerations and hematomas of the nasal septum, but was going to survive. Will worried about the child.

Tristan was started on IV-lactated ringers, provided oxygen and placed on a backboard with restraints. He'd appeared to have difficulty breathing, so the paramedics inserted a chest tube. He had bruises on his abdomen most likely from the seatbelt at the point of impact. The child was unconscious. The thoracostomy to insert the chest tube did not seem to be working. The paramedics had done all they could for him.

The ambulance arrived at the hospital and the child rushed to Will. He looked at the child Tristan lying on the backboard looking like a torn rag doll. His stomach turned sour. Will looked up for the rest of the patients, half-expecting Sean and Merry to be rolled in. But only Suzette appeared. The paramedics briefed Will on her status and moved her on to the waiting Trauma Team. Suzette was going into surgery with the orthopedic surgeon on call. She was hurt, but she was going to make it. Will had every reason to be worried about the child. Tristan's breathing still had not stabilized. Will ordered STAT Chest X-Ray and 12 lead EKG. The imaging tech finally arrived do a portable chest x-ray.

Will's fears were confirmed. Tristan was suffering from a nonresolving Tension Pneumothorax. He was going to have to take the child into emergency surgery. In Suzette's wallet, the nurses found her sister's emergency phone numbers. Sean had just returned home with Merry. Will spoke to Sean and asked for verbal permission, as the closest next-of-kin, to conduct surgery. Sean was confused. Will WAS the closest next-of-kin within proximity. But Sean knew her husband. Will was not going to perform the surgery on the child, unless no other surgeon was available. Will's replacement had an emergency of his own, and would not arrive in time to perform the emergency procedure required. Will made a decision to try to save Tristan, even though ethical protocols legally prevented it. Sean rushed to call her parents, and tell them to meet her at the hospital. Merry saw Sean reacting to the fear she felt, and began to cry. Sean realized that she had to calm down. She kissed Merry and told her to put Rex into her bedroom and to close the door. Rex managed to calm the baby, when he licked her face. Sean, then put Merry into the car, fearing the worst. Merry sat in her car seat singing the "Itsy-Bitsy Spider". The constant repetition actually helped Sean to relax a little. Price and Brittain pulled into the hospital parking lot right behind Sean. They all hugged as Price scooped Merry up, and headed for the Emergency Room to speak with Suzette's and Tristan's doctors.

Will was scrubbed and ready to go in. Tristan's color was not good. Will was prepared for the thoracic surgery he was going to have to perform. He had not stopped praying as he began to operate. It had been too long since the primary insult to the child's body had taken place. Will knew only too well that he was racing with Time. He found the problem. Tristan had suffered a bronchial rupture. Will's hands moved quickly to suture the rupture. Then the unimaginable happened. Tristan went into cardiac arrest. The EKG monitor registered a flatline. Will's concentration grew more intense. He immediately began cardiopulmonary resuscitation. He heard the vitals being recited, systematically marking the exact amount of time passing as well as EKG and blood pressure reports. Will could find no pulse. The EKG sang its out-of-tune dirge, as Will calmly, continued, doing CPR. Will knew that the known limit for oxygen deprivation the brain would survive, without irreversible damage is between three to four minutes. The vital reports continued as Will worked on. The nurses and anesthesiologist were all laser-focused on saving the baby boy. Will ordered the staff to stand clear in order use the defibrillator. Once, twice, three times, and yet once more. Will had already surpassed the four minutes. But he could not bring himself to stop. The staff were all wondering why he didn't or wouldn't call a code. The child had died, but Dr. Thorpe refused to let go.

The family waited in the OR waiting room for any news about Suzette and Tristan. Suzette's surgeon, Dr. Weintraub was the first to go see them. Suzette had made it through surgery and would be alright. She was going to need some time to recover, but her fractures had all been textbook. The miracle was that she had survived at all. The driver of the SUV had died instantly. It seems he had been talking on his cell phone and lost control of his vehicle. Suzette was still in the Recovery Room, but would be moved to the Intensive Care Unit as soon as possible. The family would be allowed only a few minutes to see her. Brittain and Sean decided to let Price go in alone. Price looked at the bruised and swollen face of his child and felt the pain only parents know. Her lips were swollen and she was coming out of the anesthesia. She was trying to tell her father something that he could not make out. He Placed his head close to her lips, but still did not understand. Suzette started to cry. Her eyelids were already almost swollen shut, but the tears found their way out anyway. Once again, she tried to communicate with Price. This time he thought he heard her say "Ian". Price frowned and said the name to himself. "Ian?" "Suzette? Is that what you're trying to tell me?" Suzette moved her head only slightly. She lifted her hand and tried to squeeze his arm. Price tried to calm her. Then he understood. She wanted Price to call Ian Adams. Of course, he thought. That is why she had not ever spoken the name of Tristan's father. It was Ian Adams. Price was not happy at hearing this news. But neither was this the time to disagree. Price whispered in Suzette's ear this time. "Honey, do you want me to call Ian?" Suzette nodded yes. "Suzette, is he Tristan's father?" This time she did not answer as though her father would disapprove. "My darling daughter, if he is, then he too, is family. You get some rest and I will call him right away. Now you get some rest." Suzette was trying to ask about Tristan, but Price knew nothing of his condition, only that he had not yet come out of surgery. Instead, he told her that Tristan was in surgery and was going to be fine. Price kissed her swollen face, happy to see it, even as it was.

Price went first to call the answering service at the firm to be connected to Ian Adams at home. Ian's machine answered. He had not yet arrived home. Price hated to do it, but went ahead and left a message to meet them at the hospital, because Tristan and Suzette had been involved in an accident. He then tried Ian's cellphone, but it went to voicemail. He left an urgent message to call, as soon as possible.

Will was rapidly approaching the ten- minute mark since Tristan had flatlined. He would still not stop the CPR. His OR staff did not know what to do. None of them could overrule the doctor and call the code. Neither could they leave the OR. So, they stayed and watched in total disbelief and amazement.

Ian had stopped to pick some extra snacks in case Tristan dropped by with his mother. Finally, home, sitting down on the sofa, he saw the blinking light of the answering machine and played the message. He grabbed his cell to check for another message, and found it. Ian jumped up after hearing Price's call forgetting all about the Cherry-Vanilla ice cream he'd just bought for the child. He jumped in his car and sped without fear of being stopped, toward the hospital. It seemed forever before he could run into the ER, hoping to see his two loves. The ER staff sent him directly to the Intensive Care Unit to see Suzette. The floor nurse on duty warned him abouther condition and what he was about to see. Ian did not care what Suzette looked like as long as she was still alive.

Suzette heard his voice and tried to open her eyes wider, so she could see him, but the swelling was becoming progressively worse. She could only hear him. Ian was devastated at what he saw, but was determined not to let on to Suzette. He kissed her swollen face and sat down next to her bed. She began to cry uncontrollably. The nurse returned and asked Ian to stay only a minute or two longer. The stress on Suzette's heart from the accident and her injuries was tremendous. All Ian could understand was "Tristan", as she fought to talk to him. Suzette still had been given no news about her baby. Ian was alarmed too, but would not let Suzette hear it in his voice. He could not bear to lose either one of them. He had somehow assumed that Suzette would already know their son's condition. The fact that she did not, scared Ian. All he could think of was that his only child had died, and he had not been there for him. The ICU Head Nurse told him how to get to the OR waiting room. Ian rushed in hoping to get some news of his son. He looked around the room at the surprised family members. Price spoke first. Tristan was still in surgery and there had been no news yet. Sean saw a different Ian in that moment. She went over to him and gave him the forgiveness he sorely needed in the form of a hug.

Will had heard the EKG Flatline for so long, his ears were ringing. Twenty-four minutes had passed. The tears ran down his face as he struggled to find strength to stop CPR. Looking up at the clock, he stopped. Will prayed for Tristan's soul, for Suzette's recovery, Sean's hurt and for Price and Brittain. They would all be crushed by the sudden death. Will called the code and asked that the time be recorded. Looking down at the child's face, he once more experienced the haunting feeling that he knew that face. Will ungloved and headed to talk to his family.

Will walked out of the OR suite slowly. The horrific sorrow of it all was beginning to weigh him down. He tried to prepare himself for the grief and hurt he was about to share in. Will prayed each step of the way. Sean saw Will first. She knew that something had gone terribly wrong. Will carried his hurt in his body, most especially in the way he walked, when he felt defeated. Sean gasped out of fear. Price and Brittain turned around to face Will as he looked down, but kept coming in their direction. Ian stood up unwilling to believe that it was Will Thorpe walking toward him. But it was.

The nurses in the OR were making arrangements for the child to be transported to the morgue. As the operating room technician reached to disconnect the EKG leads, a soft white light appeared in one corner of the room. Everyone turned in the direction it emanated from, and watched in pure amazement and disbelief of their very own power of vision, witnessing firsthand, the sight of the child being held in the arms of CHRIST. Tristan did not appear to be hurt at all. The LORD did not speak. His face was a mask of sadness, as he beheld the earthly body of Tristan Adams Butler Smith-Marshal, while holding onto the very soul, of the same. The love for this child was holding three families together. Once more the softness of that same light, this time emanated from Will's being as he walked toward the waiting family group. Will seemed to be totally unaware of it. It was the tears that ran down his face that told more. Price and Brittain stared at the glow surrounding Sean looked only at her husband. Ian stood up and started toward Will, then came abruptly to a stop. This time, he too stared in disbelief as above Will's head was the very same apparition being witnessed by those in the OR. Tristan was in the center of the brightness held lovingly in the arms of the Lord Jesus Christ. It seemed with great sadness, He Watched only Will and Ian as they moved toward each other. Will recognized Ian finally and soon understood his own feelings about Tristan's face. Embedded in the child's face was the memory of Will's old friend. This child no doubt, belonged to Ian Adams.

Will had tried his best to save Tristan because he too, loved the boy, as he'd once loved Ian. But he'd failed, the one time he was needed the most…he'd failed his family, himself and the friend he once called brother. Ian lowered his eyes and looked solemnly, and shame-filled, into the face of Will Thorpe. Ian's trespass against his old friend, Ian knew someday would carry a dear price. "whatsoever ye sew, so shall ye reap"…filled every cell in Ian's brain. Rain's death had been Ian's fault and so….this would be his cross to bear. But in paying this debt, this way, Suzette would suffer more… The mother who had had carried and loved Tristan into this world, when Ian neither knew, nor cared about his existence. The corner of Ian's eye photographed the distraught grandfather and grandmother, unable to save their own child Suzette from this pain.

This pain would most certainly take them along for the journey, and Sean holding onto Merry, lest she somehow lose her precious little one, to an undeserved fate too. Ian stopped moving and hesitated for a moment. Will never broke his stride. He'd missed his old friend whom he'd once loved like a brother. Their shared pain and hurt, sorrow and remorse, intermingled with death of the innocent child. As Will and Ian moved toward each other in forgiveness and love, Brittain, Price and Sean could see THE CHRIST smile such a sad smile, and as he did so the image of Tristan began to fade. Price cried out "NO!" Ian and Will wrapped their arms so tightly around each other, that no one else could have separated them. The two men cried a river together. Ian was trying to apologize, and so was Will but neither could talk. They could only rock back and forth as if dancing. As they held onto each other, for dear life, one of the OR nurses came running down the hall crying hysterically...."HE'S ALIVE.... THE CHILD IS ALIVE...!!!!!!

PRAISE THE LORD, HE'S GOING TO BE ALRIGHT"........

Thirty

Serenity Appleton climbed out of her car at 1112 Elm street hoping she had the right address. The search for her sister Rain had taken its toll on her. Until six months ago, Serenity had not even known that she had a sibling, much less a twin sister. They had been orphaned immediately following their birth, when their mother Lillian Meadows, died from postpartum complications. Rain had been the firstborn. Noisy and crying, she entered life. Her twin arrived quietly. Hence the names Rain and Serenity. Rain had been a colicky baby. Her constant crying made it difficult for those who cared for her at the orphanage to bond with her. Serenity, on the other hand was everyone's joy. When it came time for adoption, Serenity was selected immediately and sadly her twin left behind. Serenity had been loved from birth and Rain had only known loneliness. Serenity stood in front of the house on Elm Street, ready to meet and reconnect with the twin, life had denied her. She rang the doorbell, hoping to be greeted by Rain herself. Serenity wanted desperately to find her. No one answered the doorbell. Serenity walked around to the back of the house and stood in the garden taking it all in. It was as though, she'd found herself at home, in her own backyard. All of her favorite flowers had been planted, in much the way she'd designed her own flower garden. Serenity closed her eyes and hugged herself. There was no doubt in her own mind, that her sister lived there. Looking up across the lawn, she saw a larger version of the Cape Cod styled home at 1111 Elm. The grass had been recently cut at both homes. Serenity was hoping Rain's neighbor could tell her when Rain might be coming home. She rang the doorbell at 1111 Elm, but to no avail. No answer again. Serenity noticed a sign on the lawn, nearer to the street, next to the mailbox. It was a FOR SALE sign that listed the two properties as being available. She copied the phone number and name of the point of contact, determined to call. Even if Rain had moved, at least then Serenity could find out where she'd gone. Serenity took one last mental picture of her sister's last home and left. She took a plane immediately to Palmetto Springs.

Serenity arrived hungry and stopped to get some lunch. While waiting for her food, she decided to contact the phone number listed on the For Sale sign. "Bosch, Schuyler and Smith-Marshal" the voice on the other end said. "Yes, thank you. My name is Serenity Appleton and I'm calling to speak with whomever is handling the properties at 1111 and 1112 Elm Street", Bristol Point, Colorado". "One moment, please?" "Adams", came the reply. "Hello, Mr. Adams, this is Serenity Appleton. Ian thought some cruel joke was being played out. Serenity sounded exactly like Rain Thorpe. Ian loosened his tie and pulled at the collar of his shirt in disbelief. "We've not met. I would like to ask a few questions about the properties at 1111 and 1112 Elm Street and I'm told that you are overseeing the sales of those properties". "Not exactly, said Ian. "The firm is handling this on behalf of a special client". Daring to know, Ian continued. "May I ask the nature of your interest?" "Yes of course" said Serenity. "Are you considering the purchase of either property?" Ian countered. "No, Serenity said slowly, actually I'm trying to find the previous owner. I believe that we are family". At the speed of silence, the bullet entered Ian's head and shattered his thoughts. The voice, he realized, was Rain's voice he kept hearing and in denial refused to recognize. The old Ian found himself standing on a new precipice. Serenity's well-trained ear had measured the length of Ian's silence and knew that there was more to learn here. "Ms. Appleton, he said in carefully measured tones, would you please indulge me for a moment. I'd like to talk with you". Serenity paused, listening for the sigh Ian would surely let out, if there really was anything of importance he could share. Then she heard it, involuntarily forced out, Serenity knew that she needed to hear what this Ian Adams wanted to tell her. They arranged to meet at his office. Ian was new at facing his troubles squarely and needed all the support familiar surroundings would offer. Ian wished sincerely that he could talk to Suzette. But she had taken Tristan to see his doctor and would not return until after lunch. This time, he alone, would face the music.

Serenity returned to the table to eat lunch, but she had lost her appetite. Her every instinct trained and natural told her that she must prepare for the news to come. Instead she paid the bill and left. She took a cab to the address Ian Adams had given her, at 444 Tower Plaza, 4th Floor, the offices of Bosch, Schuyler and Smith-Marshal, Palmetto Springs, Colorado. Suzette returned to the office after Tristan's latest medical appointment. He was recovering well following the horrible accident that nearly killed him. Tristan's recovery had been a miracle and nothing less, and it had reunited Will and Ian, old friends made new.

Suzette buzzed Ian's office, but he had not returned from lunch yet. No answer. He'd probably call when he returned. Price would be out of the office for the entire day. He and Brittain were deep in planning a double wedding ceremony for their two daughters. No expense would be spared. The Smith-Marshal estate was under wedding construction in preparation. Suzette's new position in the firm as Chief Operations Officer (COO) had gone unchallenged. Even Sean had been pleased. Under her father and new big sister's tutelage, she fit comfortably. Suzette's entrance into the family provided the bridge in time needed, by both Price and Sean. Price believed someday that Sean would be made ready to take over the firm, and as his only daughter then, rightfully so. But Suzette had earned her father's admiration long ago, when he recognized the superb skills she could, and did bring to the firm. Suzette was like the son Price never had.

Serenity glanced at her watch. It was time. She approached Reception to ask for directions to Ian's office. Tabitha Jones had been promoted and assigned to Ian as his new paralegal. She stopped to say hello to her friends in Reception each day at lunchtime. She'd overheard Serenity asking for Ian's office and offered to show her the way, since she too was headed there. Serenity introduced herself to Tabitha. The two women shook hands. Tabitha checked Ian's afternoon schedule, but could not find her name listed. Serenity explained the nature of the visit. Tabitha seemed satisfied with the explanation. Once again Serenity took a seat. Ian had apparently entered his office through the side door and had returned from lunch. He stepped into Tabitha's office to let her know about Ms. Appleton's appointment and looked dead into a face identical to Rain Thorpe's. Ian was beginning to feel uncomfortable in his own skin. Extending his hand nonetheless to greet her, he could not stop the intense stare that remained plastered to his own face. Serenity smiled and nodded in return, missing none of his reaction. Ian excused himself and went to call Suzette before their meeting would begin. Suzette could hear the foreboding in Ian's voice, and wanted to help him. This time, however, Ian was determined to stand up and accept responsibility. Suzette was proud of him and told him so.

Serenity greeted Ian with a smile and followed him into his office. She refused his offer of coffee or a beverage. Ian took a seat next to Serenity instead of behind the desk. "I understand, she said, that your firm is handling the sale of the house at 1112 Elm Street. I believe it is where my twin sister Rain used to live. I am trying to find her. We were orphaned at birth. I was adopted and Rain was not. I did not know until recently that I had a sibling, let alone a twin. I only hope that it would not be improper for you to help me find her". Ian leaned forward in his chair, as though imploring

Serenity to understand. "Ms. Appleton", Ian stated ". "Please, I prefer to be called Dr. Appleton. I am a Pediatric Psychiatrist". Ian sighed heavily once more, visibly upset. "Dr. Appleton, then, I am sorry to have to be the one to tell you this, but your sister Rain..Rain Thorpe, was her full married name, is deceased". Serenity shook her head "no" in a refusal to accept the possibility. "But she can't be. She is...was. too young to have died. The house she used to live in appears to be only recently placed for sale". "Your sister died about eight months ago Dr. Appleton. She committed suicide". Ian hung his head. "There is more. She...she killed herself because of me" Ian almost whispered. "I don't understand. What have you to do with my sister? As you stated her married name was Thorpe". "Will Thorpe, your brother-in law and I went to college together. That is where we met. We were roommates. Your sister Rain worked in the college rathskellar as a waitress, and that his how we three came to know each other. Will and Rain started dating and eventually married. Rain.... your sister was never a happy person. She...we, used to joke and laugh all of the time. Those good times somehow turned into more than they should have. We had an affair. I never meant for it to happen.... Ian pleaded. Will was my best friend" .... Ian's voice trailed off as though he'd finally heard himself speak. I broke it off...but Rain didn't want it that way. She found out that I had begun a relationship with someone else....and well you know the rest now". Serenity was quiet for a moment. "How did she do it...I guess I need to know, by what means?" "She shot herself with a twenty-two caliber pistol. But there's something more that I must tell you. Rain found out that I had been two-timing her. My new relationship had actually begun while I was seeing her. I killed her Dr. Appleton. I killed her as surely as if I had pulled that trigger myself".

Serenity took a very deep and long breath. Quietly she said "Rain was killed the day she was born. My adoptive mother told me that Rain was a colicky baby and cried all of the time. That is how she got her name. Like rain falling in the midst of a storm, she just would not stop crying. That is why she was not chosen to be adopted with me. Rain was born first. She probably fought her way out. Somewhere in her being she must have understood that she was going to have to take care of herself...and it made her cry and cry until she could not stop crying". You did not kill her, Mr. Adams. She simply cried herself to death. It just took a lifetime". "Thank you for telling me your truth. I can only imagine how difficult it must have been. Whoever, you were then, you are no longer. I can see that". "If it helps at all to know, said Ian, she has a daughter. A three-year-old named Merry. Merry Adams Thorpe. She is my godchild". "You really are sorry, aren't you?" inquired Dr. Appleton. "More than you could possibly imagine and now that I have a son of my own, I only wish that I could take it all back." said Ian sorrowfully. "You can't" said Serenity standing up before him. You can only choose to learn from your error in judgment and make the world around you a better place. You owe that to Rain, to yourself and God Almighty. If you would tell me how to contact my brother-in-law, Dr. Thorpe...I would be most grateful". Serenity had lost a part of herself that afternoon, and was hoping to regain some measure of it when she got to meet Merry.

"I can help you with that. Here is Dr. Thorpe's phone number. I am sure that he will be most happy to meet you. Dr. Thorpe is engaged to my fiancee's sister. So as you can see, I will be reminded of all of my mistakes, for the rest of my days. Please don't misunderstand. I find it a meager price to pay in comparison to the one Rain had. Thank you for listening Dr. Appleton". "Goodbye Mr. Adams".

Thirty-One

Serenity had absorbed all that she could for one day. Her only sibling was gone. She rented a hotel room in town, hoping to be able to see Dr. Thorpe and Merry the next day. A long hot shower was definitely needed. Toweling the fine, curly hair that looked so much like Rain's, she sat down on the bed and turned on the television. Good, she thought, the News, just in time. She'd just dropped her head to towel dry the back of her hair, when she heard Will Thorpe's name being mentioned on the newscast. It was a News report on the emergency surgery he'd performed that literally saved the life of Tristan Adams Butler. The child had been in the backseat of the vehicle driven by his mother, when another vehicle collided head-on with it, after having accidentally crossed the center median. Adams, she thought. The name again. This must have been the son he talked about. Dr. Thorpe newly-hired, was on the staff of Palmetto Springs General. "A Miracle".

That is what the reporter called the successful surgery. The child had actually died. Some twenty minutes after loss of identifiable life signs, he was reborn. There were reports of a vision of Jesus Christ holding the child, then raising him from the dead. They were calling it "The Palmetto Springs Miracle".

Serenity turned off the television trying not to be sadder. "If only", he could have saved Rain. Exhausted, she turned off the television, the lights and went to sleep. Tomorrow she would meet the miracle doctor.

Ian decided to go straight home without seeing Suzette. He'd decided to call her later and talk. Serenity's visit had brought him face to face with himself. In the hours afterward, he wanted to share that view with no one else. Ian had gone for a walk and missed Suzette's phone call. She was worried about him. He just seemed to disappear. Ian returned from his walk feeling a little better and decided he'd better check in with Suzette. Sure enough, his machine was blinking. She had left about four messages. Ian did not feel as though he deserved her, but was so grateful to have her. They were to be married soon, and Tristan would carry the Adams name as it should be.

Suzette was not at her apartment, so he tried the Smith-Marshal estate. Ellie answered the phone and Ian could hear Suzette, Sean and Brittain talking in the background. No doubt, wedding details, he thought. Suzette came to the phone. "Ian where have you been? I was so worried about you. Tabitha said something about you seeing a Dr. Appleton. Are you alright?" "Yes, love, I am now. Listen do you have time to come over here? I need to talk with you. No, I just need to see you, to hold you…please come now????" Ian begged. Suzette heard something in his voice, she had never before, and was a little frightened. "I'll be there as soon as I can get there. Are you really alright? she asked frightened for him. "Yes, I am. I will be right here at the house. Come now please, and ask Ellie to take care of Tristan while you are gone. I just need you, right now. okay???" This was not Ian's way of doing things. Suzette knew only that she had to hurry. Something was wrong and she needed to know what.

Grandpa Price had just walked in and Suzette knew that wild horses would not separate those two now. Their bond strengthened even more after the accident. It seemed so strange to her to have the freedom to get up and go and yet know that someone else would love and protect her son. Someone other than the grandmother who had once adored him.

Suzette pulled up to the lake house, searching for Ian. Hearing her automobile pull up, he opened the front door. Ian was wearing shorts and a t-shirt. He must have left work early and gone straight home, she was thinking. He had already changed. Ian turned and locked the door to the house and putting his arm around her shoulder, walked her silently back down to the lake. Suzette could see that something had shaken him, down to the very core. She waited for him to talk. He pulled her down with him onto the grass, putting her in front of him, so he could rest his head on her back. Ian Adams, had spent his entire life running away, running fast and running far. Standing still, took far more out of him that he ever thought it would. But at least if he were still, he could rest. That is what he needed from Suzette that day. To be able to put his head down and rest. To stop being afraid..lonely…guilty…hated and hating himself. He knew that Suzette was blessed with the strength it took to protect him from even himself. In the quiet of the afternoon, they rocked slowly back and forth and enjoyed the peace that comes by and by. Later, he thought, much later when he had rested himself adequately, he would tell her all about Dr. Appleton and her twin sister Rain.

Thirty-Two

Will kissed Sean and Merry goodbye in their sleep, as he prepared to go to the hospital to work. It was agreed upon that until the wedding took place, for Merry's sake, that Sean and Merry would share Sean's bedroom and that Will would occupy the guestroom. It just felt like the right thing to do. Even though the hospital chaplain had performed a quick marriage ceremony when Emma was dying, and Brittain, a civil ceremony, Will and Sean wanted to wait for the wedding, before living as man and wife. Watching his two loves sleeping so peacefully was like meditating for Will. He felt so very blessed, and in fact, he was. Hungry, he decided to get something to eat in the hospital cafeteria. Barely six, in the morning, the dining room was empty with the exception of a woman getting a cup of coffee. Will waited on his omelet to be cooked and headed to get a cup of coffee. As he turned to go pick up his food, he looked up and seeing Rain seated before him staring, he dropped the glass cup onto the floor, feeling his nerves shatter at the very same moment. Will thought he was seeing an apparition. He knew that he'd been stressed over the events of the last year, but even he, refused to believe that he had started to see things. As she moved closer, he remained still, unable to move at all. The woman spoke to him, but he could not move, nor could he speak. As she touched his arm and he felt her touch, his senses jump-started. He began to hear sounds again. The woman who looked exactly like Rain was apologizing to him. He permitted her to offer him a seat at her table. "Dr. Thorpe", she seemed to know his name. "Dr. Thorpe", she repeated, you are alright. "I am not your wife Rain. I am Serenity Appleton, Dr. Appleton. I am your wife's twin sister". Serenity went back to the coffee machine for him. Handing him a steaming hot cup, she sat down next to him once again. "I had hoped our initial meeting would be less traumatic, but honestly I guess it could not. You knew nothing about me. I am so sorry to have upset you this way". Will apologized to the staff for the mess he'd made.

Will covered his eyes with his hands and slowly removed them from his eyes once again. In a rush of hurt and sorrow, Serenity's living presence brought him literally face to face with ghost of his first wife. Serenity began to pray, asking for spiritual guidance as she approached the close of this chapter in her life. Rain was gone. As she touched his shoulder, she could feel the presence of her sister's spirit. "Will, I am so sorry that Rain hurt you the way she did. You are an extraordinary man and father and doctor. You see Rain, never understood how to be happy and now she is in a safe place where nothing can hurt her anymore. I spent my whole life feeling like a part of me was missing and now once more my sister has been taken from me. I don't want to be sad anymore. I guess it's going to have to be enough that now she is safe. Now live your life, Dr. Thorpe and know that I wish for you and Merry and your fiancee all the happiness my sister was not able to give to you. As Will lifted his head to look at Serenity, he felt a slow calm pass over him. Serenity held out her hand to him. "Hello, Dr. Thorpe. I am sorry we met like this. I planned something entirely different. But, as I am sure you understand now, there are some things that have been planned so very long ago and no amount of detouring will change that which has already been written on the wind.

Will stood up and motioned to the cook to trash the omelet he'd ordered for breakfast. He pulled out a large bill and placed it on the cash register, in apology. Serenity stood up with him. She had the saddest look on her face. Serenity took a piece of paper out of her pocket and placed it in Will's hand and folded his fingers over it. She wanted to talk with him, but the morning had already been too much.

Will reached his office and went inside without turning on the light. He felt as though Rain had freed him completely. She had been there in the room as surely as he knew he had left home and gone to work. Somewhere in the fabric of life, through some small opening and surely by the Grace of our Lord, he had been allowed a peek at his dead wife for the few moments, she needed to put things right. Unfolding the piece of paper Serenity placed in his hand, he read "Call me please. Here is my hotel phone number."

The phone rang as Will sat in the darkness. He let it continue to ring. He was not ready to speak to anyone just yet. Will needed time, to permit the roller coaster ride of emotions settle down. But this was not to be. The phone started ringing again. Worried that it might be Sean or Merry calling, he picked up the receiver. "Good morning Will", spoke the voice of his old friend and nemesis. I guess it's time, Will thought. Clearing his throat, "Hello, Ian" came the response. "I" ....Ian stammered, but continued "I was hoping... that we could finally talk". "I'd like that, Ian.... I'd really like to try to understand", Will offered. "Lunchtime Ian. Here at the hospital. The handball court". "Alright, see you at noon". Will called downstairs and reserved the handball court and sauna.

Merry sat up in the bed and looked around for Sean. Frightened and half-asleep she climbed down off the bed and ran through the apartment crying...Mommy, Mommy, where are you? I can't find you...Mommy????? the baby wailed. Sean bounded from the shower dripping wet, barely wrapped in the towel she'd grabbed in a panic. Scooping Merry and hugging her protectively as the child ran toward her, Sean carried her back to the bed. Together they climbed back in, as Sean rocked back and forth with her. "What happened my little bird?" Sean cooed in Merry's ear. "I am here...sh-sh-sh.... I'm right here, my little one. You don't have to be afraid anymore. I will always be right here. I went to shower while you were still sleeping. Sh-sh-sh, once again, she said. My little pumpkin, I will never leave you alone. I love you baby bird. Sh-sh-sh......" Merry seemed to calm down and relax. "I couldn't find you Sean...I tried, but I couldn't find you???" Merry whispered. "I think you were having a bad dream sweetie. You were calling for Mommy", Sean smiled at her. Merry sat up in the bed and turned to look into Sean's eyes. Those huge brown eyes stretched in wonder, swallowing Sean whole. "I was calling you" ... the child said as she lowered her head, as if fearing rejection. Merry had found the little little door to Sean's heart, designed long ago for her alone, climbed in and shut it softly behind herself, and would from that moment and forever belong to Sean. Frightened too of rejection, Sean braved the elements..." Would you like to call me Mommy, Merry?" Looking down once more, she nodded "yes". Sean's heart was happy. Reaching for the baby, lifting Merry's chin, so she could see Sean's face, Sean kissed her forehead. "Let's pray and talk to your Mommy and ask her if it will be alright for me to take care of you and love you now that she is gone. Close your eyes little bird, and tell me what she says". "We have to get down on our knees first. That's how you say a prayer" Merry instructed. Sean complied and together they said separate prayers, Merry's one of request and Sean's of humble bequest. Sean peeked at the little angel beside her trying to reconcile the old with the new, in awe of the resilience and strength she saw. When Merry's head popped up, Sean took her cue and raised her own. On her knees next to Merry, Sean was eye to eye with her. "What did she say, little one???" "Mommy said to tell you, thank you". Merry watched as tears filled Sean's eyes and so she hugged Sean's head.

Thirty-Three

I t took Will's best to get through his morning. Although he tried not to think about his meeting with Ian, he could not help it. Once the best of friends, soon to become brothers, in the law of matrimony, it was time to set things right on the "manly battlefield" of his choosing and move on.

Will left his office early to change for the game. Offense was never his forte. Knowing so, this time he prepared. He'd already played a game of handball alone, by the time Ian arrived. The two shook hands and the games began. Ian's approach was defensive and tentative. Not a good position to be in with a speeding projectile determined to hit its target. Nor was it his game style. Never play anyone else's game because you won't win, he used to tell Will. The strength and power Ian used to beat Will in the past, was gone. Will stepped up the intensity of his game and the power of his strokes. Ian lost his footing and ran head first, into the ball aiming itself directly at his eyebrow. Will wanted to hurt his friend, the same way he'd been hurt, at least until it actually happened. When he saw Ian go down, a little battered around his right eye, the two became brothers again. Will rushed to Ian's aid. Ian stayed on the floor while Will examined his head. Taking off the headband, he was wearing,

Will put it on Ian's head to apply pressure to the wound. No words were exchanged. Will helped his friend to the Emergency Room. X-Rays, showed no skull fracture and to the sounds of much teasing, Dr. Thorpe, not so gently sewed up Ian's wound. Two stitches were enough. Will asked Ian if he wanted something for the pain. Ian declined. Two stitches was a very small price to pay.

Serenity had repacked her bag and sat on the side of the bed preparing herself for the call to Will. Serenity had given much thought to what she wanted to say to him. Merry was all that was left of Rain and Serenity hoped to be allowed to develop a relationship with the child. But she was a twin to the mother just lost to Merry. Serenity's physical presence in Merry's life right now would probably add even more confusion.

"Dr. Thorpe", Will spoke into the receiver. "Hello Will, it's me Serenity", as though Will could ever forget the sound of her voice. I had hoped to meet Merry and to perhaps spend a little time with her, but I can see that this would probably be the worst time for that. I am told congratulations are in order. You are going to be married again soon". "Look Serenity", he started to say, in explanation to this family stranger. "Will, please, you don't owe me an explanation. I spent quite a bit of time talking to Ian Adams. I know that you both are to be married in a double ring ceremony. Please believe that I wish all of you the very best. I am sure that life with my sister must have been extremely difficult. I only wish I could have been there for her... for all of you. My primary concern now is my future relationship with Merry. She is all that is left of Rain. I still want to meet her and to spend time with her, but I understand how traumatic that would be right now. With your permission, I would like to begin a phone relationship with her. Your new bride deserves the chance to complete her bonding with Merry. I would love to call Merry from time to time and to send small gifts, if that is alright with you. Then when the time is right, and she is a little older, I can visit. It is my personal feeling that if we could develop a relationship first, then when she sees me, she will be better able to separate me from her mother". "Thank you Serenity. Merry is fortunate to have you and I do agree with you. I want her to enjoy a relationship with Rain's relatives. Before you, there was none" Will said. "I am flying back to New York this evening Will. So, I guess this is goodbye for now". "What time is your flight, Serenity?" "No matter, she said I have made arrangements to get to the airport already". "Oh", he answered. "Let me give you my office, cell and home phone number as well, Serenity offered. I am a pediatric psychiatrist and have my own practice, so if you ever need some advice, you can get a family discount". Will smiled for the first time since their conversation began. "Then this is goodbye until then" he returned. "Until then", she repeated. Will called Sean and Merry to say hello. They were on their way to the pool to go swimming. Merry was quite excited and impatient. "Come on Mommy", Will heard her say. "I'm coming, my little bird. Will honey, I've got to go. Our child is calling and Yes... she did call me Mommy. Bye Baby, we'll talk later, for sure". "Sean, sweetheart, just one more thing, can you two meet me at six, so we can go to dinner and maybe take a ride later?" "Alright sweets, she said..kiss, kiss..gotta go". Everything was truly beginning to fall into place. A few more calls to make and Will's day would be over.

Sean and Merry arrived at six sharp in a taxi, looking happy and energetic. Will picked up and hugged his baby girl. As expected, he gave a ticklish ride back down to the floor. Upon his beautiful fiancee, he planted a great big wet one, as Merry said..."ooh-oooh-oooh", and laughed. He explained to them that they were going to the airport to deliver a gift to a friend and then out to eat dinner. Merry loved going for long rides. She never cared about the destination, as long as she could go with her Daddy. Sean did not understand what was going on, but knew that Will would explain it all later. They arrived and parked by seven-thirty. Will opened the trunk and took out a small present elegantly wrapped and put it into his breast pocket. Merry held their hands as she skipped happily between them. He took the package to the information desk and tipped the clerk generously, to overhead page Dr. Serenity Appleton.

Will left the desk and walked over to the window where Sean and Merry were watching jets take off and land. He could see the clerk pointing in his direction as he lifted his arm to wave. Serenity stood holding the gift in her hand and a handkerchief in the other as she stared at the only living blood relative she knew. Will watched her return to her seat and waited until her flight began boarding before he left with Sean and Merry. Dr. Appleton waved one last time and boarded her plane.

Serenity sat down in her seat and belted herself in. She could still see the happy child in her mind. She was the best of Rain and someday would come to know her Aunt Serenity too. She reached into her purse and took out the package Will had delivered to her. The wrapping was almost too beautiful to remove. She opened the long gray velvet jewelry box and saw inside a raindrop shaped locket on a chain. Holding her breath, she opened the cover gently. Closing her stinging eyes to clear her vision, she saw the miniscule copy of the only picture Will used to keep in his wallet of Rain and Merry together.

Thirty-Four

Brittain relented within the first week of planning and let Price persuade her to hire a Bridal Consultant. Preparing for a double wedding was going to require far more time that she had available. She still had court cases to hear. She did however agree to help Suzette and Sean select their wedding gowns and of course, to lend her considerable good taste to the selection of the clothes for the children. Merry, of course, would be the flower girl and Tristan, the ring bearer. Price's job was to sign all of the checks and help his grandchildren to practice their new duties, all of which he did quite agreeably. Price and Brittain, like all good grandparents had fallen in love with the young heirs to their legacy. "Mr. Brooks", more a title, than a name, arrived shortly after Brittain surrendered. Along with his majesty came two assistants, one each Miss Lily and a Mr. Pearl. Mr. Brooks, the consummate professional and "Artiste" was not at all disturbed by the fact that both brides had children, but Miss Lily seemed totally put off. Apparently after a stiff "talking to" by his majesty, all that nastiness took backstage priority. Both Suzette and Sean wanted Mr. Pearl to dress them. He had a deliciously wicked sense of humor and was a delight to be around. His impeccable, but daring style was immediately recognized. In order to keep the clients happy, it was decided that Mr. Pearl would handle the brides and grooms, as well as the rest of the wedding parties, while Ms. Lily, all of the formal arrangements. Truth be told, Suzette and Sean were a "smidgen" frightened of Miss Lily. A flower, she was not. The bachelor party of three, it was decided, would take place at Price's Country Club, in the billiard room. More so for Ian than Will. The miracle doctor who had saved his grandson's life and won his daughter's heart could not have been better selected. Price was, honestly in awe of Dr. Will Thorpe. Will's courage and strength were worn like humble garments, whose threads only grew stronger in the test of time and Price knew that these gifts, would Will forever share with his youngest daughter. Price had already seen the worst of Ian Adams. The file Dan Montague delivered to Price, held the sordid details of Ian's unwise life choices. Tristan's conception during Ian's brief affair with Suzette seemed to be the only saving grace. But chosen his eldest daughter, Suzette had and consequently, Price could only respect that choice. But he would be watching and Ian knew that. Somehow Suzette and Sean had managed to work through the complicated maze of emotions surrounding them. Brittain had shared this with him. Sean had come to her first, then Suzette. Brittain trusted what she knew about both of them and let the two sort it all out. A loving truce, for now, she knew had been struck. Labor pains were taking place and in time, and God-Willing, would give birth to the new families struggling to be born. No, all was not perfect but everything was perfectly alright, and sometimes that just has to be enough.

Ian was nervous. Suzette glanced over at him, understanding only too well the anxiety he was feeling. Ian's forehead was still red and bruised from the handball game. It had frightened Suzette enormously, when she'd first seen it. Ian had told her that he stumbled and bumped his head. His evasiveness told her that there had been more. But she would leave it alone for now. He would soon be facing Price, Brittain, Will, Sean and himself, when they arrived at the Smith-Marshal estate. Ian was very quiet. Tristan sat in the back seat playing with his toy jet, a present from "Grandpa". "Daddy?" said the budding jet pilot.. "Yes son", he answered. Suzette smiled. "Are we going to Grandpa's house?" "Yes, we are son" answered the father, glancing nervously at himself in the rearview mirror. Catching a view of his son playing happily in the back seat, Ian relaxed. Remembering something his father used to say to him as a child caused a smile to play around his mouth. "They can eat you, but they can't kill you son"... Suzette broke the silence and asked him what he was smiling about. "You... and him", pointing to the backseat. Suzette reached for his hand as they drove onto the palatial grounds of the Smith- Marshal enclave.

Ian drove up to the massive brick columns announcing that he had arrived in many ways. The magnificent estate sitting on 6.5 acres of lush landscaping, poised elegantly and surrounded by towering trees, beautifully manicured lawns and gardens greeting it guests approach by way of the winding circular drive, providing dramatic views of the lighted tennis court, pool, wrought iron gazebo and appropriately nestled within these prestigious surroundings, the massive brick and limestone, Georgian Revival English Country home. "The fountain, Daddy, look, the fountain" Tristan repeated excitedly. He loved to watch the water flowing continuously. It was the place he and Merry would request to go most often, when Ellie took them outside to play. Ian had only heard about the estate through office chatter, but was truly not prepared for the breathtaking grandeur of it all. The wedding would no doubt be the social event of the season. Price and Brittain Smith-Marshal moved in highly-influential circles. The guest lists for the double wedding ceremony and reception had already exceeded three hundred fifty. The grand formal dining salon provided temporary home for the innumerable wedding gifts received by the brides and grooms. Miss Lily had hired a staff of two assistants, both of whom had begun the arduous task of recording the lists of gifts and sending out thank you notes immediately. Suzette and Sean had been registered at Neiman-Marcus and Tiffany's in New York by Mr. Pearl, himself.

Suzette had never seen such extraordinary gifts. Acknowledged and welcomed as Price's daughter, she felt no slight in the generosity of the family friends and acquaintances when she saw the gifts sent to both she and Sean. Suzette had not bought anything of great value since being endowed with a part of her inheritance by Price and Brittain. She was still trying to get used to it all. Brittain and Price commissioned their antiques dealer to purchase two sterling silver tea services and punch bowl sets as well as flatware, service for twelve, as engagement gifts for their daughters. Suzette had told Ian all about it, but he had not yet seen it.

Tristan squirmed excitedly in his car seat, waiting for one of his parents to release him. He was home and wanted only to find his grandparents. Ian laughed and reminded his son that he would be released as soon as Ian could get him unbuckled. Suzette got out of the car laughing at the two of them. They had grown so close in such a short time. Both had been starving for the nurturing only "they" could offer each other. Tristan refused to wait on his parents. He knew that he belonged here and promptly ran to the front door and rang the bell. Price had seen the car pull up and was waiting at the door to greet his little man. Grandfather and grandson hugged each other happily as Price welcomed Ian to enter the family home. Suzette waited her turn to kiss her father's cheek. Price reached out his hand to Ian, saying "welcome home, son", as Suzette quickly took his other hand and squeezed.

Family is wherever you find it. In one fell swoop Price Smith-Marshal became the scion of a family he could only have dreamed. Once the father of a daughter only, by dusk, on a day soon, would gain the added blessing of two sons and two grandchildren. Had he never opened his heart to Suzette, the legacy he could now claim would have been lost.

But he had chosen well and in a double marriage ceremony the two sisters would fulfill their own destinies. Brittain spared no expense on the wedding and reception ceremonies. Her girls both wanted a sunset wedding, illuminated by candles.

Thirty-Five

Sean drove in to the office for the express purpose of seeing Ian. She knew that he preferred to arrive early, in order to organize himself. Ian had always been ambitious, Sean only hoped that it did not overextend Itself to marrying Suzette. Sean knew that her sister was truly in love with Ian. That fact alone made Sean want to insure that Ian's motives were purely emotional too. The conversation was going to be uncomfortable for both but she knew too, that it didn't need to be. Everything really depended on Ian Adams.

Sean parked Will's car in her own space and headed for her office. Will loved Sean's Mercedes, so she gave it to him. She knew that she was going to need a Sport Utility Vehicle. She just hadn't decided on which one. Price offered to help her select one and order it for her. Her life had gone from two-seater sports car to car seats and shopping for "little-people" clothes. Sean smiled. The aroma of brewing coffee made her hungry. Merry had been taken to preschool for a few hours, while Sean went in to the firm. Stopping at the buffet table, she helped herself to a croissant and coffee. Ian headed in her direction to get his breakfast. Her presence did not seem to bother him. He was quiet as he served himself. Sean hesitated. Ian stood in front of her holding his food and invited her to sit with him. As she turned to head toward his office, he nodded his head instead in the direction of the atrium. Ian wanted to sit and talk to her, in the full sunlight. To hide nothing. To leave no chance for rumor nor innuendo. Ian loved Suzette, and knew that their relationship would need time and nurturing to grow as strong as Will and Sean's. As well as Sean knew Ian, something was very different. Dinner at home with everyone last night had provided each of them with the first opportunity at family-blending. At first, Sean tried staying close to Will or her father. Both men had seen and understood, and left Sean's side whenever opportune. If they were to become a family, the ice had to be broken. Will had no fears that Ian would try to woo Sean away. Neither did Price. Suzette watched as Sean did her best to stay at Will's side. She too wanted to see what would happen between Sean and Ian. She loved Ian, but knew that this time, he had to be on his own. Ian was very attentive to Tristan, who wanted to show his Daddy everything. At every opportunity, Price joined in. When Ian finally relaxed, it was time to eat. Dinner provided relief for everyone. And now that the double wedding was coming, "time for the conversation", Sean and Ian needed to have had arrived.

"Look Suzette" …"I'm sorry, I meant, Sean, I think it would be best for us to clear the air". Sean agreed, nodding into her coffee. Surprised that he had called her by the wrong name. "I think so too". "Please, said Ian, if you don't mind, may I go first?" "Ummmm-mm, said Sean, sipping her coffee. Please go ahead, swallowing.

"I know that you know the whole story now about Will and… quietly spoken…Rain and me". Sean did not respond. "I…. Will was the best friend, no the only real friend I'd ever had. What I did to him and to you was so wrong. What I did to Suzette was equally uncaring. That was who I was then, Sean. I was selfish, immature and irresponsible. I think when I used to tell you that I loved you…I thought I meant it". Sean raised an eyebrow and frowned. Watching her face, Ian smiled and jumped back in. "No, he said, I did not say that right". Looking at his hands as though for help, he looked up at

Sean. She could see him struggling and implored him to continue. "In my own way Sean, I did love you. But I didn't know what real love was until I met Tristan and got to know who Suzette really was. Smiling, for the first time himself, Ian went on. You are beautiful and I am sure you know that. Of course, he smiled and she finally smiled back. Everyone did. "It was so easy to think that I loved you the way", he smiled again, "I love Suzette", he said in almost a whisper. Suzette did not have your kind of beauty, wealth, nor the offer of the kind of future, any man you married could expect. But somehow even when, in the face of it all, she became pregnant with my child, she carried him, gave birth and loved him so well. Beaming a little brighter, he went on bravely. "He is a wonderful little boy...My son", he said in a low tone, as he looked at Sean, "and Suzette are the two most important people in this world and I don't deserve to have either one. I intend to spend each and every day earning these riches that can only be weighed upon the scales of the heart. With tears of remorse trying to spill over, he wished Will and Sean, the same happiness. Sean allowed her own tears to fall. Wiping at her eyes with a napkin, she thanked her brother-in-law-to-be. Ian used the back of his sleeve to dry his moist eyes. Getting up from the table, he smiled and left, walking slowly back in the direction of his office. Sean watched him go.

A very tiny part of her missed him, but she believed that, in time, she would get back a finer Ian Adams, who would someday make a very fine friend and brother-in-law.

Sean felt so relieved and happy. Now that she knew that Suzette was not getting him on the rebound, she could be truly happy, for herself.... for all of them.

Thirty-Six

With only 1 week remaining before the wedding, fraying nerves were beginning to show everywhere. Brittain could finally devote all of her time to the wedding. Her vacation had finally begun. Mr. Brooks, Mr. Pearl, Miss Lily and her two assistants had managed to pull it all together.

The wedding gowns had been selected. Sean and Suzette were going to be absolutely breathtaking. Suzette selected a Givenchy original, while Sean, a Monique L'huillier. The cost of the gowns would have paid Suzette's salary for three years. Suzette was astonished by the lavish "no-holds-barred" approach Price and Brittain were taking. She felt like Cinderella once again. Just as Suzette thought she could surprised by nothing else, her father and Brittain announced the details of their honeymoon destinations.

Suzette and Ian were going to spend ten long sun-warmed days and romantic nights on the island of Martinique in the Caribbean, as they wished. Will and Sean were going back to the Hawaiian Islands, the birthplace of their love. This time however, to the seclusion of the island of Kauai, where they could make love in the midst of glittering waterfalls, and fall asleep in each other's arms before the stunning Hawaiian sunsets. Price had rented a villa on a secluded beach, complete with concierge services and cook for Suzette and Ian. Sean and Will would occupy a sumptuous penthouse honeymoon villa. The children would be staying with Grandma and Grandpa at the estate. Tristan and Merry were already making plans to play near the water fountain. The soon-to-be cousins were going to grow up together and it was evident that they were becoming friends, much to the delight of the entire family. Tristan was already very protective of Merry and it was wonderful to watch. The festivities were to take place the next evening. It would also mark the last time Brittain would have her baby all to herself. Very soon, she would become wife and mother officially and for the last time. It seemed only yesterday that Sean was only Merry's size.

Brittain had made it clear to Ellie that she was to be a family guest at the wedding. Price hired additional staff to prepare the house for the big day. Ellie was so pleased that her presence was so valued. She had been with the Smith-Marshal family for many years and had come to love them also as her own.

The two brides and mother decided to have a bachelorette party at the estate. Suzette and Sean found the idea sweet. The "girls" decided on a slumber party. Time to just laugh and watch "mushy love stories" and, to talk. Suzette and her mother used to spend many weekends just like that. They had been great friends. Suzette sorely missed those days and nights. Sean and Brittain had the same kind of relationship, but never seemed able to catch up on lost time either. Will and Ian and Price, of course would be doing the "manly" Men's Club thing, for the bachelor party. Ellie would put the children down early to sleep and everyone would be free to enjoy their parties. Tristan and Merry preferred to sleep in the same room, probably, so they could talk each other to sleep.

The next day, the estate looked like a construction site. The white straight back chairs for the wedding ceremony, as well as the tables and chairs to be placed under the tents were delivered. The giant white and cream tents were trucked onto the estate. A handful of young men set about the task of setting them up. It was starting to look like a wedding was actually going to take place. Brittain Suzette and Sean spent the better part of the day going over details with Mr. Brooks, et al. Miss Lily had sole responsibility for menus and caterers, reception logistical design and seating arrangement placement, flower orders/flower preservation artist, three-piece orchestra, photographer and videographer, airline tickets and hotel reservation confirmations, limousines, valet parking, hotel accommodations for out-of-town guests, wedding cake designers and bakers, applications for marriage licenses, appointments for medical exams and blood tests, renewal of passports, calligrapher to create hand-designed stationery, applications for name changes on driver's license and social security cards for the brides, guest book order, minister confirmation and fees, rental of the numerous aisle runners and bridal registry. As Miss Lily and her assistants confirmed completion of all arrangements, Mr. Brooks stood next to her looking appropriately pleased with her performance, offering her a "well done", as she finished her portion of the discourse. Clapping his hands twice, very quickly, he turned over the presentation to Mr. Pearl. Stepping forward, in his grand style, bowing ever-so-slightly from the waist, he began. Alterations and final fittings completed on both wedding gowns, reminding everyone of the Givenchy and Monique L'huiller selections by the brides. Flora Nikrooz lingerie for their trousseaux. Richard Tyler original for the mother of the brides, in eggshell pink. Lisa Fernandez original for Merry, Vera Wang for the bridesmaids, Father of the Brides, Grooms, groomsmen and ring bearer Tristan, to be attired in Oscar de la Renta. Accessories for Brides, Grooms, Attendants, Ushers, Flower Girl and Ring Bearer selected and purchased. Flower selection for bridal bouquets, corsages and boutonnieres would be ready for pick up, the morning of the ceremony. Gifts for the wedding party, as well as the groom's gifts had arrived at the estate and were put into the safe. Final dress and tuxedo fittings had taken place just prior to the rehearsal dinner, two nights before the wedding. Appointments for entire Wedding Party and attendants at Panache Day spa, for hairstyling, facials, manicures and pedicures. Expressly for the Brides, Grooms and Price and Brittain, body polishing and massage therapy as well, were all set. Wedding announcement sent to newspapers. "Double ring pillow" had been special ordered and received. Sterling silver Cake knives and forks from the flatware services given as engagement gifts by Price and Brittain were to be used to cut and serve the wedding cakes. For Suzette, Reed and Barton sterling service was chosen and for Sean, Towle. Waterford Crystal toasting goblets for Suzette and Baccarat for Sean, completed the last of the tiny details. Suitcases for the brides and grooms had already been packed the night before the wedding. Debra Diggsby, owner of the Day spa Panache and friend of the family would be Sean's Maid of Honor, while Suzette had asked Tabitha Jones to be hers. Will honored his new friend Dr. Bo Longmire in his request to stand as his best man. Ian asked his only friend Will, to stand for him, who would already be standing near to him and Will agreed.

Thirty-Seven

wo days remained before the wedding. The house had been transformed into an English Garden, from the front door to the rear of the house and including the pool, which was to be strewn with flower petals and softly lighted from below. Ian and Will arrived a little before the bachelor party in order to spend some time with their children and Brides-to-be. Price had not yet returned home from the office. The children were in such a state of excitement. Everywhere they looked, there were gifts and flowers and new things being built. They had even noticed Ellie's excitement, as she spoke to them about the big wedding party. They had peeked in on their mommies, as Sean and Suzette tried on their gowns to the ooohs and a-a-aahs of Grandmother Brittain and Miss Ellie. Everyone seemed so happy. Will, hearing the doorbell, smiled at Ellie, as he, standing closest to the door opened it to greet his best man, Dr. Bo Longmire. Bo entered the luxurious two story, limestone master reception hall, in full view of the dramatic and powerful grand staircase, which had two separate facing entry locations from the second floor. Hanging high above the stairs, was a twenty-four candle reproduction of a Louis XV chandelier accented with Svarowski Strass crystal drops. It was all Bo could do to keep from whistling aloud. Reading the look on Bo's face, Will laughed and put his arm around his friend as he introduced him to everyone. Dr. Forest Wethers was the next to arrive. Forest had known that Will's fiancée was an attorney, but Will had never mentioned her family wealth. Then again, Forest knew that money never really mattered to Will Thorpe. It was fitting that such a prince of a man should find his princess and kingdom, all at once. Price finally arrived, running later than he'd anticipated. After being introduced to the guests and greeting the excited wedding party members, he invited everyone to enjoy some hors d'oeuvres, while he changed. Brittain excused herself also. The sounds of love and fun filled the air. In a mere two days, everything about the lives of the betrothed would forever change. Ian watched the camaraderie between Will and his guests. Will had always been able to easily make friends, but more importantly, to keep them. Ian had no one to invite. As Will introduced Ian to Bo Longmire and Forest Wethers, he deliberately put his arm around Ian's shoulders. The shock and utter surprise Will's friends showed, went through Ian like a Scimitar. Ian realized that they knew who he was and probably all about his affair with Rain Thorpe.

Suzette had been watching and listening. Moving closer to the men, she entered their circle, quietly slipping her arm through Ian's, patting it gently. Using the edge of her finger, she quickly swiped at the tear determined to fall. Through glazed eyes, she said simply "That there should be no schism in the body, but that the members should have the same care for one another. And whether one member suffers, all the members suffer with it; or one member be honored, all the members rejoice with it". "First Corinthians, 12, Verses 25 and 26". "Hi", said Suzette, as she extended her hand to greet Will's friends. "I'm Suzette Smith-Marshal, Ian's fiancée" …. she spoke with authority. "And My Sister", said Sean proudly, as she too linked arms. Ian and Suzette smiled bravely as Sean winked at the two of them. "Please", she offered, "feel welcome to our family home". As Will looked steadfastly at his two very confused friends, a great depth of emotion transformed his face. Bo Longmire patted Will's face, smiling softly, as he nodded his understanding. Dr. Wethers followed with a hand extended toward Ian's own. As if on cue, the whole room fell into a deep quiet. "Today", Will said softly, "I am filled with a greater love, than ever I have known. As I look around this room, I see the past, present, future and am humbled. As Ian looked into the eyes of his friend, he realized that the "once upon a time", when Will Thorpe would have been first on the list, to be there, just for him, had never changed. Will and Ian had come full circle and were now once again, at a new beginning in their relationship. The opportunity for a newly-established trust had been made possible. Possible only by the enormous spirit of forgiveness and loving kindness with which Will had been blessed.

Price and Brittain, apologizing to everyone, returned to the elegantly-appointed formal living room with its 18th Century fireplace. As Brittain held the glasses, one by one, filled by Price, with champagne, she felt her heart too being filled. Holding his own glass up toward his beloved Brittain, Price offered the first toast of the occasion. "May Love ever abide". The magical clinking of the glasses welcoming destiny in her own time.

Inviting the men to join him in his double-height, cube library, with beautiful brass railings and hand-carved Italian moldings, he kissed his wife and daughters goodnight, wishing them too, a magical evening. Facing the mahogany double doors to the library was an old English marble fireplace, large enough for a full grown man to simply walk into. Even Will found himself in awe. Before him lay every man's dream. While Price took drink orders from his guests, he invited them to wander the room. Adjacent to the sitting area neatly hidden, Price opened mahogany-paneled sliding doors to reveal the large billiard room and bar that was part of his grand master study. This time, Bo let go of a long, full whistle of appreciation, as they all laughed in agreement. Price was pleased, but embarrassed at the attention. But he too, loved this very room, more than any other in the house. In this room, he felt as though he had arrived; that he had worked hard and persevered, in the face of all odds.

Ian was the first to suggest it, as everyone held up his glass to receive one of many more toasts to the occasion. With hesitation, he asked Price, if they could hold the bachelor party right there in his study. After all, Ian reasoned, the club they were going to, could offer no finer a setting, nor host. Price was touched. A finer compliment, Ian could not have paid him and the others agreed heartily. Price excused himself as he went to tell Brittain that they too, would be staying in. Ellie had made more than enough of the scrumptious morsels, he'd seen made ready for the bachelorette party. There would then, be two parties going on at the estate that evening. Deborah Diggsby and Tabitha Jones, arrived, carrying their bags. The festivities were ready to begin. Brittain suggested that the men and women as well share a drink together and head toward the breakfast room, where Ellie had laid out a spread of gourmet delights fit for the occasion. The sounds of happy chatter and good company filled the house as never before. Brittain and Price stood at the doorway, watching their daughters, soon-to-be sons, and their guests, feeling so very happy themselves.

The women, ready to begin their own fun, headed, at Brittain's request, to an upstairs gallery, leading to the master suite. The master suite encompassed the entire east wing of the second floor. There, her guests found a separate sitting room, his and her baths and dressing rooms. Brittain's bath was done in pink Italian marble, while Price's accented in polished black granite. Brittain's study was located on the second floor also. Scalamandre silk walls commanded the pure elegance of the room. Neoclassical paneling imparted order and decorum, as did her bookshelves filled with literary classics as wells as her law reference books, confirming her love of the written word. The English marquetry writing desk, opposite an eighteenth-century wingback chair invited the guests to take a peek inside her honor, Judge Smith-Marshal. In this very room, mother and daughter had shared many life-lessons and much love. Behind double doors could be found, the most astonishing of surprises, a second-floor garden nursery conservatoire. Britt had always loved flowers. Growing and nurturing them gave her an understanding of life as God made it. Brittain's fascination with the art of Bonsai, had endowed the young Sean, with an innate love and respect of the miniature and fragile, a desire to care for the innocent, the helpless and bridged, in the child an understanding of the law of life.

Thirty-Eight

Time, played master of ceremonies to the pre-wedding rituals, keeping the participants marching toward, "the big day". The day before the wedding everyone enjoyed being pampered, scrubbed and polished like the sterling silver that filled the dining room table at the Smith-Marshal estate. That same evening, Time once again called everyone to gather for the final wedding rehearsal and dinner.

The very next morning, it was Time, who had awakened the anxious parents of the brides. Brittain and Price moved quietly and lovingly from room to room as they peeked in on their sleeping daughters and grandchildren, enjoying for the very last, moments when the four would belong solely to the two of them. In terry cloth robes, they wandered the garden to see the splendor of the wedding design in the early morning dew while remembering their own humble beginnings. This day, they both hoped that Time would be merciful in allowing them to miss nothing. As expected and hoped for, Time, the consummate, brought Price and Brittain to the moment for which they had so well, prepared.

Mr. Brooks and staff arrived promptly at noon, relegated to a day of checking and rechecking countless details. By four in the afternoon, the final placement of seating place cards was being completed. The floor plan had been a good one. All seemed to be well-done under the sixty by one-hundred-foot tent, that would hold the three hundred ninety, final guest count. The brides and grooms decided to present each guest with sterling-silver engraved picture frames as gifts. The frames designed to hold the place cards at each table, would later hold copies of the official wedding photo.

Brittain and Price were determined to hold back the tears they knew would spill at any moment. Sean and Suzette had done no better. Ellie seemed the only one who'd given herself permission to cry. Though Tristan and Merry's constant questioning of her tears quickly took care of that. Will and Ian arrived together. The children seemed the only ones able to revel in the immediate joy, leaving both fathers shaking their heads in wonderment.

The wedding ceremony was set to begin at six o'clock in the evening. Everyone was getting dressed and the guests had begun to arrive. Ellie had dressed the children in all but their outer garments; waiting for the exact moments for which their roles as flower girl and ring bearer were to be called upon. Debra Diggsby's staff were confidently putting the finishing touches on the brides and grooms.

Brittain went to see her girls one last time. Sean stood in front of the full-length mirror admiring her wedding gown, as Brittain eased into the room. Sean looked so happy and excited. Hearing the sound of her mother's footsteps moving in her direction, she looked into the mirror to catch a first glimpse. Brittain was herself the picture of glamour and elegance. Her hair was pulled into an impeccable French twist, five carat mobe pearl and diamond earrings set gracefully announced the beautiful and aristocratic facial bone structure; while her barely pink, Richard Tyler ensemble whispered "haute-couture". Brittain looked remarkable. The long-sleeved hand-beaded and embroidered jacket, with victorian cameo collar, was form-fitting, stopping mid-calf in length, giving way to a floor-length skirt, made from layers upon layers of creamy pink tulle with each hem lined in satin. Brittain stopped just behind her little girl, hoping to make for herself a photographic image, she could hold onto forever.

Brittain and Price met in the upstairs hallway as Price was leaving Suzette's room, on his way to see Sean. Price took hold of his wife's hands and spun her around slowly and into his own arms. She looked so beautiful and he told her so. His heart was breaking and Brittain knew it. Suzette looked magnificent and a little sad as Brittain entered her room. Brittain reminded Suzette that the mother she sorely missed was very much nearby and very, very proud of the woman she'd become.

It was time to begin the ceremony. The orchestra's sweet violins played The Wedding March. Twenty, thirteen-branch sterling silver candelabra provided the flickering light inside the massive wedding tent, as daylight gave way to the dusk. Lighted candles illuminated the stone veranda leading down to the wedding garden. Standing at the top of the double staircase, at each end and leading down to the altar were the two brides and their escorts. Price stood at the bottom of the stairs watching and proudly waiting.

Suzette descended first wearing Givenchy. The strapless princess gown in silk-satin with full underskirt, encircled her tiny waist, as she floated down the stairs toward her father. The pearl tiara gave way in the back of her head to a delicate organza veil. As Suzette reached her father, he raised his right arm to receive her gloved one. Wiping at a tear on her face, she smiled. Sean looking elegantly sensuous took her turn descending to her future. The satin strapless mermaid hugged her incredible figure. The softly beaded lace shrug caressed her delicate shoulders, as the hooded veil of the shrug draped itself softly around her face.

Like frame-by-frame photography, the deliciously elaborate affair unfolded with far too many memories to hold onto. And once again, Time, the impatient perfectionist moved everyone along at its requisite pace, giving way to no one.

Price and Brittain had saved the very best of their surprises for last. As Price stood for the final toast, he invited everyone to raise their glasses. To his new sons, he wished Peace. As he said it, four white doves were released into the air. To his daughters, he wished love in its purest form, unselfish and caring, nurturing and instructive. As he said this, beautiful butterflies were released. To his guests, he wished, the joy of a child, and to this end, thousands of pieces of confetti fell softly blanketing all of them, like winter snow. To all present Price offered...If but one wish, could I.... Love One Another.

Thank You, GOD Almighty, for making me exactly as I am, our Lord Jesus Christ, for never Giving Up on me and the Holy Spirit, for Always Knowing How and When to reach me.

For my Beau... whose name means beautiful and my Ian, my heartbeat, thank you for loving me.

Printed in the United States
by Baker & Taylor Publisher Services